... would have I been as unprepared as I'd
thought...

ALSO BY JOHN GREGORY BETANCOURT

THE DRAGON
SORCERER

John Gregory Betancourt

ibooks

new york

www.ibooksinc.com

DISTRIBUTED BY SIMON & SCHUSTER

THE DRAGON SORCERER

An ibooks, inc. Book

Distributed by Simon & Schuster, Inc.
1230 Avenue of the Americas, New York, NY 10020

ibooks, inc.
24 West 25th Street
New York, NY 10010

The ibooks World Wide Web Site Address is:
http://www.ibooks.net

ISBN: 0-7434-7529-1
First ibooks, inc. printing November 2003
10 9 8 7 6 5 4 3 2 1

Interior design by John Betancourt
Typesetting by Wildside Press, LLC

THE DRAGON SORCERER

ONE

"Master?" Ool asked softly from behind my right shoulder.

"We're close," I said without turning. "An hour, maybe less. Keep alert."

"Aye, sir." My first mate bellowed a quick warning to the crew: "Eyes open, there! Jeffy and Squint, get aloft! Watch for Grayhaven!"

Two dozen voices cheered. I knew how they felt. It had been a long voyage; they had every right to celebrate now that our goal lay at hand. They would have plenty of short leave once we reached the fair . . . if the locals didn't hang us first.

I grinned to myself. Not that they would hang us, for I planned on giving them no cause. Foot braced against the bow's railing, I leaned forward and gazed ahead to where the Avanar River curved gently to the left. My heartbeat quickened when I saw flashes of movement—but it was only eight or ten boys busily jumping off the tree-lined bank, swimming, yelling, and splashing each other. When they spotted us, they began pointing and shouting. Then they scrambled up the riverbank, grabbing pants, shirts, and undergarments from bushes, and fled among the trees.

Ool chuckled. I glanced sideways at him. My first mate was tall, with deeply bronzed skin, a bald head, and piercing blue eyes. As always, he wore the simple yellow robes of a wizard. Mystical symbols had been stitched on the sleeves in silvered thread.

"What's so funny?" I asked.

"They were afraid of us."

"Most people are."

"They saw through our disguises immediately."

"What do *you* think?" I asked.

"My thoughts do not matter, master." He inclined his head. "Our destinies are linked. It is my job to make sure we succeed here, if success is at all possible."

"But . . . ?" I prompted.

"I think it is madness, Master, to bait these people. A needless risk."

It was my turn to chuckle. Poor Ool, no sense of romance or adventure.

I said, "You're too practical. You know I do one impossible thing every year. Bards sing of my adventures from the palaces of Zelloque to the dungeons of Pethis. After all, I *am* the greatest pirate who ever sailed the Seren Sea!"

"If you do say so yourself," he added with wry note.

"Someone has to!"

My gaze swept back over the *Pamah Reach*, taking in my ship's three tall masts, the unsavory-looking crewmen at work on the deck, and the huge stacks of crates and bales tied down to the deck. With her wide, deep keel, the *Pamah Reach* had been built for the sea, not rivers, but I had vowed to attend this year's fair at Grayhaven, and I would keep my word . . . as always. Grayhaven's lake ran deep enough, and how I got my ship past the shallows and rapids was my own business. What did I care if they called me a fool? If I wrecked my ship, I could always steal another, as I had stolen *Pamah*, and besides, everyone knew pirates were crazy. And my reputation was at stake.

"Master?" asked my first mate. "Orders?"

"Steady as we go. Prepare to make port."

"Aye, sir." He moved off, setting the men to scrubbing down the decks, trimming the sails, and generally getting things ready for docking. He was a good mate, Ool, the best I had ever had. The fact that he was a wizard helped. I knew I would need his special talents before the fair ended.

The time passed slowly. We passed two more deserted-looking villages; the inhabitants had doubtless gone to the fair already. And then, finally, rounding a last bend in the river, we came into sight of Grayhaven itself.

My heart quickened and my breath caught in my throat. Behind me, I heard startled murmurs of awe from my men. None of us had ever seen anything like the fair before.

It spread over mile after mile of land. The canvas tents and booths, the thousands of stands and displays, and the milling crowds became a dazzling patchwork of colors, reds and blues and golds, pinks and greens and bright yellows. More people than I had ever seen before in any one place surged through the streets and alleys. Everyone who was anyone in these parts came to Grayhaven for its annual month-long fair.

Beyond the fair rose thick stone walls belonging to the city of Grayhaven, with hundreds of white stone towers capped in gold jutting up from inside like so many fingers. The fair proper lay outside of the city, completely circling it.

Ool called more orders, and the sails came down. Slowly we eased forward, nosing in among all the smaller river-craft tied at Grayhaven's numerous docks. To my right and left bobbed the small, single-masted boats of fisher-folk; ahead I saw the flat, empty beds of river barges whose cargoes were already up for sale at the fair's various stands and booths.

We had not arrived unnoticed. People swarmed along the dock, following the *Pamah Reach*'s course. I recognized a half-dozen or so of them: Ophir the Cat, Vern Nuli, Jaster One-eye, others, all former sea-captains whose cargoes I'd . . . *liberated* . . . on more than one occasion. Several of them shouted curses at me. Others shook fists or knives. The bright-plumed helms of the Grayhaven guardsmen bobbed up and down above the tumult as the soldiers did their best to preserve order.

"Ease a bit to port," I called.

The mate at the wheel shouted, "Aye, sir!"

Ahead I saw an empty berth on the inside of the third-most pier, where thick oak pilings had been sunk deep into the lake's clay bed. Seizing the end of the mooring rope coiled beside me, I waited. Thirty feet, twenty . . .

"Drop anchor!" Ool shouted.

"Aye!"

I heard a splash as the anchor dropped, and the squeak of rigging as sails were lowered.

"I'll see you hang, pirate!" Ophir the Cat shouted.

I just smiled coldly. I had special plans for him.

A red-faced man in blue robes called, "Hanging's too good for him—death by torture!"

The guardsmen drew their swords and pushed the people back thirty feet—a safe-area for me and my ship. The last time I'd seen such a mob had been in Zelloque, when the Prince Neb of Coran had come to visit. He had been possessed by a demon at the time, it later turned out, and he had tried to murder the Great Lord of Zelloque, Narmon Ri himself. There had been riots in the street and the Coranian Embassy had been burned to the ground.

The dock crept closer; I felt the *Pamah Reach* beginning to slow. A boy of perhaps eight slipped through the line of guardsmen and ran to the edge of the dock. I tossed him the mooring rope, which he looped around the end of a piling, cinching it tight as my ship eased closer.

With a shudder, the anchor caught and eased the ship to a halt a half foot from the dock. I couldn't have asked for a better arrival. While the crew began to stow the sails away and see to a hundred-odd shipboard tasks, I stepped calmly onto the dock. Ool, my tall, dark-skinned first mate, bellowed orders with a cheerfulness I'd always found disconcerting, considering I had found him half-dead in the hold of a slave ship.

I gave the boy a silver coin and off he ran. Watching him go, I felt a bit nostalgic. Once I, too, had worked the docks in my native city of Zorvoon. It had been one of the happiest times of my life, when I'd had no cares in the world and known nothing of pain or loss.

"That's him!" the red-faced man shouted again. "That's Fel Blackmane, the pirate! Grab him!"

The crowd surged forward, but the guardsmen kept their swords up and the people in place by sheer force. They lashed out with their fists, and soon the men drew back nursing bloodied noses and blackened eyes.

A captain of the guards pushed his way through to the safe-area and shouted for silence. He was a large, heavily built man dressed all in brown, from his leggings to his steel and leather helmet. With his thick black beard and bushy black eyebrows, he looked like someone I wouldn't want to meet in a fair fight. I made a pretense of smoothing my yellow silk shirt and black silk pants that puffed out from ankle to waist, then ran my fingers through my dark beard, setting the jewels clipped there jingling and flashing in the sunlight.

"Are you Fel Blackmane, the pirate?" he demanded. His eyes narrowed as he studied me with obvious disdain.

"No, good sir," I said. "I'm Fel Blackmane, the trader. And you?"

He blinked.

Slow-thinking lout. I'd have no trouble getting in, I knew then. I almost felt a twinge of disappointment. *Almost.*

"I'm Galvan Blickling, Captain of Grayhaven's Guardsmen."

"Ah, sir, I'm pleased to make your acquaintance!" I clapped him on the back as if we were old friends. You could talk your way out of almost any minor dispute by making friends with the local guards . . . and if that didn't work, gold often did. "I've studied the laws of Grayhaven, and under them I'm entitled to protection against needless harassment from thieves and cutthroats such as those assembled here." I waved to take in the crowd assembled on the dock. "I wish merely to attend your fair. I've come to set up a small booth and sell various items I've taken on during my last voyage."

"He's lying!" Ophir shouted. "He robbed me and my ship of twenty thousand in silks and spice six years ago! I demand *justice*!"

"Jealous competitor," I murmured so only Blickling could hear.

Blickling shrugged my hand from his shoulder. "Let me see your fair pass," he snapped.

I took a small silver medallion from around my neck and held it up for him to examine. It carried the emblem of Grayhaven Fair, a complex sword-and-snake pattern inscribed with certain mystical wizard-marks that were supposed to be impossible to counterfeit. I'd found a wizard who could copy them anyway (it always amazes me what gold can buy), and I knew my medallion would pass any test Blickling could come up with.

I could see Blickling weighing all the evidence in his mind. I could tell that, despite my pass, he wanted some excuse to arrest me, to throw me to those who called for my blood.

"The guards at the foot of the Avanar River didn't have any objections to my entering the fair," I quickly pointed out. As if I'd given them a chance to object. All barges had to be inspected before sailing into the harbor, and the blockades made it impossible for anyone to pass unnoticed. Any boat on the water, that is . . .

"I must ask the Fair Council," Blickling said reluctantly. "Wait aboard your ship."

I bowed my most impressive and sincere bow. "As you wish, good sir. I trust the matter will soon be taken care of." With that, I turned and boarded the *Pamah Reach* again. I went straight to my cabin without looking back.

Inside, I began to laugh.

TWO

When I was ten, an unscrupulous trader took a sudden liking to my mother. He accused my father, a poor dock worker, of stealing from his ship. When the city guards searched our home, they found a few small jars of expensive Varanian wine—planted, my father swore, by the guardsmen. My father's protests came to naught; he was imprisoned, sentenced by the Council of Justice, and sent to work in King Ornay's copper mines. He soon died after, broken and despairing, or so I am told. My mother disappeared the day the trader set sail—kidnapped, I am sure—and I never saw her again.

I had no relatives who would take me in, and nobody on the docks would hire a child to work when he could have any of a dozen good men for the same few coppers. Rather than wander the streets and steal food from merchants like other orphans and vagabonds, I stayed on the docks and watched the ships. Every trader became a secret enemy. I hated them all and wished myself a man that I might kill them as they had killed my father.

It was then that I began living by my wits. I stole whatever food I needed from the traders' warehouses. I put worms and mice in their bundles of fine silks, and I dropped dead rats into their costliest jars of wine. Such petty revenge kept me satisfied for a time.

Then a pirate ship, the *Golden Sword*, made port. King Ornay had an open port in those days, inviting all the world to commerce with his people, from the richest of merchants to the lowest of slavers. The *Golden Sword*'s black flag called to me like a beacon, and from a nearby alley, I studied all those aboard as they stowed away the sails, let out the hawsers, and fastened the ship's fenders in place. Their captain, a grizzled, gray-haired old man, tall and broad, with muscles just starting to go to fat, strode among them, his crimson cape a striking contrast to his sea-green shirt and bright blue pantaloons. He bellowed orders, his sharp voice carrying even to where I stood on the docks. His commanding presence impressed me greatly; here was a leader of men, someone who fought the traders I hated so much! I had to join his crew and learn his trade.

After they finished tying up the ship and wrestling the gangplank into place, their gaudily dressed captain strutted down to the pier. I shadowed him at a safe distance, studying his every move. He walked with his head high and his shoulders thrown back, as though he owned the world. Traders looked at him and cringed with fear. That was the reaction I wanted from them!

When he pushed his way through a crowd watching a cock fight, I saw a daring cutpurse nick his money pouch with practiced ease. The captain never suspected a thing.

Without even a glance into the contents of the pouch, the thief turned and casually threaded his way out through the crowd. He didn't notice a vagabond in tatters following. After all, he had just made the theft of a lifetime—a pirate captain's purse had to be a fabulous prize.

He headed for Cutpurse Alley, where his kind liked to gather and brag and drink to their successes. I ducked down a side street, raced ahead, and bided my time just inside the mouth of the alley. When he turned there, I was waiting. With a length of wood, I struck him on the back of the head. He fell, unconscious, and swiftly I retrieved the pirate's gold.

"Hey, Sonny-boy!" one of the other thieves farther up the alley called, starting forward. "Give me that!"

Barely giving him a glance, I darted into the street and into the crowd. He probably would have given chase had he known my prize, but he didn't bother. When I glanced over my shoulder, he was busily relieving the man I'd knocked out of his valuables.

I reached the cock-fight just in time to see my pirate captain leaving. He entered a large, boisterous tavern called the Sailor's Jig. The place rang with shouts and cheers, and over the noise I could just make out the sounds of a lyre. It was a notorious den for pirates and slavers, and under normal circumstances, I would never have gone near it. Swallowing nervously, I followed him in.

In the wide, dim common room, I paused, letting my eyes adjust. The air held the rich, fruity smell of expensive wines and the tang of old urine and other, more unpleasant odors I couldn't readily identify. Turning, I looked the patrons over until I finally saw the pirate captain sitting alone in the corner, at a small table, sipping wine from a heavy silver goblet.

Pushing aside my fears, I walked boldly up to him and demanded a place aboard the *Golden Sword*.

"Who are you to order me about?" he snarled, drawing his knife and slamming its point into the table between us. He scowled fiercely, blue eyes flashing. And yet, somehow, I thought I saw a trace of amusement in the set of his jaw.

I threw his purse on the table. It made a loud jangling noise and came open, spilling more gold coins than I'd ever seen before.

"Where did you get that!" he cried, snatching it up.

"From a thief at the cock-fight. I believe it's yours?"

He gave an angry growl. "How do I know *you* didn't take it?"

"If I wanted your gold, I would have kept it."

"Then you don't want a reward?"

"I didn't say that. I do. I want a place on your ship."

He laughed and tossed a single gold coin onto the table. "Off with you, boy, while I'm feeling charitable."

"I don't want your gold."

"You earned it."

"I want a job," I repeated stubbornly. "Give me a place on your ship!"

He studied me for a long minute. "You look fit enough, I suppose," he muttered. "Do you dance? Maybe you can entertain the crew for a few coppers more."

"No." I folded my arms and glared. "I want a place in your crew."

He chewed his lip for a second. "But I don't need any more men—and I certainly don't need *children!*"

I flushed. "Maybe you need me to take care of your money. You certainly can't do it yourself!"

Suddenly the room shook with laughter. Startled, I glanced about us. Every sailor and barmaid had turned to watch us. No longer so sure of myself, I shifted uneasily.

"Captain Frago, how 'bout givin' the lad a chance?" a

sailor called from a nearby table.

"Shut up, you!" Frago growled, "I decide who berths on my ship." He turned to me. "Where's your father, boy? And your mother?"

"My father is dead, and my mother was kidnapped by traders two years ago."

His expression softened a bit. "Why don't you see the captain of a merchant ship, if you want to go to sea? You might find one who needs a cabin boy or a cook's helper."

"I hate traders!" I said. "I will never serve them!"

"There's many a worse man in the world."

"I want to be like you. I want to kill traders and take what's theirs!"

"Do you know what sort of a life a pirate leads?" he asked almost gently. "We live for blood and gold, and everywhere we go—except Zorvoon—people hate us, and fear us, and try to kill us. Could you live such a life knowing that, if you are ever caught, you will be hanged? *Could you?*"

I knew he spoke the truth. I had heard stories about what the kings of Murical and Varania and Pethis did to pirates their warships caught, and yet it didn't matter to me. I was young and foolish and full of anger. Why should I worry about the future? I *knew* what pirates did to traders, and that more than made up for any risk. To kill the trader who'd murdered my father and kidnapped my mother . . .

Slowly I nodded. "I know."

"You still want to come with me?"

"Yes."

"That's yes, *sir,* when you speak to your captain!"

"Yes, sir," I said. Then, suddenly realizing what it meant, I grinned happily. He grinned back.

There was laughter and applause around the room. Then the lyre music started again, and all the other sailors turned back to their drinking and gambling.

"Sit here, lad, by my side." He motioned at the chair next to his. While he called for another goblet, I sat and studied him. He had a firm chin beneath his whiskers, a large red nose, and a broad, deeply lined forehead. When he smiled, it was with wicked merriment. Here was a man who relished life. Here was a man I would follow to the ends of the world for my revenge.

*　　　*　　　*

We sailed from Zorvoon three days later, after Frago sold his cargo of stolen Almanthian spices and took on fresh provisions. True to his word, Frago made me the new cabin boy. He already had a cabin boy, but it caused no ill feelings since Jost, three years my senior, got the promotion to active seaman he'd always wanted, and he moved his few possessions belowdecks to join the rest of the crew. Jost was sixteen, he told me, and had been at sea with Captain Frago for four years now.

"A better captain I've never seen," he said proudly. "He takes care of his own."

Over the next few days, Jost instructed me in my new duties, which mostly consisted of keeping the captain's quarters in a tidy mess instead of its usual jumble, swabbing out the cabins twice a week, and helping anyone who needed simple work done. Mending sails, scrubbing pots, and polishing woodwork filled my days—a pleasant enough existence, though hardly a promising start to my new piratical life.

So it went. Over the coming months, I witnessed fierce battles, helped bandage our wounded, tasted rum for the first time, and worked harder than I had ever worked before. I spent long hours learning to read with Largo, the second mate; boxing with Ket, the cook's helper (to the amusement of the crew, who took to betting on us); and learning the rudiments of swordplay. Frago himself was my instructor in the arts of war, and a more demanding master I never could have had. Still, his teaching paid off, and my swordplay improved.

Six months out of Zorvoon, rewarding my hard work and diligence, Frago gave me my first saber.

"You earned it," he said.

"Thank you, sir!" I just stared at the blade, hardly knowing what else to say. Now I would join the crew when we attacked traders, I thought. Now I could avenge my father's death and my mother's abduction.

Frago must have suspected my intentions, since he said, "That saber is just for show. I will let you know when I think you're good enough to fight beside my men."

"But—"

"No!" His hand slashed through the air, ending the conversation.

"Yes, sir." I bowed my head. I knew better than to argue; my ears had been boxed often enough during our voyage that I now listened and obeyed instantly. Still, I had a sword. That was the main thing. Soon I would fight and kill traders alongside him.

A year passed, then a second. I grew taller and stronger.

My skills with a sword continued to improve until I could hold my own against most of the crew. Ket no longer boxed with me, since I had broken his nose and laid him out unconscious, near death, in our last bout. I could read and write passably, and Frago had begun to include philosophy and science in my studies. Under his rough exterior I discovered a quick, brilliant mind that always surprised and challenged me. I learned to navigate from the stars, predict the wind and weather, and read his maps of the Seren Sea. Important lessons, all.

One day, I found myself abruptly promoted to reconnaissance duties in the crow's nest. "Young, sharp eyes," Frago muttered. It was a sign of his growing confidence in my abilities.

Within a year, I fought in my first battle—against a Varanian wine merchant we caught off the Lystian coast. Frago's crew called me a madman with some affection afterward. I remember little of the battle myself; just bits and pieces, flashes of scenes, glimpses of men's horrified faces as I, a stripling of fifteen years, cut them down with wild abandon, laughing like a demon all the while.

That day I became a true pirate.

One memory stands out from my years with Captain Aldenius Frago. It was a singular event—and a realization—that changed me more profoundly than anything since the loss of my parents.

At dusk one hot summer day of my sixteenth year, we came upon a small, unescorted trade ship from Varania, a two-master which had no hope of outrunning us. Her captain put up every yard of sail in hope of losing us in the coming darkness. Yet Frago's men were the best in all the Seren Sea, and keep up they did. At dawn we threw grappling hooks over her rails and pulled our ships together.

"Now!" cried Captain Frago, and we leapt across to do battle.

I was the first to reach her deck, the first to bloody my sword. I screamed my battle cry in pleasure, in sheer joy, as I attacked without fear or regard for my own safety. Before more than a minute had passed, though, the captain called for his men to lay down their arms and surrender, for he saw no chance of defeating us. It infuriated me that such a coward would escape with his life so easily, and I would have slaughtered them all anyway, but Captain Frago called for us to put up our swords. Reluctantly, I did so.

As soon as Frago examined the hold, which held a cargo of rare spices and jars of fine wines, he swaggered back up onto the deck with me beside him. He smiled, as happy as I'd ever seen him. And why not? He had a rich cargo, and he hadn't lost a single crewman to get it.

He clapped me on the back. "A fine haul, Fel my lad, wouldn't you say?"

"Yes, sir," I said. "But we only killed five of them!"

He snorted. "Blood? I've had enough of it to last me a lifetime. Gold, now *that's* the heart of a trader, my boy. Get your lusts in order, like any good pirate—gold, then women, and only then killing. It's the way of things."

And what he truly meant came to me in a sudden rush of insight. Gold truly *was* the heart of every trader, more important than life itself. There were, of course, a few rare exceptions, like this ship's captain, who cared more for his crew than his cargo. But greedy merchant-captains, who ordered their crews to fight to the death, were far more numerous. These were suitably punished. Frago would maroon them and their surviving crewmen on some remote shore and sink the ship, or he'd marry their daughters off to his officers (our second mate had a collection of seven after only four years with Frago—one wife for each port we frequented).

Once, when we took a ship full of noble-born women bound for the Almanthian court, Frago made presents to the women of a good bit of his treasure. He did this, of course, after murdering most of the crew and all the officers. In the end, even after looting the hold, I think he lost money on the deal. He gifted those women with a fortune in jeweled necklaces and rings and bracelets before setting them free in Zorvoon.

"Why bother?" I demanded. "We will never see them again."

He sighed. "Fel, my lad, some things you do because it's the right thing. These are beautiful noble-born women. They will tell all the world what a gentleman I have been. My reputation among ladies is forever made! From the lowest whore to the greatest lady, all will swoon when I pass by and long to be held in my arms!"

That was the second most important discovery of my young pirate-life: A man's reputation mattered. A pirate like Captain Frago actually *cared* what the world thought of him.

That very day, in my seventeenth year, my thoughts and dreams and aspirations came together. I would be the King of the Pirates, I decided. My reputation would spread far and wide, and my very name would caught traders' hearts to skip in fear.

For I would rob instead of kill. I would steal the gold that so inflamed the hearts of such traders as Jaster One-eye, Ophir the Cat, and others like them. Death is too quick, too happy an end. If you want to hurt someone, take away what they love.

I had lived by that rule ever since.

After Frago retired to Zelloque—which had recently opened its ports to pirates—to live the life of a ladies' man, I inherited his ship and crew, for he had adopted me as his son and heir. I plundered traders' again and again. I even managed to put a few of the most corrupt out of business. No more would they hurt innocent people—like a certain boy who'd lost his mother, lost his father, because of them.

And as for becoming the King of Pirates? To that end, I had begun doing one impossible thing each year.

Two years ago I fought three of King Ornay's best Zorvoonian warships in the space of one week, seized all three, and sent them back to the king's wife draped in red roses with my compliments, "for inspiration rendered."

Last spring I had led the first successful raid on Bar Altibb, the best-defended, supposedly impenetrable island fortress of the Countess of Fleurin. I had breached her defenses, surmounted her walls, and stolen—a single kiss.

This year I intended to set up shop at Grayhaven's fair and sell precious goods back to those from whom I'd stolen them. In the bargain, I was going to keep a certain long-standing vow to myself. Yes, they would remember Fel Blackmane's trip to Grayhaven fair for many years to come. My reputation was already spreading from Zelloque to Coran to Pethis and beyond.

After I finished at Grayhaven Fair, bards across the world would sing of the King of Pirates and his daring men.

THREE

Her name was Alna Savina, and her titles would have filled a book. She preferred to call herself simply the Countess of Fleurin. In her childhood she had been beautiful, with skin as pale as new-fallen snow, hair long and black and soft as a raven's wing, and eyes like emeralds, deep and green and mysterious. When she spoke it was like the softest whisper of wind; when she sang it was with the voice of a dove.

So it had been.

Alna Savina still considered herself beautiful. The faint lines around her eyes and mouth, the thinness of her lips, had only added to her stature.

Once many men had tried to win her hand. But it had been many years since the last suitor had departed, and these days no more strangers came to woo her, nor did princes send gifts of silks and furs and rare fragrances. It had been her decision, she told herself, to thrust them from her. When she studied herself in one of her many looking glasses, she knew the reason she had never married: she had never found the man good enough. She had broken many hearts, and she often smiled secretly at the memories: all those foppish princes and rich merchants who had longed to hold her close, or strived to win her favor, only to be rebuked and made a fool before her court. They had left, always in anger and sometimes in tears, and she had continued to rule alone.

Bar Altibb—the fortress at the crossroads of the world, on the western shore of Fleurin, the largest island in the Seren Sea, where the nearness of the trade routes between the Northern

Kingdoms and the Southern Kingdoms made easy pickings of ships—this was her home.

She had grown rich extorting money from traders who sought only safe passage, yet she no longer enjoyed her wealth. Life had been endlessly monotonous for the last few years until a man—a savage, exciting man—had dared attack her keep. She had been lax, unprepared when he came, and he had escaped with a sizable share of her fortune. She wanted it back, and she wanted the pirate who'd stolen it dead.

As she stood on the highest battlements of her fortress, she looked out across the water far below. Two hundred feet down, waves crashed and foamed on jagged black rocks. The scent of salt brine carried up to her. It was a long drop, and quite deadly.

Smiling a bit, she stepped back from the edge and turned to face the spymaster called Palamar. He was a tall man, with the narrow face, blue eyes, and white-blond hair of all Varanians. His dressed immaculately, from his wine-red robes to his red doeskin boots to the round hat he now carried politely in his hands.

He bowed low to her, then rose at her nod. Caneel and Ril, her two uniformed bodyguards, shifted uneasily, watching Palamar's every move. Their hands never left the hilts of their swords.

She folded her arms. "What news?" she asked.

"Good, Countess. I found the one you seek, the pirate Fel Blackmane."

She leaned forward eagerly. Finally! Scarcely could she believe her luck.

"Where?" she asked.

"In Grayhaven. At the fair."

She drew back in disgust. "Impossible!"

"I would have said the same about his attacking Bar Altibb."

"He could never go there. The rivers aren't deep enough for his ship, and he would never dare leave the safety of the sea. He is nothing if not careful."

"Nevertheless," Palamar insisted, "he *is* there. Perhaps because of your age," he paused for effect, and Alna Savina felt a horrified tightening in her chest, "you don't realize what romance and adventure someone young and bold would find in Grayhaven."

Her age! She managed to restrain herself. *Find out everything he knows first.*

"Do you have proof?" she demanded.

"My man in Grayhaven sent word. In ten years of service, he has never failed me."

Alna Savina turned away suddenly, sharply. *He's lying to me,* she thought. *Blackmane would never leave his ship.*

She had made it her business to study the pirate, to know all there was to know about Fel Blackmane. They said his genius showed in the boldness of his plans, each one worked out in such detail that it could not possibly fail. They said he always got what he wanted. Once, she thought idly, she would have welcomed such a man as Blackman as her suitor. Perhaps she might even have let him win her hand. But now she had made him her personal enemy.

"Countess," Palamar said softly, "I am telling you the

truth. You paid me to find him. I have done so. And . . . there is the matter of my pay."

"No." She shook her head. Then she motioned to her bodyguards. "Show Palamar the way back to his ship," she said. "The shortcut."

"Yes, Lady," Caneel said with a grin. He and Ril stepped forward, seized Palamar's arms, and threw him over the stone rail in one quick movement. The man barely had time to yelp in surprise.

Alna Savina stepped forward to watch the trader fall. She said not a word; her face revealed not the slightest trace of emotion. Palamar spun around and around like an acrobat in a tumble. His fall seemed to take longer than usual. But finally, when he struck the water between two sharp black teeth of rocks, she let out a sigh. A white plume of spray rose for a second, and then Palamar was gone.

"I am," Alna Savina said, "still young and bold. Let that be a lesson to you."

Caneel and Ril said nothing. But then, they never did. It was almost a game they played.

"Do you like killing people?" she asked suddenly.

Ril looked up at her in surprise. "Lady?"

"You heard me. Do you like to see men die?"

"We like to serve you, Lady," Caneel said, and he and Ril bowed.

That was enough to satisfy her. As she gazed out across the sea, again she smiled secretly to herself. "Of course you do," she murmured. "Just as you love me."

Grayhaven, indeed! A river-port, and the most secure one

in the world at that. She cursed Palamar for a fool. Fel Blackmane would never dare go to Grayhaven, she told herself. At the annual fair, his enemies would recognize him instantly. He would have no friends, no hiding places to run to, no allies to draw upon. . . .

And yet, something about the trader's report bothered her. As she turned and headed back toward her quarters in the heart of Bar Altibb, flanked by Caneel and Ril, she wondered what it was. Assuming Blackmane *did* go to Grayhaven— why? What purpose could it possibly serve?

They say his genius lies in the plans he makes, worked out in such detail that they cannot fail.

As she entered the large arched doorway to the audience chamber, she let her gaze travel around the room. Rich tapestries covered the walls; thick carpets covered the floor. Overhead hung a huge chandelier, but instead of candles, tiny balls of wizard-fire floated among the intricately cut dewdrop crystals, lighting the room more brightly than sunshine. Few could look at the chandelier itself for more than a few seconds at a time, such was its brilliance.

Guards in brightly polished armor stood by the doors, holding steel-headed pikes stiffly upright. Their plumed helmets and wine-dark capes made them as decorative as the tapestries and carpets. When they saw Alna Savina, they snapped to attention.

She climbed the twelve steps to her golden throne and sat, stiff-backed, regal. She took her duties as the ruler of Fleurin seriously. Already a line of supplicants had formed. Motioning to the first one, a burly, bearded trader whom she dimly remembered, she pretended interest in his case. It was expected of her.

*   *   *

The afternoon passed with painful slowness. Time after time she had to ask supplicants to repeat themselves, since she hadn't been paying attention. Their voices droned in her ears, monotonous, boring. She tried to concentrate but could not get Fel Blackmane from her mind.

At last she called an end to the day's session and withdrew to her private chambers. She needed to rest. She needed to think.

They say his genius lies in the plans he makes, worked out in such detail that they cannot fail.

As veiled maids bathed her in warm mares' milk, she remembered the day Fel Blackmane, the pirate, had come to her.

He had arrived on a sunny afternoon, sailing into Fleurin's harbor with three ships bearing the flags of Zorvoonian traders. Like any other captain, he gave his crew leave to visit the various gambling houses, taverns, and brothels along the waterfront, then came ashore himself. Alone, dressed in the finest silks, he walked up the long, winding road to her huge stone fortress, Bar Altibb, to pay his respects and his taxes.

The guards admitted him without question. After all, hundreds of seafaring captains sailed into Fleurin every month, and they saw nothing different about this one. Blackman strolled into the audience chamber and joined the line of visitors waiting to speak with her.

Meanwhile, his crew had, one by one, disguised themselves as noble-born men of rank, garbed in rich silk robes of bright hue, adorned with gold pendants, diamond rings, and silver pins. Throughout the afternoon they passed, one by one, through the open gates and into Bar Altibb. No one suspected they were other than what they seemed. No one noticed the swords and knives they carried concealed in their clothing.

The pirate's crew wandered the labyrinthine corridors of her fortress until sunset, unchallenged. Then, as one, they drew their swords and attacked the guards, slaughtering the few that resisted, taking the rest prisoner.

Fel Blackmane had nearly reached the head of the line when Alna Savina heard sounds of fighting in the hallway outside. As her bodyguards rushed to defend the door, Blackmane leaped forward, laughing in triumph. He leaped to her throne three steps at a time and placed a silver dagger against her throat.

As the cold steel pressed into her flesh, she gasped in shock and began to murmur a death-prayer. But Blackmane maneuvered himself until her body shielded him from her bodyguards. Leaning on her shoulder, he whispered in a suave, soothing voice:

"Do not be afraid, my lady. We mean you no harm. I am Fel Blackmane, and Bar Altibb is completely mine. Order your guards to lay down their weapons, and you will all live to see me depart."

She had looked at the pale, frightened faces of her bodyguards, at Caneel and Ril, and she had seen the love and horror in their eyes. They would have died for her, and gladly. But this was a fight which could not be won.

"Do as he says," she called. And they had done so—grudgingly, haltingly. She had breathed easier when Fel Blackmane removed the dagger from her throat.

"A wise decision," he said. "I expected no other."

More furious than frightened, she said nothing. Only her trembling hands betrayed the tension within her.

He sat on the arm of her throne, lounging there like a common ruffian. His every word, his every gesture, seemed designed to mock her. As his men paraded through the doorway in triumph, cheering, *"Blackmane! Blackmane! Blackmane!"* she swore to see him dead.

And then, laughing, he made her move aside. He sprawled in her throne, wore her golden crown like laurels of triumph to celebrate his victory, then made her kneel before him like a commoner.

"You have won," she said, concealing her fury through clenched teeth. "My fortress is yours. Is it gold you seek? Take it. Jewels? Women? They are here, too."

He laughed, as though it were all a great joke. "I have come to rule," he said, "for a time." Rising, he lifted her to her feet and set her beside him on the throne.

And then she knew he was mad.

The pirates locked her guards in the dungeons. They allowed Fleurin's petty nobility free run of the fortress and island, as always. Messengers were sent to the ships of various traders in the harbor proclaiming a new Count of Fleurin—Fel Blackmane. Business would continue as usual in the morning.

That night, in the banquet hall, acrobats tumbled and jugglers tossed balls and plates and flaming knives for the amusement of all. Fel Blackmane sat at the head of the banquet table, with Alna Savina to his right. Many other nobles sat at the table as well, their faces grim and unpleasant. Humiliation consumed her, but Alna Savina did not show the slightest hint of anger or resentment. She would not let Fel Blackmane know he had vanquished her. Always she felt his eyes upon her. Feigning interest in the entertainment, she ignored him and his men as best she could.

Toward the end, old, gray-bearded Joran, who sat to her right, stood and raised his cup as though to offer a salute. Instead, he threw back his ceremonial cape and whipped out a small crossbow, which he aimed at Fel Blackmane.

"Death to rogues!" he shouted and pulled the trigger.

Alna Savina felt a rush of excitement. As she leaped to her feet, she began a rallying cry, a call to action which would set her followers on the pirate and his men.

The cry died on her lips as she looked at Fel Blackmane, then at the single white rose which had struck him in the chest.

Magic!

She cursed under her breath. Who had saved him? She glanced about the room for the wizard who'd obviously just saved the pirate's life, and she spotted a bald, dark-skinned man against the far wall. He wore yellow robes with mystical symbols stitched on the sleeves and a smug expression. He must have been Blackmane's savior. Alna Savina cursed them both.

Fel picked up the rose, smelled it, and grinned at her. "For you, my lady," he said, dropping it onto her plate.

His men laughed and cheered. Alna Savina flushed, feeling a helpless rage building inside her. Damn Fel Blackmane and his smugness! He infuriated her more than any man she had ever met.

Beside her, she felt Old Joran trembling with shame and helplessness. She picked up the white rose, threw it to the floor, and ground it to pulp under the toe of her beautifully sequined dining slipper.

To make things worse. Fel Blackmane ascended her throne at dawn, once more with her at his side. There he stayed all morning. Alna Savina was obliged to advise him, humor him, smile at his foolish jokes and too-obvious witticisms.

Undeniably Blackmane had a great personal charm that she found difficult to resist. Physically, he was devilishly attractive; his body was deeply tanned and muscled from hard work on the open sea. His penetrating gaze bespoke a man who had seen much of the world.

Still, she reminded herself, she was his prisoner. He had stolen everything of hers she valued, her people, her throne, her lands. And then her hatred was rekindled.

At sunset that evening, exactly twenty-four hours after he'd conquered Fleurin, Blackmane gave the fortress back to her. His men had emptied the island's treasury into his three ships' holds. He'd had his little adventure and now he was moving on. He took her—alone, without a single maid in retinue—to a hilltop overlooking the bay.

They stood there, side by side, and watched his ships. The triumphant shouts of his men mingled with the keening of the gulls. A black flag signaled their readiness to depart.

She waited for him to act, to say something, to explain himself. He merely watched her with an infuriating boyish grin.

"What would you have of me?" she finally demanded, nearly choking on the words.

At that moment he pulled her close and kissed her passionately, as though they were lovers. Her whole body tingled. She felt like a girl again, young and alive—somehow exhilarated by his touch. And then he'd bowed low, bade her farewell—and left. He'd been smiling as though his triumph were complete.

His men set fire to the town and sank several ships in the harbor to keep her from following with warships. That had been the last she'd seen of him, but she had followed the tales of his daring exploits with interest, waiting for her revenge, until now—exactly one year later.

As she lay in her bath of mares' milk, brooding, one of her maids combed her silky black hair. It felt pleasant just to soak, and her mind began to wander. She thought once more of Fel Blackmane's kiss. It had been one last touch, the perfect touch, to make his name a legend throughout the world, and to make her a laughing stock.

She stood suddenly, and two maids hurried forward to wrap her in soft towels. She spoke to the girl who had been combing her hair.

"Send one of the guards to summon the Karnekash. I will meet with him tonight."

"Yes, Lady," the girl said, curtseying. She turned and half-ran to the door.

Alna Savina, the Countess of Fleurin, smiled. But there was a grimness to her expression that hinted at the simmering hatred within.

Precisely one hour later, Alna Savina entered a conference room followed by Caneel and Ril. The two bodyguards stopped at each side of the doorway.

An old, gnarled man stood waiting there for her, gazing out through the open window at the sea. A small gray-green dragon, scarcely an arm's length from nose to tip of tail, perched on his shoulder. A small puff of steam rose from the dragon's mouth as it shifted from foot to foot, looking toward Alna Savina with large sea-green eyes. A puff of smoke curled from the wizard's mouth as well.

"Karnekash," Alna Savina said. "Your trip was pleasant, I trust." She had summoned him from far-off Janjor after one of her spies had spoken well of his talents. He was—if the reports spoke truly—among the most powerful and ruthless wizards in the world.

Karnekash turned slowly to face her, and only then did she see the small clay pipe he held. It had been wrought into the shape of a dragon.

"No more or less so than any other, Lady Savina," he said. She thought she saw a faint gleam of amusement in his eyes. "I do not complain. What is it you seek of me?"

"I have finally located Fel Blackmane, the pirate. I want you to kill him."

"So?" He drew casually on his pipe. "Where is he?"

"Grayhaven."

Karnekash nodded thoughtfully, blowing smoke rings.

Alna Savina could smell the heavy, bitter-sweet aroma of herbs and dried rose petals; the smoke seemed to twine itself around her. As she breathed, she felt dizzy. For an instant she saw Karnekash as an old gray dragon himself, only infinitely folded and coiled within a human body. She blinked and the illusion was gone; he stood before her as a strange old wizard once more.

"And so?" he said again. "What would you have me do, exactly?"

"Kill him," she said again. "Destroy his ship. Destroy his crew. But do it where no one can come to his aid. And I want it known that *I* am the one responsible."

As the wizard continued to puff on his pipe, he scratched his tiny dragon under its chin. It stretched out its neck and flapped back its wings for a second, twin plumes of steam jetting from its nostrils. Slowly its great green eyes closed. Had it been a cat, Alna Savina thought, it would have purred.

"Well?" Alna Savina demanded after several minutes.

"It *is* possible . . . but it will be expensive."

"How much?"

"A thousand pounds of gold ought to cover it."

She gaped at him, scarcely daring to believe her ears. "How much?"

"A thousand pounds of gold. For this amount, of course, you also receive a guarantee."

"I've never heard of a guarantee on magic—either it works or it doesn't."

Karnekash shrugged. "So? If you can find a better deal . . ."

"I could buy ten good warships for that amount!"

"If you thought you could kill Fel Blackmane with just ten warships, you would not have considered my services, Countess. Magic is an art. And an expensive one. And so is revenge."

She hesitated, studying him. Still he puffed on his pipe and scratched his dragon's scaled neck, ignoring her for the moment.

"You pledge his death?" she asked.

"Of course. By this time tomorrow."

"Very well." It would be worth whatever it cost, she thought.

Since Fel Blackmane's attack, two other bands of cutthroats had tried to capture her fortress. Both times her guards had slaughtered the attackers—but at great expense. As long as Fel Blackmane lived and boasted of his conquest of Fleurin, others would try to imitate him. Yes, Fel Blackmane certainly had to die. Honor and safety demanded it.

"Very well," she said. "Half payment now, half when I have confirmation that Blackmane is dead."

"Agreed," Karnekash said. "I will take the gold tonight."

"My guards with deliver it to any ship—"

"No." There was a calmness to his voice that disturbed her. "I need no help with it. Have it delivered to my quarter, Countess. My creatures will remove it."

FOUR

Late that afternoon, Grayhaven's Council of Elders came to interrogate me aboard my ship. They were three old men swathed in black ceremonial robes (which meant they held their errand in distaste), wearing ivory masks over their faces. The masks were supposed to make them remote, uninvolved with the world, but their eyes gave them away: they hated me, feared me, and wished I had never come.

Ool ushered them in. The three old men grouped themselves in front of chart table where I sat, surrounded by gilded wooden furniture and rich tapestries. Deliberately I ignored them for the moment, pretending to study a sea chart.

A chandelier jangled overhead as the ship shifted a bit. Finally one of them cleared his throat.

I glanced at Ool, who had busied himself studying the tapestries. He had little intention of helping me with these negotiations, I saw. At times my first mate seemed to take an almost perverse pleasure in watching me squirm my way out of tight situations.

"Am I to be deprived of seeing your faces?" I finally asked the Council, glancing up.

"That is not why we have come," said the one on the right, a deep-voiced man. "There are those in this city who say you are Fel Blackmane, the pirate. They have warned us of your deeds. Still, our laws protect everyone. If you wish to set up a booth to barter your goods, we will not deny you. But be warned: many here hold grudges against you. Our guardsmen cannot guarantee the protection of you and your ship. We advise you now to sail back to the sea, to ply your dark trade elsewhere. You are not welcome at Grayhaven."

I shook my head. The jewels in my beard spun and twinkled in the dim light, hypnotic, soothing. "I will stay here a while longer, I think . . . though not for the whole fair. I've missed its first week as it is."

I smiled enigmatically. I could see by their narrowed eyes they found my mere presence offensive. Deciding to draw out their stay and discomfort as long as I could, I leaned back, set my feet on the table, and—in my best long-winded way—said:

"That reminds me of a story I once heard from another captain. He had sailed beyond the Seren Sea, into lands far from any regular trade route, to a country unheard of by any Zorvoonian. He called the place Shekara, after the woman who ruled there. Now this captain was a crafty man, and he knew a good thing when he saw it. He smelled a profit. And let me say more about Shekara. It was a beautiful place, with fruit trees growing everywhere, game bountiful, and fields yielding harvests greater than any seen in these parts. As you can well imagine, the people were happy and content, wanting for nothing. But that was before the captain arrived."

"Get to the point," the deep-voiced man said.

"Patience, patience, my friend. The story isn't over yet. As I was saying, this captain gave lavish gifts to a few of the lesser-born nobility—strings of beads, gaudy bits of jewelry, ivory fans, beautiful ribbons, and silken gowns. Envy spread. Before long every noble in Shekara lusted after the captain's gifts—fought for them, stole for them, even threatened to kill for them. Then, just before the fighting got out of hand, the trader set up shop and traded his baubles for a fortune in Shekaran spices. Brilliant, wouldn't you say?" I laughed. "Yes, brilliant!"

The three members of the Fair Council just stared at me. They obviously didn't understand.

"So?" their spokesman finally demanded.

"A good trader can always find—or make—business," I said. "I plan to do the same."

There was a snort of derision from the man on the left. "We have yet to hear anyone remark on your trading skills."

"Are you saying I came for another reason?"

"It cannot be revenge—you have no weapons aboard. Our spells have checked."

"I would never dream of bringing weapons here." Only Grayhaven's citizens were allowed to bear arms; wardens on the Avanar River took and stored all blades longer than a knife from barges headed to the city. I had carefully stashed our weapons on the coast, in a secret place known only to me and my crew.

Laughing, I said: "Did you think I slipped through when your wardens weren't looking?"

"That is impossible. The river is always watched."

"Then why did you check to see if I had weapons aboard?"

They said nothing for a time, but looked at each other uncomfortably. At last the deep-voiced man spoke. "Will you abide by the rules of our fair?"

"I have come to sell my goods, not to fight and not to steal."

"So be it. You have been warned."

"For that, I am grateful." My lip twisted.

"There remains the matter of your seller's fee . . ."

"Here." Without hesitation, I tossed a small pouch onto the table. It clinked softly, filled with Zelloquan silver royals. It was ten times the normal seller's fee, but I thought a small bribe might help smooth things over. "See? I am nothing if not honest!"

He scooped it up. And he had the discourtesy to count it in front of me. He took four coins and threw the others back onto the table.

"You may keep the rest for any other miscellaneous fees," I offered. "I know how little public servants earn."

He ignored me. "Your booth number is 9605. Ask at the city gates and you will be shown to your area. You must provide your own stand."

"Of course." I smiled my most winning smile. "Thank you for your time and attention."

*   *   *

"You told a truly inspirational story," Ool said solemnly after they had gone.

"Indeed. But I don't think they took it to heart."

Ool couldn't help but sigh. "Ah, but Captain . . . trading is the smallest part of your mission here. We both know you don't care about money."

"Oh, but I do! I live to take it away from traders."

Laughing, we went up on deck together. My men lounged about, talking and joking, waiting for orders. A wineskin circulated among them.

I seized the skin and threw it overboard. "I'll have no drinking here. You'll need clear heads before the night's over. Now get moving—carry the wood ashore. Ool will find out where our booth goes. I want it built before dawn."

Grumbling good naturedly, they set to work.

I sat on the hatch-cover and stared out across the docks to the fair. Lanterns on the ends of long poles glowed with wizard-light, but most of the booths had closed and much of the crowd had vanished. Only those selling food and drink or offering games of chance still seemed to be open.

A few passers-by stared wonderingly at me and my ship. I recognized none of them, but that meant little. Spies for my enemies? Almost certainly.

I knew I'd be hearing again from those who had called for my blood. I chuckled. Fools, letting their tempers get the better of them . . .

I felt excitement and tension beginning to build inside me.

*　　　*　　　*

"It looks good," I said, standing back to survey the work of the ship's carpenters.

My booth had been assembled in the center of the fair, next to a small tent where fine goods and bolts of silken cloth were sold. It was a large square wooden building with a red silk canopy in front, and the outside walls had been painted a brilliant green, the color of the *Pamah Reach*.

"Are we ready to bring everything ashore?" Ool asked.

I nodded. "Tonight, when it's dark."

"Captain . . ."

"I know what you're going to say, and yes, I expect someone to try and stop us—perhaps even try to kill me. But I have everything planned. You know I leave nothing to chance, so trust me, Ool, trust me."

"Aye, Captain." But I could see he still had doubts.

I wandered among the various stalls, acting interested in what the other merchants had for sale, apparently doing my best to be just another inconspicuous fair-goer. Since I wore a bright green silk shirt, yellow silk pants, a cape of sky-blue velvet trimmed with red fur, and dozens of sapphires in my beard, I found a lot of people staring at me. Indeed, I cut quite a striking figure . . . exactly as I had planned.

Some booths were little more than wagons with piles of furs or tools or carvings set before them; others were huge, ornate tents made of rustling silks and colorful canvas. A puppet show was going on, and I stopped to watch the colorful wooden figures going through one of the age-old comedies. Good and evil clashed, dark and light, storm and sun. I felt like the sun today, shining hot and confident in my power. Good, like me, always won. Tossing a copper coin into the puppeteers' money bowl, I meandered on.

Word about me seemed to have spread. Everywhere I went I drew strange looks—some wondering, some hostile. I wanted everyone to know I had come to the fair . . . and that I wasn't afraid to show myself.

I kept running into the captain of the guard, Galvan Blickling, wherever I went. He was sitting in the back of the taverns I visited, examining merchandise at the various wagons and booths wherever I paused to shop, or just strolling through the crowds a few yards behind me. I ignored him utterly. He was as incompetent as he was stupid.

Once I found him skulking behind a bundle of silks I was examining. I pretended not to notice him as I set a bolt of red silk back onto the pile and prepared to leave.

On the way out I turned to the dark-haired weaver in charge and leaned forward conspiratorially. "My compliments," I whispered. "Your merchandise must be of the highest quality for the captain of the guards to be trying to pilfer a few yards for his own use."

"What?" the man squawked.

"Why," I said, all puzzled innocence, "he's over there, behind that bundle, trying to work out a length of it!"

The weaver took a long, thick, heavy weight from his loom and headed, grim-faced, for the bundle of silk behind which Blickling crouched; I raced out the door. I never laughed so hard as I did imagining Blickling's face, red and sputtering, as he tried to convince the weaver of his innocence. In any case, I had the feeling the captain of the guard would be too busy to bother me for a while. Now I had shopping to do . . . presents to buy for certain lady-friends in Zelloque and Zorvoon. . . .

Later that afternoon, as I continued to wander through the fair, I became aware of men following me. There were two of them—no, *three*—all raggedly-dressed and carrying portions of roasted meat on steel skewers. Such skewers could also serve as crude dirks, I realized. The men were eating at a leisurely pace, pretending to examine various wares whenever I turned around. Never mind that their eyes followed my every movement.

My heart began to beat faster, and I quickened my step. I glanced around for Blickling and his guardsmen, but didn't see them. Good. I'd be able to take care of these three myself.

Casually, like any shopper taking a shortcut, I turned down a narrow alley between two huge tavern-tents, stepped over a dead pigeon, then turned and leaned casually against the wooden support-pole to my right, waiting for them to catch up.

They started down the alley, saw me waiting, then froze in surprise and suspicion. For a moment I thought they were going to bolt away, expecting a trap, but they just hesitated, whispering among themselves. What were they waiting for? I'd just given them the perfect opportunity to murder me! Didn't they see it?

"Well?" I said when none of them advanced. "Hurry up! I've been waiting for three men like you." I stood up straight and motioned them forward. "I want to hire you."

"Aye? Hire us?" The one in the lead, a slim, dark-haired man of perhaps twenty, moved forward with a chuckle. He held his skewer like a rapier now. The other two would-be cutthroats lingered in the alley's mouth, watching expectantly.

"That's right," I said. "I have a job you'd be perfect for. So put down that toothpick before you get hurt."

Slim lunged. I stepped back a half-foot, grabbed his arm and jerked him forward, then broke his wrist in one quick move. After slamming his head into the wood post, I let him drop to the muddy ground, unconscious.

The other two just stared, open-mouthed. I stepped over

the body, still smiling.

"Well, my offer still stands. I'm looking for a couple of people such as yourselves to do some work for me. Are you interested or not? I'll pay you fifty silver royals each—no, make it a hundred! I'm feeling generous today!"

"Uh . . ." mumbled the one in front. He, too. was young and thin, but light-haired—probably from Tázgul or Varania. The one behind him was light-haired too, but taller and of a heavier build, perhaps Narian.

"First, put down those ridiculous skewers," I said.

They dropped them at once, looking bewildered and frightened. I'd never seen a more hapless pair of hired killers. Any of *my* men could have done better blindfolded.

"Now let's go get something decent to eat while we talk. How about Varanian sweetmeats?" Smiling, I stepped forward, put my arms around their shoulders, and led them off toward the best food shop I'd seen.

*   *   *

In a private booth, over syrupy cakes of cold, spiced meat, we sat and talked. Their names were Tane and Barran, I found out, and from their description I recognized the man who'd hired them to kill me: Jaster One-eye, captain of the *Silver Squid*. One-eye never was a man for subtlety. I knew him too well—his practice of killing his partners and taking their share of the profits had become legendary in certain circles. More than once I'd gone out of my way just to rob him. Of course he'd never stopped trying to get even.

One murder attempt down—how many more to go?

I sighed and took out my money pouch, poured out a

handful of coins. Tane and Barran's eyes bulged. I counted out four gold royals for each of them and pushed the money over the counter. They grabbed the coins and tucked them away.

"Remember what I told you to do," I said. "At noon tomorrow you begin spreading word that my goods are fake and that I've cheated everyone I've sold them to. Right?"

"We'll remember," said Tane.

"Right." I smiled sweetly. "Forget and I'll have you gutted."

He swallowed hard, suddenly looking like a frightened rabbit again. I could see he remembered the encounter in the alley.

Rising. I nodded cordially to them, then headed back toward the *Pamah Reach*. Night would soon fall. I needed to supervise the unloading of my cargo.

*　　*　　*

"Put it there," I said.

Dane set the crate down with a sigh. "That's the last one, Captain."

"Good." I looked around my booth. Crates and bundles of various sizes had been stacked everywhere. Silks . . . spices . . . jewelry . . . wine. It was all here, a small fortune in merchandise taken from the cargoes of a dozen different merchants who were in Grayhaven.

"Anything else, sir?"

"No, that's the lot. Go on back to the ship. Baden will get you when it's your turn for the watch."

"Yes, sir." He turned and jogged off into the darkness.

We'd worked three hours to unload everything. Now the

only problem would be keeping it safe until morning. I certainly expected One-eye and the rest to have hired thieves—or worse—to try to rob me: such petty maneuvers would be just like them.

"Captain," Ool said.

I turned, but had trouble seeing him in the shadows. "Yes?"

"You can go back to the ship. I'll keep watch with the others. You need your sleep for the morning."

"And you won't?"

"My needs are . . . different from yours."

I hesitated; he was a wizard, but also a man. "Very well," I said slowly. "You know your own limits."

"Shh!" he hissed suddenly, holding up one hand. His eyes were closed. "Two men are placing oiled cloths against the back wall," Ool announced. "They have flint and steel. I believe they hope to burn the booth down."

With a growl of anger, I motioned for the four crewmen I'd assigned to guard my goods to follow me. Silently we padded out the booth's door. Baden, Marzan and I circled around to the right while Vila and Bull moved to the left.

We reached the back at nearly the same time. Sure enough, two men crouched there, striking sparks from flint and steel as they tried to light the oil-soaked rags. Baden and Marzan seized the first one while I grabbed the other by his collar. He yelped in surprise and tried to jerk away. Bull and Vila grabbed his arms and I let go.

"Stop struggling," I told the two. I folded my arms and glared with all the menace I could manage. "I have no intention of killing you. Yet."

They stared sullenly back at me.

"Who hired you?" I demanded.

Neither spoke. Clearly they feared their master more than they feared me.

I drew my knife and fingered the blade. Time to get a little more threatening. Slowly I circled them.

"Do you know what they do to arsonists in Pethis?" I asked.

The man on the right shuddered. *He* knew.

I had no idea, but I could make a good guess. The king of Pethis believed in making punishments fit crimes. Cutpurses got their hands cut off. Swindlers and frauds didn't have a leg to stand on—literally. And arsonists? Burned at the stake, most likely.

"I don't take kindly to having my possessions burned," I said coldly. "Start talking or you'll wish you were in Pethis. I'll have my men break a bone for every heartbeat you delay. They will begin with your legs. Marzan—"

"No—*wait!* It was Captain Nuli!"

Vern Nuli—former captain of the *Green Witch*. I should have known. For a supposedly legitimate trader, he had a strange penchant for arson: whenever he sailed into port, his competitors' goods had a habit of burning up in warehouse fires. I had no love for him or his kind.

"Of course," I muttered.

But now—what to do with them? I knew we were being watched; Galvan Blickling was out there somewhere, spying on me, waiting for me to make some mistake. And murder might

be just what he needed to get us thrown out of Grayhaven . . .
or into prison.

I nodded to my men. "Find the guardsmen and turn this
scum over to them. I will sign whatever complaint is needed
to see them properly punished. After all—" I grinned. "I *am*
an honest, law-abiding citizen!"

"Aye, sir," Baden said with an unhappy look. Clearly he
trusted our own justice more than Grayhaven's. He and my
other men dragged the two would-be arsonists off into the
dark.

"A wise decision, Master," Ool said.

"Glad you approve. We can't take any chances, after all.
I've come too far to fail now. Can you handle things here by
yourself?"

A look of glee crossed his face for a moment. "Of course,
Master!"

*   *   *

In the early hours of the morning I sent runners to various ships' captains. They carried beautifully inked invitations
to visit my booth and promised a gold coin to the man who
couldn't find something to buy. Gold was the bait I knew
would lure them to me.

I came ashore at dawn, breathing deeply of the fresh
morning air. Today I'd chosen more conservative garb: a white
linen shirt, black silk breeches, soft gray boots. Not a single
gem decorated my beard. To all appearances, I might be any
shopper moving among the booths. One young woman even
smiled shyly at me as she passed. No doubt she would have
fainted away had she known the true name of the object of her

affections.

Finally, I reached my own booth and glanced inside. Bundles, bales, and jars still present—everything looked in order. Stretching, Ool rose and came out to greet me. He looked more irritable than tired, but as bright-eyed as always. Magic, no doubt.

"What happened during the night?" I asked him.

"About what you expected, Master." He smiled faintly, remembering. "Two clumsy thieves tried to cut their way in through the back wall. Someone else tried to toss a torch onto the roof. And some drunks threw rocks at the walls, all the while shouting various unimaginative insults, but they gave up soon enough and wandered on."

"That's all?"

"Aye, Master. Is it not enough?"

I laughed. "I thought I had more enemies than that!"

He arched an eyebrow. "The day is young yet, Master."

I grinned, and he grinned back. We were much alike, Ool and me. We'd been together for almost six years, and we both had reason to hate merchants and traders and their kind. The slavers who had kidnapped him from his home in Zorvoon had planned to sell him in Murical—where magicians are despised, feared, and often burned in public spectacles for the amusement of the people. Doubtless that would have been his fate.

"What did you do to the luckless ones who threw the torch onto the roof?" I asked.

"I almost set their clothes on fire—but then I remembered what you said about using magic." He shrugged. "They were beaten and given to the guards."

"Good. Any reply to my runners yet?"

"I think one is coming now, Master."

Turning, I saw Captain Ophir striding down the street toward me. He was tall and emaciated, with dark eyes that always seemed to stare down on the world. He wore a huge powdered white wig, the latest fashion in Zorvoon, and equally fashionable gold robes and slippers. Two large, heavily muscled men flanked him—his bodyguards. That was just like him. They called him Ophir the Cat, but he was a coward; he wouldn't have dared hire anyone to kill me. Somehow, it figured he'd be the first to come for a coin.

Ophir the Cat's *Sea Snake* was one of the most notorious trade ships ever to sail the route between Tázgul and Zorvoon. His crew consisted of dozens of teenage boys he'd bought at slave auctions or kidnapped from small towns—the only sailors he felt certain wouldn't mutiny against him. Whenever I'd raided his ship, I'd stolen not only his trade goods, but most of his crew—they would beg me to save them from his abuse. I'd always rescued them, and dropped them off at the nearest free port.

Yes, I had plenty of reasons to despise Ophir the Cat . . . but he had many more reasons to hate me. Nevertheless, I put on a pleasant expression for him and extended my hand in greeting as he entered.

"Captain Ophir!" I said. "How good of you to come! You're looking well these days. Life at the Fair must agree with you."

He stared at my hand until I withdrew it. So much for

pleasantries.

"I'm here for that gold coin." He produced the invitation and threw it at me. "Pay up, thief."

"Ah, but you must play by the rules, my good Captain! First come into my booth and see what I'm selling. Leave your friends here," I added, glancing pointedly at his bodyguards.

"Very well," he said, sniffing with disdain. "And if this is some sort of trick . . ."

"Would I do that?" I asked with feigned innocence. "Honest trader that I am, I take deep insult from such remarks!"

"Hah!"

Smirking, I turned and led the way inside my booth.

It took his eyes a moment to adjust to the dim light. Suddenly he gasped, ran forward, and knelt before a dozen clay jars that bore his personal mark, a pair of sea-snakes rampant. When he tore away the wax seal on one, the fruity smell of a fine Varanian red wine filled the room. He dipped out a taste with his fingers, sucked them dry, then rose and turned to me.

"You stole this from me!" he cried. His face purpled and his hands trembled with outrage.

"You must be mistaken," I said. "This wine is part of my trade goods. You're welcome to buy it, if it appeals to you."

"But it's mine!"

"Not," I said, "anymore."

That made him pause. "How much?"

"Oh, two hundred in silver ought to cover it."

"That's . . . that's—"

"About half what you can get for it. Are you interested, or should I look elsewhere for a buyer?"

Cursing softly, he produced a pouch from some hidden pocket, then proceeded to count out my money. "There, thief!"

"You should be more grateful," I said. "Where else could you have found such a bargain but at the booth of Honest Fel Blackmane, the world's greatest trader?"

"Dakar!" he shouted. "Limn!"

"Sir?" His bodyguards ran into the room, hands on the knives at their belts. They glanced suspiciously at me.

Ophir pointed to the jars.

"Take those back to my booth," he ordered.

With grunts and puzzled expressions, the two men hoisted two jars each and carried them away. Ophir the Cat took the last two and stalked after them, giving me a look of great venom. I would have thought he'd be more grateful, but some people just wouldn't let you help them. Clearly he didn't appreciate a bargain.

Ool stuck his head in the door. "Master, Captain Vern Nuli is here."

"Send him in." I took a deep breath. It was beginning to look like a very busy morning indeed.

*   *   *

By twelve o'clock, the my booth had been stripped completely bare. Thirteen traders had stopped by over the last five hours. They had taken away everything from boxes of rare spices to pouches of rubies, from silks and furs to small ivory statuettes of the thirteen gods. They had left enough gold and silver to fill two small chests.

As Ool and I carried our well-earned profits back to the

ship, Ophir the Cat ran up and planted himself firmly in my path. I saw Galvan Blickling hovering not fifteen feet away, pretending to examine a great crock of cheese, and I knew he could easily overhear what was being said.

"Return my money!" protested Ophir. "That wine you sold me wasn't real—it was an illusion!"

"Nonsense!" I said. There was nothing wrong with the wine. It was exactly what I'd said it was. "You're just paranoid."

"You *cheated* me!" he howled.

"You tasted it, as I recall," I said dryly. "Illusions don't have taste or smell. Don't make a bigger fool of yourself than usual, my friend."

"You used magic! *Cheat! Cheat!* You're nothing more than a thief!"

I snorted and kept going.

"Wait, Blackmane," said a new voice from behind me. "This man's charges are quite serious. I must look into them."

Sighing, I turned and found Galvan Blickling had finally worked up his courage to join us. This time three of his men accompanied him. About time. I was wondering if he had the conviction to carry out his duty.

"The shadow speaks!" I said. "How is the cheese today, Captain?"

"Don't mock me, pirate. I've heard stories about you. How you use magic and trickery to get what you want. I can easily believe you'd sell illusions to unsuspecting customers. What have you got to say for yourself?"

I couldn't believe he would take Captain Ophir's claims of fraud seriously. He really was as slow-witted as he appeared.

I said, "That wine is as real as you are." Most of it, anyway. I squinted at Blickling. "At least, I *think* you're real." I reached out and pinched his cheek.

He shrugged me away angrily. "Stop that!"

"But—" Ophir began.

"And" I said, talking over him, "you know very well that I have no weapons on board my ship. If I were to try to cheat people, would I come here unarmed? Of course not! I have more important things to do than steal a pittance from traders."

"Then you deny his charges?"

"Of course!"

"You're a cheat!" Ophir shouted.

"Be quiet," Blickling told him. Finally, some sensible orders!

I went on, "Why doesn't Captain Ophir bring the wine I sold him down to the dock? If you aren't satisfied after you've both opened the jars and examined their contents, I'll give him double his money back. Does that sound fair to you?"

"Quite," Blickling said. He seemed hesitant now. "Double your money back, Captain Ophir? What do you say?"

"Yes!" agreed Ophir. I could tell he thought he'd be doubling his money . . . and having me arrested. He hurried off toward his own booth.

"Why don't you send your men along to make sure he doesn't empty the jars before bringing them down to the docks," I told Captain Blickling. "I don't trust him."

"*You* don't trust *him*?" He laughed at that. But he nevertheless motioned a couple of his men to accompany Captain

Ophir.

"Poor fool," I said sadly, gazing at Ophir's back. He would regret his actions.

Blickling accompanied me to the dock, where I called to one of my crewmen. "Put the chests of gold and silver in the bow of the *Pamah Reach*. Prepare to cast off."

"Are you leaving?" Captain Blickling asked.

"As soon as my business with you is concluded," I said.

"Good." He smiled smugly. "We don't want your type here."

"Because, of course, you'd rather have honest, upstanding traders like Captain Ophir."

He shifted uneasily, but did not reply. I snorted. At least he realized Ophir the Cat was no great prize.

"It really *is* his wine, isn't it?" Blickling asked me quietly.

"Yes."

"Of course it is," Ool snapped. "We have made every effort to obey the rules here—"

"Relax, old friend," I said, shifting my money-chest to one hip and placing my right hand on his shoulder. "It will be Ophir's loss. Once the seal is broken on those jars, he's only going to have a day to drink or sell all that wine. The finest Varanian wines spoil fast, remember."

"Just so." Ool gave a satisfied chuckled.

"Now, Captain Blickling," I went on, "it's been a long and tiring morning. May we proceed to the docks? I want to get my profits safely aboard my ship. After Ophir the Cat has been dealt with to everyone's satisfaction, I will take my leave of Grayhaven Fair."

"Very well."

Blickling followed me to the dock where the *Pamah Reach* lay. I handed my chest to Ool, and though he staggered a bit from the weight, he managed to carry them up the gangplank.

"Put both chests in the bow," I called to him. "Then prepare to leave."

"Aye, Master!"

Everything was going exactly as planned.

By then Captain Ophir and his two bodyguards were hurrying toward us, burdened with the wine. Blickling joined him a few feet away, and together they began unsealing the jars one by one.

Cautiously, I glanced over my shoulder. My men had removed the gangplank and untied the *Pamah Reach*. We could leave at a moment's notice.

Blickling and Ophir the Cat were opening the final jar of wine. Without a moment's hesitation, I turned and vaulted gracefully over the rail.

"Now!" I called.

Crewmen shoved hard with poles, and we began to drift away from the dock ever so slowly. Blickling and Ophir didn't notice; they were too caught up in tasting the wine. How long would it take? When would they notice my slow escape?

Suddenly the first jar exploded with a bright flash and a thunderous roar. The force knocked Blickling and Ophir and everyone around them off their feet. Someone screamed in horror, someone else in pain. I threw back my head and laughed.

"Revenge is sweet, Ophir!" I shouted.

Smoke roiled up from the shattered remains of the jars. Slowly it drew together into the shape of a beautiful woman—tall, slender, with high cheekbones and long golden hair swept back with twin ivory combs. The woman who had been my mother.

Ophir must have recognized her, for he screamed her name and raised his hands to ward her off. Smiling, the figure reached forward, embraced him, flowed over him.

I heard him gasping, trying to breathe, trying to shout for help. No one moved, not Blickling, not Ophir's bodyguards—they stood frozen in shock and fear.

Still we drifted away. Ten feet from the dock. Twelve. Fifteen.

Ophir the Cat collapsed, clutching at his throat. His face grew black and his tongue protruded. Shuddering once, he lay still. Dead, finally dead. A burden had been lifted from my soul.

I found I had been holding my breath and let it out in a happy sigh. His body lay still, then crumpled in upon itself, turning to dust. A beautiful, poetic spell . . .

After a moment, the smoke-woman grew fuzzy and indistinct as the breeze scattered her image to the winds.

I threw back my head and laughed with wild satisfaction. I'd waited half my life for the right time to destroy the trader who'd framed my father and stolen my mother. A note inside the jar would explain my revenge to Blickling, and the ten gold coins wrapped inside it would pay for any accidental damages to persons or property. No man would blame me for what I had done, once the truth came out. It had taken nearly two decades, but it had been worth the wait.

*   *   *

Blickling and his guardsmen ran up and down the docks frantically, shouting and cursing as the *Pamah Reach* continued to drift out toward the center of the harbor, sails ready but unraised. They could have chased us with any of the fishing ships, but for some reason they did not . . . waiting for reinforcement? Or Grayhaven's wizard? That had to be the answer.

People gathered by the hundreds. Boys threw rocks at me that fell a hundred feet short. Shouts and taunts carried over the water.

"Thief!"

"Pirate!"

"Murderer!"

"You'll be hanged for this!"

I waved and blew kisses to the women until I saw a boat casting off, then another, and another. In the first stood the same three Councilmen who'd come to see me the day I'd arrived, and with them, straining at one of the oars, sat Galvan Blickling himself, along with five of his sturdiest men. Unsheathed swords lay beside them. In the other boats stood several dozen more well-armed guardsmen—all carrying drawn swords. So much for a peaceful departure.

"Now!" I shouted to my men. "Raise the sails! Ool! To your task!"

The men ran up yards of billowing canvas. The sails snapped out at once, catching the wind, cracking and snapping loudly. The *Pamah Reach* began to move.

Ool stood in the bow beside me, wind rippling his robes.

He raised his hands wide as though to embrace the world, then began to speak in an odd, sing-song voice, working the spell that had brought us safely to Grayhaven, working the spell that would take us away.

He seemed almost in a trance, gaze distant, focused on something not in this world. I knew better than to disturb him now, in the midst of a spell, so I said nothing—just stood aside and watched and wondered at the powers within him.

The sky overhead grew darker. Phantom breezes began to whisper. The air shimmered, and for a second the world reeled. Magic always unnerved me, and now I could feel the atmosphere around us changing, growing heavy and charged with anticipation. I gave an involuntary shiver as gooseflesh broke out on my arms and neck. Then the air took on an odd glowing quality, as though I gazed through an amber-colored glass.

The guardsmen rowed faster as the *Pamah Reach* turned. They seemed oblivious to Ool and his magic.

"Now! *Now!*" I gripped the rain until my knuckles turned white.

For a second the world reeled dizzily. Then the deck tilted and we began to rise, slowly at first, then faster and faster. I felt my heart skip. The *Pamah Reach* moved a dozen feet above the lake, beyond the reach of any guard.

My men let out a cheer.

"We're not done yet!" I shouted. "Hard to port!"

"Aye, sir!" called Marzan, from his place at the wheel.

We moved to the left, circling around, back toward the docks. Still we rose higher—twenty feet, thirty—

I leaned over the railing to see the world below. We swept over Blickling, the three Councilmen, and all the guards in their boats. They had grown silent, staring up at us with gaping mouths and bewildered expressions.

We passed them and moved over the docks. I picked up the chest of coins I'd bargained from the ships' captains, flipped open the lid, and began scattering the contents. It rained down on Grayhaven Fair, a veritable shower of gold and silver.

Below, people swarmed across the docks and streets and alleys, scrambling to pick up the riches. My ship was forgotten.

"Not that one, too!" Ool pleaded when I picked up a second box of treasure.

I grinned at him. "There's plenty more where it came from." I emptied the second chest as well, save for a single gold coin I slipped into my pocket, for luck and for the pleasure of revenge.

By that time we'd passed over all of Grayhaven and its fair and turned southward. A thick forest lay directly below, and ahead stood the majestic Skyreen Mountains, their jagged, frozen peaks capped in white. A day's journey by air beyond waited the Seren Sea . . . and home. Now that I had finally avenged my parents, I felt a rising contentment. It would be good to return to our home waters, see old friends and lovers in Zelloque, and give the crew a well-deserved rest. They would spread word of Fel Blackmane's trip to Grayhaven Fair in every tavern they visited. I had done my impossible task for the year. Yes, it felt good to be me right now.

"Captain! Look!"

The shouts of alarm came from one of the men in the stern. What now? Had the Councilmen magicked some fishing boats and sent them after us?

Baden was pointing dead astern. I followed his finger.

A black dot moved across the sky with the speed of a falling star. It had wings, I saw as is grew steadily closer, but there was something odd about them.

It grew closer, larger, impossibly large. I gasped at the thing's size. Its wingspan was greater than my ship was long.

Dragon. I realized it with a sick feeling inside.

It glided past the *Pamah Reach*, scarcely thirty feet overhead, eclipsing the sun for a split second. I glimpsed teeth sharp enough to rip a man to shreds, a shiny blackish-purple underbelly with scales so hard that only the strongest steel blade or arrowhead could even hope to penetrate them.

Now its dark, leathery wings flapped once. It twisted around, gaining height, gaining speed for its attack. Grayhaven's Fair Council hadn't been as unprepared as I'd thought.

FIVE

"To your places!" I shouted. "Prepare for battle!"

A dozen men leaped valiantly into the rigging and began to climb, knives clenched in their teeth; others seized whatever lay close at hand—belaying pins, stray pieces of wood, hammers, an axe—and moved to the rails.

"Can you do anything?" I asked Ool.

"I am sorry, Master," he said. "My will is focused on keeping the ship aloft. If I let go of my concentration, we will fall to our deaths!"

"Bring us down!" I commanded. "I don't care if we crash! We cannot hope to find it in the air!"

"It will attack at once if we do that," he said. "We must not flee."

I hesitated. It hadn't attacked yet . . . perhaps it was merely curious. After all, how many flying ships could it have encountered before?

"Then stick to our course," I said. "Use your best judgment. If there's trouble . . . do whatever you must to save us."

"Aye, Master."

I left him in the bow and moved toward the center of the ship. Meanwhile, the dragon wheeled overhead, studying us. Its eyes glittered, and whenever that gaze rested upon me for an instant, I felt my heart lurch in panic. Such creatures, according to every legend I had ever heard, were old beyond human measure, and more cunning and intelligent than any man. This one's attack—if it meant to attack us—would be careful, guarded, and deadly.

I cursed myself for a fool. Why had I risked my life and ship when I could just as easily have killed Ophir the Cat at sea? Why hadn't I been content with a common, everyday sort of revenge? I never should have come to Grayhaven. I never should have cached our weapons on the coast. How could we possibly fight off a *dragon* without so much as a sword or an arrow?

A desperate answer came to me. Grappling hooks. If we could somehow pin its wings and make it fall—

I shouted, "Break out grappling hooks and lines!"

Several hands immediately ran below deck to fetch them from the ship's stores. As they did, I turned to study the dragon once more.

"A good idea, Master," Ool said from behind me.

"Thank me if it works."

The dragon banked overhead again, its shadow flashing across the ship. The creature had a sinuous grace to its movements, and its presence commanded a certain horrific fascination like a spider or a bat, only a thousand times more powerful. I turned slowly, following its course. Still it circled, and slowly it started to descend toward us, closer, closer. I could see each individual scale on its belly, so sharply etched they might have been carved in ebony. I could see the tough, hard leather of its huge wings. I could see the fire and bloodlust in its eyes. It opened its mouth, and smoke streamed out. Then, powerful wings surging, it began to fly up and away.

I let out a sigh. Perhaps it had only been curious about us after all. What did I care, as long as it left . . .

But no, I realized suddenly with growing alarm, it hadn't

left. It had flown away, climbed higher, and turned toward us. Then, closing its wings, it dove straight at us.

Several of my men screamed in terror. I felt my own stomach twist. Nearer came the dragon; it threw back its head to let loose a blast of flame.

As if in reply. Ool mumbled something in his sing-song voice. Abruptly the deck jolted and the *Pamah Reach* swung hard to port, canting so sharply my men lost their balance and slid across the planking.

I clung to the rail, wind ripping over me. The dragon passed not six feet to my right. I glimpsed gouts of flame, and then the heat of the monster's passage rushed over me in a burning wind. I had to close my eyes and turn my head away.

Slowly the deck righted itself. I stared at Ool, at his singed hair and half-burnt robes; he seemed completely unaware of them. He spoke again in the language of magic, working another spell, and the *Pamah Reach* began to sail faster, rising higher. Had he lost his senses? We should be heading for the ground and safety—

Then the first wisps of cloud passed between us. He was trying to hide in the clouds, I realized. Maybe—

"Captain!" I heard Vila call.

Turning, I found him behind me. He held six strong steel grappling hooks. Cal and Baden stood beside him with heavy coils of rope slung over their shoulder. They vanished in thick clouds for a second, then we passed through and I could see again.

Glancing at the dragon, which beat its wings and rose into the air ahead of us, I hurried over to my men. It seemed to be preparing for another dive. We had a minute or two.

"Do something, Ool!" I called to my first mate. "Stall its attack until we get the grappling hooks ready!"

"Let me do my work, Master." He said it calmly, as a man would close a window to keep from being distracted. "I will do what must be done."

Quickly my men and I ran rope through the grappling hooks' eyeholes, knotted the lines securely, and tested their strength. They would hold.

"Volunteers to help grapple the creature!" I called out, and every crewman on board leaped forward.

"Cal, Vila, Bull, Lobito, Baden—spread out along the rail." I passed out the hooks and line, giving a quick glance forward.

Just then we entered the clouds again; a thick fog surrounded everything, and I couldn't see more than a foot or two in any direction.

"Hang on!" Ool shouted.

The deck canted to the left. Wood creaked and groaned as the ship turned sharply. I grabbed hold of the railing again and clung to it.

To the right, a brilliant glow burned partly through the cloud-cover, and a scream of rage came from the dragon. We hadn't been where it expected to find us.

The deck straightened, and we burst into the open again. The clouds had given way to clear blue skies.

"Ool!" I howled. "Get us back under cover!"

"I am trying, Master," he said.

My ship banked to the right, heading back toward the

clouds. We would be in the open too long, I realized. The dragon had seen us. It circled up and prepared to dive again. I didn't think we'd make it in time.

That left our defense up to me. My five grapplers had joined me again, hooks and lines ready, grim determination etched into their faces.

"We'll cast our lines the next time it passes," I said calmly, trying not to panic them. They couldn't ever see their captain afraid, not even facing a dragon. If we won . . . if we did manage to best this creature . . . I knew they would follow me to the edge of the Earth itself!

"Aye, sir!" They hurried to their places, hefting the hooks, preparing themselves as best they could.

I returned to the bow and stood next to Ool. The dragon drifted overhead like a leaf in the wind. It was toying with us now, a cat with a mouse. We could not escape.

As the clouds neared, Ool raised his hands and began casting a new spell. His attention seemed to slip from the *Pamah Reach,* for her bow nosed toward the ground; we started drifting downward. I wondered, for an instant, if this was part of his plan—to land us where we might be able to abandon ship and scatter for cover.

Then I saw him shape something in the air between his hands. A silver disk appeared—no—a burning sphere that flared with a cold, silver light unlike anything I had ever seen before.

When he spoke a single sharp word, the sphere arced up into the sky like an flaming arrow, streaking toward the dragon. When it struck the creature's side, it was glowing as brightly the sun.

Such a missile, which would certainly have killed any man, barely staggered the beast. The dragon gave a bellow of rage, plumes of steam and smoke jetting from its nostrils, and folded back its wings once more. Eyes gleaming, it dove straight for us. Smoke streamed back from its nostrils. It roared.

Ool paid no attention, continuing to work his magic. The effort of controlling the ship and fighting seemed to be taking its toll. He wheezed for breath, and sweat soaked his face and robes. He shaped a second ball of light between his hands, then made it leap away at his command. The ball streaked up toward the dragon, but the monster saw it coming and dodged.

The dragon's change of course took it past the side of our ship—exactly as Ool must have planned.

"Now!" I shouted to the grapplers.

We cast our hooks. Mine circled a wing but failed to catch anything; Vila's snagged in a fold of scales and held securely; Cal's caught as well. The others missed.

Two lines were enough. Caught, the dragon jerked back and beat the air with its huge wings, screaming. It almost went over backwards.

My men let out a cheer. We had the creature!

Unfortunately, I had underestimated its strength. Regaining its balance, it beat the air and rose quickly. Vila and Cal gave startled yelps as they were yanked off the deck and into the air. I dove for Cal's rapidly unwinding coil of rope, thinking I could tie it to a stanchion, but it snaked through my hands, leaving my fingers raw and burning.

"Hang on!" I shouted after them.

I could only stare with shock and dismay as the dragon carried my men higher and higher. What could I do? How could I possibly save them?

I glanced at Ool, but he could barely stand. The *Pamah Reach* trembled and shook as his concentration failed. Pale and trembling, he clung to the bow railing and barely kept his feet. The only time I had ever seen him so exhausted was the day I had rescued him from the slaver's hold. I wouldn't be able to depend on him for much of anything now, I realized.

At last, when the dragon and my men had dwindled to tiny specks overhead, I saw a sudden gout of flame. A few seconds later, two charred, smoldering corpses plummeted past me.

The dragon circled around for a third attack. We seemed unable to do more than enrage it.

"Tie down your ropes," I said grimly to my three remaining grapplers. "We'll try again."

"Sir—" Baden gasped. "The weight of the thing—"

"Nothing we can do but trust Ool to save us, if it comes to that," I said. I glanced forward at my half-slumped first mate, but I couldn't see his expression.

The *Pamah Reach* drifted lower. I hadn't realized how close to the ground we were. The Skyreen Mountains rose directly ahead of us, imposing stone walls. We would barely clear the foothills if Ool didn't find some hidden reserves of strength.

"Uh, Ool—" I began.

"Not now, Master." He knelt, hands trembling, and

shaped another sphere of light.

The mountains were getting dangerously close. Treetops began to strike the bottom of the hull with thumps and scraping sounds. I shook my head in frustration, then, scowling, tightened my grip on the rail. My knuckles grew white, my hands aching from the tension.

Roaring in triumph, the dragon dived at us. When I glanced back at my men, I found them paralyzed with fear, their faces pale, their eyes wide. I could not blame them.

Ool sent off his third missile. It hurtled toward the dragon, which tried to dodge, but couldn't. The ball of light struck it full in the face, exploding into sparks and a blaze of white flames.

For a moment the creature tumbled through the air and I thought Ool had killed it. Behind me, my men began to cheer. But then the creature jerked open its wings, turning its fall into a long glide, and passed to the side of us, wings pounding like thunderous bellows. When it roared, I could hear the rage and bloodlust in its voice. All we had done was anger it.

Then it drew back its head and let loose a blast of fire. Flames engulfed the rear of the ship. The masts and sails blazed like candles. Half the crew died instantly.

The ship jerked and pitched. Chaos reigned as my surviving crewmen ran wildly across the burning deck, screaming in fear, looking for cover, looking for anything that might be used as a weapon. Several dove off the ship and plummeted, screaming, to their deaths a hundred feet below.

The land flowed beneath us. The mountainside was growing close, ominously close. Grabbing Ool's arm, I forced his attention away from the dragon for a *second*.

"Look!" I shouted, pointing. "We're going to crash!"

He blinked in surprise and muttered, "Damn careless of me." Struggling to his feet, he reached into one of his robe's hidden pockets and drew out a small silver flask.

Unstoppering it, he took a long pull, then passed the flask to me.

"Drink this. Quickly!"

"But the ship—"

He seemed infinitely old, infinitely tired. "I cannot control it, Master—I cannot stop it in time. Drink!"

A cold, numb feeling of impending disaster swept through me. Grabbing the flask, I tipped it back and took a long swallow. I'd known Ool too long not to realize he had something in mind, some last desperate trick. It had better work.

The flask didn't contain alcohol. The liquid inside was cool and fruity, spiced with cinnamon; I couldn't stop swallowing. It warmed my stomach like ale, and a pleasant glow spread through my body. I wasn't drunk, and yet I felt strangely removed from the world, as though I floated high above it.

The mountain hazed in front of me. Distantly, as though through waves of light, I saw Ool moving. He took my shoulders, shook me until he had my attention. His expression was grim.

"Go on," he said, motioning with his hands. "Fly to safety, Master. It is your only hope." And then he stepped back.

Suddenly his body melted and ran like hot wax, shrinking, reforming. I just gaped; I'd never seen magic like this before. In a sudden shimmer of light he was transformed into a small brown-and-white hawk.

Hopping onto the railing, he spread his wings and, with a shrill cry, took off. He darted away, below the ship, out of sight.

I bent my head and looked down. I had a bird's clawed feet. When I tried to spread my arms I found I had wide brown wings. Hopping up onto the rail, I spread my new wings as Ool had done, then leaped—

My stomach lurched as the world twisted and turned, but my wings seemed to cup the air and stop my fall. It became a glide, down and away. I was small, fast, invisible to dragons. What mattered a small bird, when it had a ship full of men to destroy?

Hitting a fast air-current, I soared through the sky, higher and higher, faster, circling up and away.

A ripping, grinding, tearing noise came from behind; I realized my proud *Pamah Reach* had crashed into the mountain. I reached out my claws and landed awkwardly atop a pine tree. I hopped around in time to see my flame-engulfed ship twisting around and bounding across the mountainside. Planks and beams snapped like toothpicks, the hull buckled and burst, and the remnants of the masts crashed down. Flames seemed to explode. Wood and flesh and metal sprayed in all directions.

It all seemed to be happening impossibly slowly. And my men—my faithful, valiant men—all gone—

Debris rained down around me. I hadn't flown far enough, I realized. An instant later something sharp pierced my wing. I screamed as waves of pain pulsed through my left side.

Clawing at the place where my elbow should have been, tumbling wildly, my whole body shaking from the agony, I fell from the tree. Branches whipped at me, and I caught at them with my claws, catching one. I hung there, upside down, dizzy with pain. Never had I felt such excruciating hurt; it burned through my mind, obliterating all else.

My beak finally caught the two-inch splinter of wood lodged in my wing. I pulled it out in one quick motion, and blood spurted across my eyes, blinding me. Somehow, I held on. My talons seemed incredibly powerful.

After the worst of the agony had passed, I managed to climb back up onto the branch. Just a splinter, just a splinter. I would live. That was the important thing.

I sat in the tree and watched as the dragon landed, rooted through the burning remains of the ship, and feasted on the blackened bodies of my crewmen. There could be no looking away from this grisly scene, for I vowed to learn everything I could about this beast. Somehow, if it took me the rest of my life, I would track it down . . . it and its masters. And I would have my revenge.

It spent perhaps twenty minutes in the wreckage. After it had made sure no one had survived, it took wing . . . but instead of heading north toward Grayhaven, it headed south, toward the Seren Sea. Perhaps it hadn't come from the fair, I realized.

I took a deep breath and tried my wing. It still hurt like anything, but I couldn't stay here. After a few minutes' rest, I decided to try to fly again. Spreading my wings gingerly, I thrust myself from the branch.

An updraft caught me and bore me skyward, but with every tiny movement I felt something tear in my wing. Little needles seemed to jab my muscles, and at times the pain grew so intense I couldn't breathe.

I went as far as I could—following the mountains, soaring miles from the wreckage of the *Pamah Reach*—but the pain got the better of me. My mind was spinning. I couldn't think, couldn't really steer, and let the wind carry me where it would.

Finally I reached a small valley where a river tumbled and frothed from its snowy origin somewhere high in the mountains. I headed for a clear spot on the far side of the river. As I glided a scant two feet above the water, I felt something give in my left wing. It twisted behind me, useless, and I fell like a stone into the icy water.

The current dragged me under once, twice, again. From ahead I could hear the roar of a waterfall. Thrashing, I fought my way to the surface and took a last wheezing breath of air before the water closed over my head.

SIX

"My Lady," the guard said from the doorway. He saluted. "Pardon the intrusion, but . . ."

"What is it now, Pranton?" The Countess of Fleurin looked up from her book of poetry impatiently. This had better be important.

"Lady, the wizard Karnekash is here. He demands your immediate attention."

"Karnekash," she said, musing. Only a day had passed since she contracted with him for the pirate's death. Perhaps he had news for her, or perhaps he wished to share the details of his plan. She would enjoy that, she decided: knowing every detail of Fel Blackmane's death would make it all the sweeter.

Leaning back on her pile of pillows, she motioned the serving girl to fan her more quickly. Though impatient, she could not appear too eager. Let the wizard wait a few minutes more. He should know he could not demand her attention.

"Lady?" Pranton asked. "What do you wish done with him?"

"Wait twenty minutes, then show him in. Be polite. Remember, I need him—at least for now."

"Yes, Lady." The guard saluted again, then turned and marched down the hall. Alna Savina could hear his armor jingling. *I really must do something about him,* she thought. *He's much too noisy. Perhaps a tour of duty with her mercenary forces . . .*

Sitting up, she motioned her servants from the room. They set aside whatever they were doing and left quietly. When only her bodyguards remained, Alna Savina slowly stood and stretched, returned her book to its place on the shelf, then strolled out onto her balcony.

Tonight the heavens were dark with clouds, and a strong wind from the east made the sea rough and choppy. She smelled brine and fish, the usual smells of the sea, but for some reason they seemed more intense than usual. Far below, waves beat against jagged black rocks, tossing white ribbons of foam high into the air.

For a moment Alna Savina fancied the foam made a picture—the face of the pirate. She saw his wide eyes and wild hair, his beard, the sharp line of his jaw and cheekbones. An omen? Fascinated, she watched for a time longer, but no more images appeared.

She looked toward the heavens. The sky seemed to grow darker still, the black clouds lower. She could taste salt on the wind and smell rain in the air. Far off, lightning flickered like the tongues of serpents.

Again she looked across the water, letting her thoughts turn to Fel Blackmane, to their last parting kiss. Had he truly enjoyed it? Smiling, she let her imagination provide the answer: Kissing her had been the most exciting thing he'd ever done; the memory of her touch haunted his every waking moment. He longed to hold her once more, longed to kiss her, longed to caress her silken hair.

She smiled. Thunder rumbled nearby; the storm would soon arrive. She stepped back under the balcony's overhang and forced all thoughts of the past away. Duty called; she had to see Karnekash.

Still she hesitated, though she didn't know why. *Perhaps,*

she puzzled, *I dread the wizard's news.* Somehow, she found the thought of Fel's death more than a bit disturbing. Still, it had been her duty as countess to order him executed.

"Good evening, my beautiful Lady Savina," a low voice rumbled.

The Countess of Fleurin whirled and found Karnekash standing in the middle of the room. The wizard was dressed in blood-red robes and a cape of a darker hue. He seemed amused for some reason, and that annoyed her; she couldn't tell what he was thinking.

She also hadn't heard him enter—why hadn't the guard announced him? She looked around, but didn't see the oaf anywhere.

"Where's my. . . ?" she began.

"One might say . . . *indisposed.* He didn't want me to see you, for some reason, and attempted to detain me. But perhaps he will join us later, when he can breathe again."

Alna Savina swallowed. Unconsciously her hand moved to her throat.

Karnekash stepped forward, red cape drifting behind him. "Doubtless you've been anxiously awaiting my report, my beautiful Lady Savina?"

He's baiting me, she thought.

"Yes—" She stepped forward. "What news do you have? What of Fel Blackmane?"

"The matter has been dealt with."

"Is he dead?"

"Dead? Oh quite, I assure you."

Something turned in her stomach. "How?"

The wizard smiled. "A dragon happened across his ship this afternoon. The beast is still there now, bloating itself on roasted man-meat and gathering gold and silver for its lair."

"Good." Alna Savina turned away from Karnekash and stepped out onto the balcony so he couldn't see her face. Her eyes burned a bit—some pollen in the air, she told herself, or a bit of dust on the wind. Silently she cursed the pirate for all he'd done, for all he'd made her feel. She wished she'd never heard of Fel Blackmane.

The wizard followed her. "Are you well?" he asked. "Should I call your physicians?"

"No, no. I'm fine."

Thunder rumbled again. A drop of rain, warm as blood, touched her cheek. *Thus,* she thought, *do we weep for the dead.*

"This storm," Karnekash said, "is a suitable omen to our black deed."

"Oh?"

"Such murderous deaths are always black deeds, witnessed by the gods, noted by the rulers of men's souls. It does not please me to kill. Such things attract attention I could do without."

The Countess of Fleurin laughed. "The executioner confesses!"

"Perhaps I am weak. I see that you have none of my, shall we say, human flaws? Still, it is over and done with. We have nothing left to discuss. Now only the matter of my payment remains."

"You are too bold, wizard. Have you forgotten our agreement? You get the rest of your gold when I have proof Fel

Blackmane is dead—and not a second before."

"You have my word."

"That is not sufficient."

Karnekash stepped to the balcony's railing and gazed up into the cloud-swollen sky. For an instant lightning lit the clouds as though it were noon. The wizard's face seemed to glow a bit in the dark. "Assassination," he said, "is not murder. It's a profession like any other, and older than most. It is not my chosen line of work; certain financial requirements make it a necessity from time to time. I regret debasing myself to serve humans such as you."

"Is it a hobby, then?" she prodded. "An affectation unique to you?"

His voice was sharp. "At times a pleasure."

Suddenly Caneel and Ril closed around him, hands on their swords. Their warning was apparent enough.

Karnekash laughed. It was not a pleasant sound. "You are right, we had an agreement, my beautiful Lady Savina. The terms were quite clear. I will return with proof enough to satisfy even you."

"Do so and you will be paid."

The wizard stepped up onto the balcony railing. As he stood there, gazing up into the sky, a dazzling bolt of lightning leaped down from the heavens—and seemed to strike him. Sparks flew in all directions, leaping and dancing.

Gasping, Alna Savina jumped back, trying to protect herself. The air around her flickered. She couldn't see for a moment and cried out in alarm and fear.

Then she heard a laugh, long and deep, and a whisper of

leathery wings. Blinking quickly, rubbing her eyes, she found her vision abruptly clear.

Karnekash was gone.

She ran to the rail, her bodyguards beside her, and looked over the balcony's edge. Water seethed in the darkness. No trace remained of Karnekash. It had all been so much theatrics, designed to awe and impress her.

A warm, misty rain began to fall. The Countess of Fleurin retreated indoors to safety.

She didn't like the wizard and the liberties he took in her presence . . . arriving unannounced, jousting with words, prodding her with innuendo and double-meaning. And her guard—She turned to Ril. "Get Pranton," she said. "Bring him here." She had to discipline him. Wizards couldn't be allowed to barge into her private chambers whenever they felt like it.

"Yes, Lady." Ril saluted, then turned and strode quickly through the open door.

Alna Savina turned and gazed out onto the balcony. Rain pounded down now, a gray curtain that hid the world from view. What had the wizard said? *Such deaths are always black deeds, witnessed by the gods, noted by the rulers of men's souls.* She shook her head. More the fool for believing such nonsense. The gods cared little for men and their petty disputes, she knew. Here in Fleurin, power was all that mattered.

Only why did his news hurt so much? *Perhaps I did love Blackmane,* she thought. Now that he was dead, she could let herself feel something for him, some hint of love. His touch, his lips against hers . . .

Ril reappeared in the doorway, breaking her chain of

thought. He was dragging Pranton by the heels.

"What's the meaning of this?" Alna Savina demanded.

"He's dead, Lady," Ril said. "I found him this way. Look at his neck. I thought you would want to see what killed him."

The Countess of Fleurin drew closer. Around her late guard's neck twined a small gray serpent with vestigial wings along its back. The creature drew back its head and hissed at her.

"Kill it!" Alna Savina said, backing away, one hand touching her throat. "Kill it!"

Ril and Can drew their swords and stepped forward, but as they did, the snake melted into the air like fog beneath a hot morning sun. It vanished as though it had never been.

Unsettled, Alna Savina sank down on a pile of pillows. She felt her heart beating, heard it in her ears. A lump in her throat made swallowing difficult. It had been a very unpleasant evening. Never again, she promised herself, would she deal with wizards.

"Bring me wine," she said softly.

SEVEN

After an eternity of tumbling through foaming, roaring rapids, I came up gasping for air and found myself floating in calmer water. Somehow, despite the persistent ache in my hawk wing, despite all the water I'd swallowed or tried to breathe, I managed to swim to the riverbank. I crawled up onto the dirt and gravel and sprawled there, half-dead, letting the sun's rays dry my feathers and spread its warmth through me like a healing balm.

Later, after the sun had moved across half the sky and long shadows from the trees began to stretch over me, I heard distant voices getting louder, closer.

A boy and a girl were approaching, both barefoot, dressed in rough, patched shirts and breeches with the legs rolled up to the knees. Laughing, they waded and splashed each other, playing as young children will. They looked enough alike to be brother and sister—some farmer's children, I guessed, for work in the fields had tanned their skin a deep brown and bleached their hair almost white.

The younger girl, perhaps eight or nine years old, stooped and pulled a rounded stone from the riverbed. "Gare, watch me!" She threw it sidearm-style.

Gare laughed as the stone sank with a loud plunk. Though he couldn't have been more than two years older than his sister, there was an air of superiority about him I didn't like, the same sort of condescension I'd seen in traders like Vern Null.

Gare finally said, "No, stupid, you need a flat stone, not a marble." Bending, he picked up another rock and showed it to his sister. "Like this one, Wirna, see?" He skipped it across the river once, twice, three times before it finally disappeared.

But Wirna wasn't looking, I noticed with a sudden tremor of apprehension. She was staring straight at me. Maybe they won't bother me if I don't move. I slowed my breathing as best I could, closed my eyes to mere slits.

"Look!" Wirna said, running forward. She stopped almost on top of me. "A dead bird!"

Gare joined her and they both loomed over me, giants blocking out the sun. I tried not to move, not to breathe, but still they didn't go away. The sun silhouetted them, making them look like shadow cut-outs rather than people. I couldn't help myself; I began to tremble. Against the coolness of the mud and gravel my body seemed ablaze with fever. "What is it, Gare?" Wirna said slowly.

"An eagle?"

"A hawk, stupid. Look, it ain't dead—I can see it breathin'. There! Its eye moved! It's got a busted wing's all. The dumb thing must've flown into a tree or somethin'. Find a rock and we'll put it out of its misery."

I jerked, startled and frightened, trying to get to my feet, trying to get to safety. Somehow, by sheer dint of will, I managed to stand. My side throbbed. I took a half step forward, spreading my wings as best I could, looking as threatening as possible. But pain burned through my thoughts like a branding iron, sharp enough almost to make me pass out again. I tried to talk, but barely managed a feeble cry. Unable to help myself, I sank down onto the riverbank again.

Gare put one foot on a small boulder. "Come on, help me lift it. We'll drop it on him."

"No!" Wirna cried. "I found him, so he's mine! I'm going to take him home."

"Stupid, hawks ain't no good to eat. Cook'd just as soon pluck you."

"I'm going to make him my pet."

My thoughts were collapsing around me, vague relief and gratitude all I could manage. It would have been ironic, in a way, to die at the hands of Gare and Wirna. It would have proved children more deadly than dragons. In pleasanter times I might have laughed at the thought, but now it seemed all too real, all too grim a possibility.

"What do you want a beat-up old hawk for?" Gare said with a slight sneer. "It's not good for nothin', stupid. Papa'll boil you alive if you try to bring it home. It's probably crawlin' with bugs."

"I'm going to call him Dero," Wirna said, "after the hero of Strafferd."

Never heard of him, but thanks. I'd always fancied myself a hero.

As the girl slowly moved forward, holding her skirt like a net to snare me, I fought down my senseless panic and tried to remain calm. Wirna's hands seemed too large, suddenly, her fingers too blunt and blundering. She might crush me by accident and never realize it.

"Careful!" Gare said. "He might peck your eyes out."

"Dero wouldn't do that!"

"He's a hawk, stupid. How's he going to know you're

tryin' to help him?"

I hissed at Gare. He laughed at me.

"Looks like it's tryin' to say somethin'," he said.

Wirna scooped me up in her skirt. "Got him!"

The world swayed as she lifted me higher. Her hands felt surprisingly gentle as she pressed me to her chest. Through her blouse I could feel her pulse, the beat too hard, too fast. Gare had made her nervous with all his talk of lice and my pecking people's eyes out.

Despite her fear, Wirna avoided touching my wounded wing; she certainly seemed more understanding than her brother. There was a kindness in her I liked. It would not go unrewarded.

"Come on," I heard Gare say. "Supper will be cold . . ."

*   *   *

It was a warm room full of good smells—newly baked bread, roasting meat, fresh fruits and vegetables. It had to be the kitchen. I also heard the burr of talking voices, but the words sounded odd, distant, indistinct. They seemed to be discussing me, but I didn't really care; I felt sick and feverish, as near to death as I'd ever been outside of battle. I lay on my side and panted for breath.

At last I felt hands lift me—not Wirna's this time, but larger, stronger hands, hands calloused from work in the fields—then set me down again in a soft pile of cloths. Someone whisked the skirt from over my head, and I could see.

I blinked in confusion. The world swayed this way and that, sliding around me, making me nauseous and dizzy. My wing throbbed. Pressing my eyes shut, I whimpered in pain.

Blackness swept over me like a wave, and I lay there senseless for a time.

* * *

When consciousness returned, I found myself in a tiny wooden cage that stank—of what, I couldn't say. Perhaps it was chicken, perhaps pig. I'd seen similar cages used by farmers bringing livestock to market, so I had little doubt as to my status: I was now definitely a kept animal. A bowl of water and a handful of seeds had been set in one corner. I lay in straw which had been formed into a small nest.

Seeing the water made me realize how thirsty I'd become. When I tried to stand, I found something had been tied around me. When I twisted around a bit I discovered that it was a soft white cloth that smelled sweetly of healing herbs. Someone had spent a good deal of time cleaning and bandaging my wounds.

I moved to the water and drank thirstily. I eyed the seeds, but wasn't hungry enough to try them yet.

"He's awake," I heard Wirna whisper from somewhere over my head. "Papa! He's awake now."

I glanced up. Through a hole between the slats I saw two ice-blue eyes, the bridge of a nose, and a forehead covered with tight curls of pale hair. Her skin was deeply tanned, unwrinkled, and as she bobbed up and down excitedly I saw her cheeks still carried a bit of baby fat. Wirna was even younger than I'd first thought, perhaps seven or eight years old.

"Let's see," her father said, and the door to the cage swung open. He was a tall, broad-shouldered man with hair just going to gray, a firm chin, strong brown eyes. Lines from laughter creased his face; he smiled now, and I saw he was truly kind.

Wirna's father reached in to my cage with hands rough from labor, but gentle with experience. Lifting me, he looked me over briefly, nodded, and set me down on the table.

Slowly I turned and looked left and right, examining the kitchen. There were rows of rough-hewn cabinets, counters loaded with jugs and jars, barrels on the floor. Overhead, the high rafters were hung with bundles of dried fruits and vegetables. There were only two windows, both screened, and several doors, all closed and latched. They'd made sure I couldn't escape before letting me out of my cage. Not that I could have flown away—or even tried to—with my wing bandaged so securely.

Wirna was staring at me, fascinated, along with Gare and their father. I hopped toward them and cocked my head to the side.

"Can I keep him, Papa?" Wirna asked. "He seems tame enough," Papa said slowly. "He probably belongs to some rich noble who lost him during a hunt. I see no reason why you couldn't keep him, at least for now."

"He's pretty," she said, reaching for me. I let her scratch me under the chin. It felt surprisingly good, like a cat must feel when its ears are rubbed. For a second I forgot myself and arched my back, bristling my feathers contentedly.

"Aww, Wirna, leave him alone," Gare said. As Wirna started to draw her hand away, I hopped up onto her wrist, just as I'd seen trained falcons do. Papa would be more likely to give me liberties if I acted like a civilized bird, and this seemed the ideal opportunity to prove myself to him.

"Don't move," Papa told his daughter, who had tensed. Slowly he extended his wrist to me.

I stepped onto it. Wirna grinned happily. Gare just looked at me with jealousy.

Papa nodded once. "Yes, a trained bird. That was a lucky find you made, Wirna, a very lucky find indeed. He'll bring us quite a few pheasant dinners when he's strong enough to fly again."

"May he sleep in my room?" Wirna asked.

"No!" Gare barked. "It oughtta' stay in the barn—"

"Gare," Papa said in a warning tone, "don't yell at your sister."

"But—"

"That's enough! She found him, so he can certainly sleep with her tonight."

"But—"

"And," Papa cut him off to add, "I seem to remember you hadn't finished your chores when you went down to the river. Now . . ."

Gare looked down and scuffed at the floor. "Yes, Papa."

"Thank you," Wirna said, hugging her father.

Papa smiled and ruffled her hair. "It's bedtime now. Run and tell Mama goodnight. I'll put Dero back in his cage."

He lowered his arm to the table, and I stepped off. Though I hated to do it, I went back into my cage. Whistling, Papa slipped the latch and locked me inside for the night.

In a moment Wirna returned. Papa carried me to her room in another part of the house and set me on a table by the window. Through it, in the moonlight, I could see a glistening line of silver that could only be the river. We were on flat land a good day's hike from the foothills. How I longed to leave this farm, to run to the river and follow it back into the mountains.

Wirna's mother, a stout, kind-faced woman who looked much like both her children, entered the room and tucked Wirna in for the night. She sat on the corner of the bed and started to tell one of the old faery tales, about a poor maiden who meets a prince who has been changed into a giant fish by an evil witch.

So much like me. If only she knew.

With that, I slept.

*   *   *

Sunlight woke me. Papa and his family were already moving about outside, at the morning chores. They seemed to have forgotten me. I didn't mind overly much; farmers are not the most interesting companions under the best of circumstances. The time alone let me think of all that had happened.

I settled down unhappily to wait and spent a boring day just looking out the window.

Finally, evening came. Again, Wirna took care of me for the night. I think it had something to do with Gare forgetting to tend to the chickens, but since hawks are seldom privy to the inner workings of family relationships, I couldn't say for sure. I was happy for any excuse to be rid of him.

I stood in my cage, breathing quietly, trying to sleep, when a sharp tingling started in my claws. Was this it? I wondered. Was I changing back into human form? The tingling spread to my legs, my wings. I shifted uneasily.

Then, with a sudden jerk, I stood up, shattering the cage. Little bits of wood rained down around me, striking the carpet with soft jarring noises. To my surprise I felt no pain in my arm—the wound seemed to have vanished with my transformation.

Wirna sat bolt upright in bed, her eyes wide, her sheet clutched protectively up around her throat. She opened her mouth to scream.

I had to keep her quiet, or she'd alarm the whole household. I didn't fancy the idea of trying to explain myself to a mob of angry servants and her father, all out to avenge her honor.

"Hush, sweet child," I whispered hastily. "I am Prince Nikor of Serconia, and your love has freed me from a terrible curse." It was the first thing that came to mind—I remembered the faery tale her mother had told her the night before.

"Really?" she squeaked.

I bowed low before her, as I would have to any noble-born lady. "I am forever in your debt."

"What—what happened to you?" Wirna managed to whisper. She pulled her sheets still higher, covering her mouth and nose. Her eyes were wide with awe.

"An evil witch placed an enchantment on me. She turned me into a hawk until a woman loved me in that form. You are that woman, and you have freed me from the witch's curse. Soon, fair Wirna, my followers will come here, and you and your family will be rewarded for your service to me. But I must ask one more favor of you, slight though it may be."

"Oh, yes!" she breathed. "Anything!"

I smiled. "Do you have any food in the house? I'm starving!"

"I'll call Papa."

"No!" I said. "Pray you, do not disturb your parents or your brother. This must be a secret between us until my followers come. Will you do this for me?"

"Anything!" she said.

Wirna rose and put on a long red dressing gown, then took my hand and led me into the hall. In the next room I could hear her father snoring loudly. Pressing her fingers to her lips, she pulled me to the left, toward the staircase.

I breathed easier when we were finally in the kitchen, away from the sleeping chambers. If we spoke here, we wouldn't wake anyone.

"Momma made cookies," Wirna said. "They're on the counter, in that jar. I can't reach them myself. And there's ale in that jug. Papa says visitors should always get the best ale."

"I need to travel to the city to find my friends," I explained. "I'll need more than cookies and ale. May I take some dried meat with me, and perhaps, if you can spare it, a skin of wine to last through my journey?"

"Of course," she replied, and in a very businesslike manner she went to a storage cabinet and pulled out a large cloth sack. To the sack she added fruit, bread, cheese, and carefully wrapped meat. She seemed to have a rather exaggerated idea as to how much one man could eat in a week. Five could have lasted on what she gave me.

"Won't that much food be missed?" I asked, a bit concerned. I didn't want her getting into trouble.

"Yes, but Cook won't know who took it. She'll think Gare or one of the other servants swiped it."

Still Wirna took more food. I began to have doubts as to whether or not I'd be able to carry it all.

"You are *very* kind," I said, "but surely that's enough?"

I saw a faint blush spread across her cheeks as she found a bit of string and tied up the end of the bag. I patted my pockets, looking for something which I could give her, some token she could treasure.

I found a gold coin. After a moment I remembered where it had come from—I'd taken it in Grayhaven. It seemed suitable that this stolen money should go to Wirna and her family. I pressed it into the child's hand. She looked at it without understanding what it was.

"You must give that to your father tomorrow, when he asks what happened to the hawk. When you do, he won't be angry with you. In fact, he'll be happier than you've seen him in a long time."

"What is it?" she asked, eyes wide.

"A present from me to all of you. After you've given it to your father, tell him what happened tonight. Tell him . . . tell him a poor hawk thanks him for his hospitality and wishes to repay him for all he did to help me in my time of trouble. Will you do that for me?"

"Yes, Prince Nikor." Again she blushed.

I kissed her on the forehead. "You are, without a doubt, the most wonderful child in the world." Hefting the sack, I strode to the door, slipped the latch, and went outside. The night air was cool, fresh; I breathed deeply.

"Good-bye," Wirna called softly.

I waved cheerfully to her. Then, turning, I set off.

In human form, the world seemed a much smaller place; the trees which had seemed so enormous now stood no higher than the *Pamah Reach*'s masts, the river I'd thought a raging torrent was now a swollen, muddy creek.

The moon and stars provided scant light, but I could see that to my left, far beyond the river, far beyond the foothills, loomed the shadowy peaks of the Skyreen Mountains.

Soon, I'll be home on the sea.

*   *   *

I followed the river for the next two days, climbing rocks, pushing through thick tangles of reeds, skirting swampy patches of land. Finally the ground rose, and I found myself in hilly country once more. I passed a series of rapids, then came to a small waterfall that looked familiar.

Surely I couldn't have floated this far downstream; the fierce rapids, the waterfall, the submerged rocks all seemed different when I was in man-form . . . smaller, much less terrifying.

Even so, I figured this had to be the waterfall I'd been looking for, the one I'd fallen into. Turning from the water, I hiked through the trees, toward the huge gray mountains looming directly ahead of me.

It took another day to scramble through the pine forest, and I was cut and bruised from forcing my way through thickets and up small cliffs. The sea was my chosen life, not land, and I found it hard adapting to the ways of a mountain goat. I cursed my fate again and again.

But at last I reached the timberline, above which grew only grass and weeds and a few small, twisted scrub trees. I breathed deeply of the cool, crisp air, then set off once more at a brisk pace.

Late that afternoon, I found what was left of the *Pamah Reach*—burned timbers, burned bodies, the cargo in the hold scattered across half the mountainside.

I wandered through the wreckage, shocked, grieved by what I saw. Here a bit of map stuck on thistles, there tatters of canvas from the sails, and all around were the remains of my men lying twisted on the ground. Everything was utterly, utterly silent; not even the wind blew.

After an hour of searching, I'd found nothing of interest. Save for me—and, I hoped, Ool—there were no survivors. I sat in the wreckage and wept for those I'd lost.

Toward evening, as the sun began to settle to the west, I heard a strange, high-pitched whistling sound. I was on my feet in an instant, straining to hear. The noise seemed to be getting louder.

I dove for cover, afraid the dragon might be returning. I belly-crawled under a section of the hull and lay there, hardly daring to breathe.

As I watched, a huge silver ball materialized and hovered in mid-air, shimmering brightly, like the sun. It moved through the wreckage, stopping here and there over a body or a particularly large piece of deck or hull as though examining it in detail.

I didn't like the thing; it stank of dark magic. Its mere presence made me distinctly nervous—someone was taking interest in the carcass of the *Pamah Reach*. Ool? I didn't know, but I had no intention of taking any chances.

I still had some of the food Wirna had given me, and I munched on a piece of cheese and drank water from the skin as I waited, hiding under the wreckage.

At last the whistling noise faded away, and the silver ball vanished.

Suppose my suspicions were right and some wizard other than Ool controlled the magical sphere? Could that someone also be responsible for the dragon attack? It made sense. Dragons did not live in these parts. They were rumored to roam the far north, thousands of miles away. But who could control a dragon? I'd never heard of anyone—wizard or not—who had such power.

Whoever sent the dragon also sent the silver ball, and now that he'd seen the destruction, I doubted he'd spy on the *Pamah Reach* again. I'd be free to bury my men and take what I could find from the wreckage.

After locating a shovel, I began digging a mass grave. And, as I worked, I plotted my revenge.

EIGHT

Alna Savina suspected a trap. She had developed an instinct for that sort of thing, an instinct finely honed from years of dealing with treachery and deceit. Some of the treachery and deceit had been other than her own.

Now, as she studied the three warships disguised as traders in her harbor, she knew with uncanny certainty that the attack would come soon, perhaps that night.

Even dead Fel Blackmane haunts me, she thought. Before he'd come, no one would have dared attack Bar Altibb. This would be the third attack in the last six months. She cursed Blackmane's ghost, wherever it roamed.

"Lady?" one of her servants called from the doorway.

"What is it?"

"The wizard Karnekash is outside. He wishes to see you."

"Very well. Show him in." With a sigh, she turned away from the balcony. She didn't feel like playing games today. She would hear whatever Karnekash had to say, then get rid of him as quickly as possible.

A moment later the wizard entered the room. As before he wore robes of red, and a small yellow-green dragon, scarcely a hand's width from wingtip to wingtip, perched on his shoulder.

He bowed slightly. "Lady."

"I assume you've come about the final payment," she said. "Remember, you are to have it only after I receive proof of Blackmane's death."

"I have proof."

"Oh?" She stepped closer, eager to see it for herself. "What is it? Show me!"

Karnekash drew a small, intricately scrimshawed ivory box from some hidden pocket and handed it to her. "Look inside," he said softly.

Alna Savina threw back the lid. The box was empty. "There's nothing here!" she said, frowning. "What is this, some trick?"

"Keep looking, my beautiful Lady Savina, keep looking. It takes a moment for the magic to work."

Once more she looked. After a moment the bottom seemed to recede into infinity. Slowly the whiteness grew clear as glass and she gazed down through a tiny window onto a rugged mountain scene. Her view moved, soaring birdlike over the ground.

"Blackmane used sorcery to fly his ship to and from Grayhaven Fair," Karnekash explained. "One of my pets caught up with him over the Skyreen Mountains. It is not a pretty sight, the ruination. But I know you have gazed upon far, far worse."

Alna Savina saw *Pamah Reach* now, how it had been smashed on the mountain like a fragile piece of glass. The masts had shattered like toothpicks, the deck and hull had been charred almost beyond recognition, and the hold's contents lay scattered across the ground for a hundred yards in all directions.

And bodies lay everywhere. She could not help but smile. Yes, this was the fate she had wished on Blackmane and his men, for any fool who coveted Bar Altibb. No one who sought to humiliate her or plunder her treasure.

The device lingered over every charred and blackened body. Each man had been burned beyond recognition. If Fel Blackmane lay among them, she could not hope to identify him. Without any way to identify the pirate, the wizard had no proof he'd done his job. She frowned. A tricky problem . . .

She looked up. "Which one," she asked, "is Blackmane's body?"

Karnekash frowned. "How would I know? I've never seen him before."

"All I see here are faceless corpses. How do I know this was the right ship? How do I know he's among the bodies? Our agreement was clear—no payment until I have proof Blackmane is dead. I won't know until I have seen it for myself. I want to see his body."

"He is dead," the wizard said firmly. "I have no doubt about that, and neither do you."

"I have every doubt!" she said. "Blackmane lives a charmed life—one could almost say the gods look after him. If anyone could survive such a disaster, it would be him. And, beyond that, how do I even know he was aboard his ship when you destroyed it? No, Karnekash, this is not proof. You know it as well as I do."

She flung the box at him. He caught it easily and tucked it into his sleeve.

The wizard's eyes narrowed. At last he nodded. "I will return later today," he said. "Have the other half of my payment ready."

"Of course," Alna Savina said, "if you have proof I will

gladly pay. Have I ever given you reason to doubt my word?"

She laughed to herself as the wizard stalked from the room, red robes fluttering. The dragon on his shoulder threw back its head and hissed at her, its emerald eyes flashing.

*   *   *

As the day wore on, she almost forgot about Karnekash. Word reached her of yet another plot to seize Bar Altibb. It would come at dusk.

At the appointed time, she stood on a balcony and gazed down at the harbor below, where one hundred and fifty men, dressed as rich merchants, rowed ashore from three Pavanian ships. Her spies had been thorough; she knew how every detail of their plan.

Sixty feet below her, inside the fortress battlements and out of sight of the sea, crouched a hundred archers with bows. She waved down to Larran, the bowmen's commander, a dour-faced old man who had served her almost as long as she could remember. He gestured back impatiently.

By her orders, the harbor area had been left all but deserted; there were almost no guards in sight. She wanted the invaders to grow confident and reckless. As soon as they revealed their true intentions, they would be overpowered.

At a subtle command from Larran, who was the sole man visibly patrolling on the battlements, a small band of lightly armored guards began making their rounds along the docks, checking each tavern for trouble, talking to each shopkeeper, generally acting as though today were a day like any other.

The first few boats reached the dock and tied up. Richly dressed men swarmed onto the pier by the dozens. The fading light of the sun glinted off of half-concealed swords.

"Hurry up," she whispered. She wanted the bloodshed over quickly, efficiently, and brutally.

Though they could not possibly have heard her, the patrol marched out onto the pier toward the newcomers. Alna Savina knew the plan: "Hold!" they would be saying now. "In the name of Alna Savina, Countess of Fleurin, identify yourselves!"

After the challenge, things happened almost too quickly for her to follow. In the growing-darkness, the hundred and fifty-odd men drew swords and rushed the patrol with fierce war cries. Her guardsmen quickly dropped their weapons and jumped off the pier into the harbor as they'd been instructed to do.

"Now!" shouted Larran from the battlements. The bowmen leaped to their stations, notched arrows, and began to fire at will.

Breathless, Alna Savina leaned over the railing to watch. The men below began to fall. More arrows hissed down at them. Screams of the dead and dying rose to her ears, as sweet as the sound of birds, more satisfying than the laughter of children. The screams meant her lands and possessions would be safe for a while longer. The screams meant one more threat to Bar Altibb had been eliminated.

"Enjoying the slaughter?" a low voice said from close behind her.

Startled, she whirled about. Karnekash stood there, arms folded. He should not have been there. How had he gotten into her private rooms unannounced?

"Caneel! Ril!" she called. Where were her bodyguards?

"They are too busy choking to death to answer," the wizard said. A trace of a smile flitted across his face. "I have come for my gold. Pay me what you owe, my beautiful Alna Savina, or you will join your bodyguards."

"Caneel!" she cried again, pushing past Karnekash into the next chamber. Both her bodyguards lay near the door, their faces blue-black, tongues protruding, expressions of terror and pain frozen in place. Around their necks coiled small serpents with vestigial wings. The serpents hissed at her, and she drew back with alarm, one hand rising to her own throat.

"No . . ." she whispered.

"I am in something of a hurry, my darling Lady Savina. I told you to have the rest of my payment ready. Since I am not known for my patience, I trust you have obliged?"

"You have given me no proof that the job was done," Alna Savina gasped.

"Must I kill you as well? That would be unfortunate . . . but it can be arranged, as you must realize."

"Guards!" she screamed.

"They can't hear you any more." Karnekash stretched out his arm, revealing a serpent coiled around his wrist. He moved steadily toward her.

"Perhaps we could compromise," she said hastily, retreating toward the door. "I am not an unreasonable woman."

"Oh? And what sort of compromise do you suggest?"

"A year's wait. I know Fel Blackmane; if he *is* alive, he won't remain hidden for long. He will be back at sea with a new ship and a new crew, looting and killing. If he is alive," she repeated, "we will know soon enough. I should think that you, as a wizard, would wish to protect your own reputation."

"Indeed," said Karnekash. He stroked his chin thoughtfully.

"You offered me a guarantee," Alna Savina said. "If Fel Blackmane is still alive, then you must kill him as you promised—and give me proof of the deed. Return in a year, and the second half of the money is yours."

"Very well," Karnekash said. "I am not unreasonable. I agree to your conditions—but I add one of my own."

"What's that?"

"If Blackmane does not reappear in the space of one year, you will double my payment."

"What?" she cried.

The wizard smiled. "Let me finish, my beautiful Alna Savina. If Blackmane does not reappear, you will *double* my payment. But if he does turn up again—as you seem to think he will—I will kill him and accept what you have already given me as payment in full for my services."

"You have a bargain," Alna Savina said.

The next time you come, I will see you dead, she thought, turning to look at Caneel and Ril's bodies. She would miss them. They had been more than mere employees to her—they had been . . . *almost* . . . friends.

Karnekash backed from the room, bowed, then said, "I will return in one year." With a bow, he stalked down the hall.

Alna Savina went back onto her balcony to watch her bowmen slaughter the few remaining men from the warships. It had been a terrible day, a terrible, terrible day. Not even the bloodbath below could cheer her up.

NINE

After I finished burying my crew, I wandered from the *Pamah Reach* to a secluded place by the river. I felt odd, immensely old, and tired beyond my years. The knowledge that I was responsible for the deaths of so many of +my comrades depressed me beyond measure.

"Fell" I heard a distant voice calling. "Fel Blackmane, where are you?"

I jolted to my feet, suddenly alert. Who could be calling my name? A scouting party from Grayhaven, come to steal what was left of my ship and bear it back to their city as a macabre trophy?

Taking to cover, I crept back toward the wreckage. I drew a dull carving knife I'd salvaged and held it ready to defend myself as I slowly peered around the edge of an enormous boulder.

"There you are," said a familiar voice from overhead.

I glanced up and found my wizard first mate standing on top of the rock. Grinning happily, robes fluttering,

Ool hopped down.

Weary, I told him all that had happened, how as a hawk I'd been struck and wounded by a bit of wood, how I'd been washed downstream and almost killed by Gare and saved by Wirna, and how she'd helped me escape from her father's farm.

"But enough about me," I finished quickly. "What happened after I left?"

"I, too, drank the potion and was transformed into a

hawk," Ool said. "After flying away from the ship, I could do naught but sit in a tree and watch the dragon kill everyone else." He shuddered a bit at the memory. "It was a terrible slaughter."

"Were there no other survivors?"

"None. The fortunate ones died in the crash. The dragon burned the rest. After that, the monster spent half a day rooting through the wreckage, eating the gold and silver and whatever valuables it could find."

"Eating them?" I said in surprise. "Why—"

"Dragons can't carry treasure," Ool said. "They eat it, then regurgitate it in their lairs, like cows chewing their cud."

I shook my head. "I've never heard that before."

"How often are people alive to see dragons carting off treasure?"

I conceded the point. "I lost everything in the *Pamah Reach*. Damn Grayhaven's Council!"

"What?" Ool asked, puzzled. "The dragon didn't come from Grayhaven. It came from Fleurin."

I stared at him. "How do you know?"

"It had a short message painted on one wing, a few gloating lines about how Alna Savina always avenges herself on those who steal from her."

"No!"

"Oh, yes, it was her doing."

I had a sick feeling inside. I saw it all now: the pettiness of the Countess of Fleurin, obsessed with her lands and her money and her fading beauty.

I felt her revenge more sharply than she ever would have

guessed. She'd succeeded all too well, accidentally using my own strategy for making people suffer. Rather than killing me, she'd taken away that which I loved most: my ship and my crew. I cursed her for it.

"Buck up," Ool said, sounding, as always, unbearably cheerful. "You're alive, and as long as you are, it will be business as usual. This is but a momentary setback."

"I'm ruined!"

"Nonsense."

"But don't you see?" I cried. "Without my crew, without my ship, how can I hope to continue?"

"You always said you could steal another ship."

"And who would sail her?" I asked bitterly. "All the men who are loyal to me are dead."

"There are ways to get a crew," he said. "Why not take someone else's?"

"Why not? I'll tell you why not. Because I hand-pick my men. It took me five years to get the crew of the *Pamah Reach* together, and they were the best and the bravest in all the Seren Sea. No others would come even close."

"But it would be a fresh beginning," he said. "Think of the challenge . . . consider the possibilities . . . Or are you growing too old for a young man's sport?"

Ool knew how to tempt my pride. Could I begin anew? Could I start with a new crew and all the plans and adventures I hadn't yet dared? There was something immensely appealing about the idea. With everyone believing me dead, the navies of the world would give up searching for me; I could take risks as I'd never dared before.

Slowly I began to nod. "It might be for the best after all. I could shave off my beard, take on a new name. No one would ever know me." I smiled as I began to think of revenge. "I'm going to take over Fleurin again," I said, "And this time Alna Savina won't get off so lightly."

"But why disguise yourself? If you attack Bar Altibb, surely you want Alna Savina to know you're responsible."

"If Alna Savina wants me dead so badly that she arranged for a wizard to stalk and kill me, she's going to try again when she finds out I'm still alive. It'll take a long time to plan an attack against her that will succeed. I'd rather not have her assassins chasing after me in the meantime. And there are other advantages. Yes, it's best if I go into hiding . . . at least for now."

"Where do we start?" Ool asked promptly.

"Zorvoon."

"Aldenius Frago!" he said, as though he'd been reading my thoughts.

We grinned at each other. I knew my old master, my old mentor, would help me. He was someone I could trust.

"Help me gather some of my belongings from the wreckage," I said, "and then we'll set off. We have a long trip ahead."

TEN

There is an old saying in Fleurin: Fear keeps a king alive. Paranoia had kept Alna Savina alive through countless assassination attempts and innumerable failed rebellions. The slightest trace of doubt was enough to set her mind in motion, and since Karnekash had left the week before, she had been thinking quite a lot. Mostly her thoughts concerned the wizard and what he had done to Caneel and Ril.

Glancing at her new bodyguards, four of them this time, all trained Sethian assassins hired from the Assassins Guild, she began to smile. Next time Karnekash called on her, she'd be prepared.

She had also been thinking, worrying really, about Fel Blackmane. Her own words came back to haunt her: she *hadn't* been able to identify his body among the debris of his ship, among the corpses of the crew. Blackmane *had* lived an almost blessed life. What if he'd escaped?

Despite all of Karnekash's assurances, she began to wonder if perhaps Blackmane was still alive. If he knew she'd sent the dragon, he would swear vengeance against her.

She remembered his kiss once more, how passionate he had seemed. His ready smile, his quick wit, his fingers brushing her cheek in a gentle caress—had all that been a mockery of her? Had it all been an act? She recalled how her body had tingled at his embrace, how she had felt like a young girl again in his arms.

No, she told herself, *he must have loved me.* He must have! *But what if . . . ?*

Suppositions had kept her alive through twenty years of rule; she always tried to anticipate the possibilities. She had to know for certain whether Blackmane still lived. There was a madwoman, a fiend with the eyes of a cat, some said, who lived in a cave at the far end of Fleurin. Some of the nobles in Alna Savina's court went there on weekly pilgrimages to hear prophecies. Perhaps this madwoman could determine Fel Blackmane's fate.

Suddenly decided, Alna Savina gathered her robes around her and stood. "Prepare my coach," she said to one of her attendants. "I will hear the madwoman prophesize today."

Her four new bodyguards slipped quietly and efficiently into position around her. Praemir, their leader, whispered in her ear. "I advise you not to leave Bar Altibb, Lady Savina. It will be easier to keep you safe here. On the roads . . ." He shrugged.

She turned to him, haughty and imperial. "I hide from no one. The world must know that."

He bowed. "As you wish."

*   *   *

Five hours later, a train of twenty golden carriages, each pulled by matching teams of white stallions, headed north through Bar Altibb, toward the rich farmlands of Fleurin, toward the tall mountains in the distance. The Countess of Fleurin knew it had been too long since she'd made a public appearance.

Peasants lined the city's cobbled streets to shout her name and cheer; though she thought they overdid it, she was pleased, and smiled and waved to them. Already she felt better;

escaping the politics and intrigue of court life, even for a short time, would do her good.

The procession left the city and passed into the flat, fertile farmlands where most of the kingdom's food was grown. Looking out the window, Alna Savina saw a checkered pattern of green and yellow, marking the fields of wheat and rye; further away stood apple and peach orchards, the trees in neat rows like soldiers in formation. The moist smell of humus and growing things was sweeter than her finest perfume. From all signs there would be a record crop this year.

Houses and barns, some large and rambling, some small and neatly whitewashed, stood among the fields like lonely sentinels. Smoke rose from chimneys. Raising their hands in salute, shouting her name effusively, workers in the fields stopped their toil as she rode past. They had better!

Fleurin looked well and prosperous, she decided, and the people content. Kept apart from the machinations of state, they were secure from all the intrigue of court life. They did not have to worry about anything except devoting their lives to her well-being. Satisfied with the way of things, she leaned back and closed her eyes.

When next she looked up, it had grown dark outside, and the fields had given way to rocky hills. The madwoman's cave was not far from here, she knew.

A few minutes later the drivers began calling to one another and the procession slowed. Abruptly, a coachman opened her carriage door and helped her down. Praemir and the other three bodyguards already stood beside her door. Beyond them, milling about like sheep, were all her ladies-in-waiting, several dozen minor nobles, a visiting prince from Serconia, a pair of bards who were the court's current favorites, and a couple of others whose faces were vaguely familiar but whom she could not quite place. The babble of excited voices was loud and oppressively cheerful.

Alna Savina stepped forward. As though drawn by a magnet, the people began to move toward her In eddies and swirls. A moment later they had surrounded her.

"Where is the cave?" she asked, trying to sound light-hearted.

"A little bit of a walk up the path to your right, Lady," said one of her ladies-in-waiting, Pinia Pompora, chief among the court gossips. "The cave is a perfectly *ghastly* hole. You won't be able to believe a person actually lives there."

"We shall see." Smiling tolerantly, Alna Savina turned and saw the path, little more than a goat-trail, which led up a hill and seemed to vanish over the top. "Go first and see that it's safe," she whispered to Praemir.

He nodded. "Yes, Lady." After edging his way through the giggling throng, Praemir drew a knife from his belt and proceeded up the hill and out of sight.

Servants were setting up a large canopy and laying out chairs and tables. Trays of sweetmeats circulated, and everyone gathered to joke and laugh and tell the shallow sort of stories such occasions always demanded. Alna Savina made light of her trip and listened to one of the bards sing a few satirical verses he had composed especially for the occasion; all the while she kept an eye out for Praemir. Minutes later, he reappeared atop the hill and motioned to her that it was safe to proceed.

"Wait for me," she said to the others, then, with her three remaining bodyguards, she started up the hill. She let them help her over the path's rough spots, and in a few moments she stood beside Praemir.

"There is a child playing in front of the cave, and an old woman spinning yarn inside." His voice held a note of disgust. "Neither looks at all like a prophet."

"We shall soon see," Alna Savina said. "Lead the way."

Praemir turned to the left and marched forward. She followed close behind.

The trail led down into a steep ravine, and from there, the path curved to the left, around the edge of the cliff.

"How much farther?" Alna Savina asked a bit petulantly. She wasn't used to such exertion and was already feeling the strain.

"Not far," said Praemir. "Another hundred feet."

"Wait here, then," she instructed. "I want to see the madwoman by myself."

"Lady—"

Alna Savina turned to him. "You said it was safe, did you not?"

Praemir sighed. "Yes. As you wish, Lady. You are in charge."

"And don't you forget that." Taking a deep breath, she pressed on.

Soon she came to a dark opening in one side of the ravine. A child, a girl of perhaps thirteen, sat outside and played a complicated game with colored pebbles. Alna Savina watched her for a moment, then stepped forward.

The girl looked up. Her eyes were yellow and had slit pupils, like a cat's. Alna Savina shifted uneasily beneath the child's strange gaze.

"Do you know who I am?" Alna Savina asked.

"I know why you have come," the girl said at last. "The prophet told me you would be here today. She did not have to tell me your name—that I knew, for I share her gift in some small measure. Wait here, Lady. I will get her."

"Thank you," Alna Savina said.

Rising, the girl set aside her colored stones, and brushed the dirt from her clothes, then went into the cave. A moment later she returned, leading an old woman by the hand. Half blind and feeble, skin the color of clay, white hair in a wild tangle, she looked every bit a madwoman.

"I am told you already know why I have come," the Countess of Fleurin said softly.

The old woman smiled, showing toothless yellow gums. Slowly her eyes opened; they were covered with a thin white film, but behind the white Alna Savina could see that she, too, had cat's eyes. "Yes," she said, and then she gave a cackle of laughter that made Alna's skin crawl. "Yes, yes, yes!"

"Tell me then—is Fel Blackmane dead?"

"Fel Blackmane is no more; he thinks of you yet." She paused. The old woman lisped. "His strength is on the wane as the moon but will swell in the belly of the world to be born anew. In one year a dead man shall rise. He shall come to your wedding." Then, she was silent.

"I don't understand," Alna Savina said, distraught. "Will

you say no more?"

The blind woman shook her head. "There is nothing else for you this day, my Lady."

Fel Blackmane is no more. That was certainly an answer to her question. But 'He thinks of you yet'—what did that mean? Was his ghost plotting against her?

And how would a dead man come to her wedding? What wedding? No suitor had sought her hand in over five years.

More bewildered than ever, Alna Savina pressed a gold coin into the old woman's calloused hands. "Thank you," she said in a subdued tone. "I shall consider your prophecy carefully." With that she turned and headed back toward her caravan. The others were waiting to see the prophet, she knew, and she felt uncomfortable without her bodyguards.

From behind her came the old woman's cackling laugh.

ELEVEN

The room was dark and shadowy, full of strange devices whose purposes I could only begin to guess at. Some were mechanical models of strange animals which whirled and clicked and moved all by themselves, others were collections of tubes and bottles which bubbled and made little popping noises. On the ceiling was painted a map of the heavens with the constellations and zodiacal symbols.

We had come posing as wine merchants. Ool and I, to the house of Malmortu, Seer Extraordinaire. It was our first day in Zorvoon, and I wanted to learn the name of the wizard who worked for Alna Savina.

A month had passed since the *Pamah Reach*'s destruction. We'd journeyed through the Skyveen Mountains to the Seren Sea, then along the coast to the city of Calachi. There we found passage to Zorvoon by working as crewmen on a freighter.

I had shaved off my beard, cut my long black hair, and adopted Serconian-style clothes: plain white breeches, a gray linen shirt, and leather sandals that laced almost up to my knees. And I had learned to answer to my new name, Dray Sorrel. Thus disguised, I had come to the Seer.

Suddenly a white hot light flared before us. I blinked and shielded my eyes, unable to see. Beside me, Ool chuckled in amusement; he had obviously been expecting something of the sort.

"You could have warned me!" I whispered to him.

"But that would have taken all the surprise out of

Malmortu's entrance," he whispered back. "You know I would not dream of interfering."

I growled back a reply.

When the light died down, a man dressed in rich blue robes stood behind the table in the center of the room. The palms of his hands rested on a crystal ball.

"Good evening," he said in an unnaturally deep voice. He stroked the crystal ball with his fingers, and it began to glow with a pale yellow light. "I am Malmortu, Seer to the noble-born. Please, gentlemen, I bid you be seated. Together we shall plumb the mysteries of the universe."

I glanced over at my first mate; he looked very solemn and wouldn't meet my gaze. I knew he was having trouble keeping a straight face. Malmortu's bad theatrics might have struck me as amusing, too, under different circumstances, but now I needed information I felt certain he could provide. He was said to know all the gossip about magic-users in the lands bordering the Seren Sea, and it would be worth almost anything to me to learn what he knew.

Humoring the man, I sat in one of the uncomfortable wooden chairs that had also materialized. Beside me, Ool did the same.

"Thank you for seeing us on such short notice," I said.

"It was . . . nothing. I know how merchants are often in a hurry to gain rivals' trade secrets, and I make myself available accordingly. Now, what is it you wish?"

"There was a pirate, Fel Blackmane by name, who was killed recently by a dragon. He robbed several of my ships. I wish to know the name of the wizard responsible so that I may reward him as he richly deserves."

Malmortu sighed. "Is that all? You must have been at sea quite a while not to hear of it. The whole world is talking about Blackmane's most horrible demise. The Countess of Fleurin is behind it. She pledged fifty thousand ounces of gold to hire a wizard."

I leaned forward, intent. "And what was that wizard's name?"

"I don't know. I don't think anybody does. He calls himself the 'Master of Dragons,' or some such nonsense. Killing Blackmane made his reputation. I hear the King of Almanthia has already engaged his services to kill some of his . . . shall we say . . . former friends and allies in neighboring countries, if you know what I mean."

"So this Master of Dragons is in Almanthia?" I asked. "Look into your crystal ball. Make certain he's there!"

The Seer gave me a strange look, and I realized I'd let my anger show itself. Despite this, he obeyed. A paying customer was, after all, a paying customer. He gazed into his crystal once more, stroking it softly with his fingertips, whispering words in the lilting tongue of magic.

A glowing gray mist swirled inside the crystal ball. I glimpsed faces, strange cities, impossible designs. My head swam; I had trouble focusing my eyes. At last a clear image appeared: a man's face, old and weatherworn, with thick black eyebrows and hair just going to gray. The Master of Dragons! He seemed to be sitting in some nobleman's garden, for around him were sculpted bushes and flowerbeds and golden statues of the gods.

Behind the wizard thrust the proud buildings of a city. I saw gleaming white towers, fluted columns, arched doorways, and windows filled with multi-colored glass. And far on a distant mountain crouched a huge, sprawling, magnificent palace built all of white marble: its King had sent his navy after me more times than I could count. Almanthia.

Rising, I thanked the Seer warmly for his help.

"It was . . . nothing," he said with a grand gesture. "I am always eager to serve such as you. Do recommend me to your friends, won't you?"

"Certainly," I said.

He smiled. As he made a quick motion with one hand, a flash of blinding light came from where he was sitting. When I could see again, he was gone.

A door behind us had opened. The Seer's manservant stood there, silhouetted in the doorway.

"Follow me," he said.

*   *   *

I pondered Almanthia as Ool and I sipped wine in a small, pleasant tavern near the docks. Almanthia lay halfway across the world, at the far edge of the Seren Sea, hundreds of miles beyond Fleurin. It was just my luck the wizard who'd sent the dragon had gone there. The trip would take two months by ship.

"Fel," Ool said softly.

I glared at him. "It's Dray now," I whispered fiercely, "and don't forget it again. A slip like that could cost me my life!"

He laughed. "Oh, you will endanger your life without any assistance from me."

I had to laugh as well. "I'm an impatient man. I want everything at once. But it looks like this Master of Dragons is going to have to wait until we have a ship once more."

"You'll have one soon enough."

"Then you have more confidence in Frago than I do."

Ool smiled knowingly. "He'll back you. He knows he can count on you. You'll see soon enough, in the morning when we visit him."

"I can't wait that long—I've got to know now!" I stood. "Let's call on him tonight, sound him out."

"All right." He stood, too, then raised his goblet in one last toast. "To your impatience!" Ool downed his drink with gusto.

"Let's go."

A couple of drunken sailors lounged in the doorway, mugs of hot, spiced ale in their hands. As I pushed my way between them, one of them bumped into me, and I felt a clumsy attempt to pick my pocket. Without looking, I reached down and back, grabbing the man's wrist, then twisted and yanked it as hard as I could.

With a startled shout, the fellow stumbled through the doorway and into the street. I leaped forward and kicked his legs out from under him. He fell heavily, facedown, and an instant later I was kneeling in the small of his back, pressing his face into the gutter's dirt.

"It's not nice to pick pockets," I said. I drew his knife and slit his purse strings, then tucked his heavy wallet into my shirt. Releasing him, I stood.

The sailor's two companions were staring at me from the

doorway. Too much wine had slowed their thoughts; they had-n't had time to react. Now, though, all that I'd done sank in. I saw the anger in their eyes. They drew their knives and charged me, growling like animals.

"Ool!" I shouted.

"Yes, Dray?" he called.

"Do something!"

I heard him laughing. "What do you suggest?"

And then the sailors were on me. Fortunately, one hung back, and the fellow who attacked first was well on his way to being falling-down drunk; his swings went wide of target or were so clumsy and obvious that I avoided them with ease. I feinted, then kicked the knife from his hand. Stepping close, I punched him as hard as I could in the stomach, and when he doubled over in surprise, I hit him again. He collapsed half atop his friend, the would-be pickpocket, wheezing and gasp-ing for breath.

The other man, the one who'd stayed out of the fight, studied me shrewdly. He sheathed his knife and retreated a step toward Ool, who watched us both with an amused smile on his face. "You don't need me," Ool said finally. "You're do-ing fine!"

I grumbled a bit but felt pleased with myself. I hadn't lost my touch.

"Who are you?" the one remaining sailor demanded. "You fight like a pirate I once knew."

"So?" I asked guardedly, studying him. Even allowing for the dirt and bristle on his face I didn't recognize him. Had he been a crewman once?

"You ever sail with Blackmane?" he asked.

"Blackmane's dead."

"Maybe you used to know him, huh?"

I shrugged. "I sailed with Fel Blackmane, and he was the finest captain I ever knew." It wasn't a lie—I was the finest. Humility had always been the greatest of my many virtues.

Grinning, the sailor stepped forward and offered me his hand. I shook it cautiously.

"Why didn't you say so, brother?" He laughed. "We had you pegged as merchants, you and your friend, both out slumming. Never would've bothered you if we'd known you'd sailed with Blackmane."

"What's your name?" Ool asked him.

"Graff," he said. "And yours?"

"I'm Captain Dray Sorrel," I said, "and that's my first mate, Ool."

"What's your ship?" asked Graff.

"I don't have one at the moment—we lost her three months ago on the Shark Reefs. I'm in Zorvoon to get a new one."

He made sympathetic noises. "Tricky, those reefs, if you don't know what you're doing. Many a time I've been through there myself, and I didn't like it, not a bit. Still, it's nothing compared to navigating the Muju Islands without a chart, like I did a couple of years ago . . ."

"Oh?" He was obviously a braggart. I motioned to Ool and started up the street. Unfortunately, Graff followed us. His companions, drunk or unconscious, were left behind in a heap.

"I'm a good man in a fight, Captain," Graff persisted. "How about hiring me? I'm the best navigator ever to sail the Seren Sea."

"I don't have a ship yet," I reminded him. "I haven't any business hiring people yet. Can't afford it."

That made him pause. I could tell he was considering things carefully. "I'll stick with you anyway," he said at last. "I have a feeling about you, and I've always been one to follow my instincts. You're a born pirate, like the great Fel Blackmane. I can see it in you."

I laughed. "Me—like Blackmane? Come, now, what flattery!"

"It's true!" he insisted. "When you hit Clattie back there, I could have sworn I was watching Blackmane all over again."

"You knew him, then?" Ool asked.

"Sure." The sailor stuck out his chest. "Me and Fel, we went way back. I saved his life once, you know."

"Really?" I asked dryly.

"Oh, sure," he said, launching into one of the most improbable tales of daring and adventure I'd ever heard. It was almost as wild as some of the things I'd actually done. Unfortunately, none of it was true.

But I took a liking to Graff as he'd talked. Perhaps it was his boldness, or perhaps his self-important style of storytelling. Anyway, it seemed to me that I could use a man who knew the locals; I'd been away from Zorvoon for too long. If he had a tenth of the talents of which he boasted, he would make a fine navigator.

"Can you read and write?" I asked.

"Certainly!" Graff said. He produced a small book from his pocket and proceeded to read from it.

"That's enough," I said after a few minutes. It was bad verse, and he read it with an almost painful seriousness. "Where did you learn to read?"

"My mother was noble-born. She was captured on a raid and sold into slavery. Eventually she ended up in a tavern, and there I was born. She taught me letters and counting and almost everything else I know."

"Counting?" Numbers were something I'd never mastered; the intricacies of cargo manifests and shipping orders were a riddle to me. I could certainly use someone like Graff to help tally my plunder.

I glanced at Ool, curious as to his opinion. My first mate nodded slightly.

"Very well," I told Graff. We had our first man. "You're hired."

*   *   *

It took half an hour to walk to Aldenius Frago's palatial home in the better part of Zorvoon. We stopped before the wide marble steps, and I studied the place with a critical eye. It seemed little changed since I'd last been there, but I knew the guards would be in new locations. I wouldn't be able to barge in as Dray Sorrel and expect to see him—I'd be thrown out at once. There was bound to be a fight, or at least a scuffle. Ool and I could probably handle it ourselves, but a third hand wouldn't hurt, and it would give me a chance to see Graff in action.

I stepped up close and, scowling, stared Graff in the eye.

"You're coming in with us. Whatever you see or hear, keep your mouth shut. If you mention anything about what happens to anyone—anyone—I'll gut you. Understand?"

My words were hard and cold, deadly cold. I'd practiced that tone of voice for long hours.

Graff paled and began to tremble. "Y-yes!" he said.

I could see he understood well enough and would obey. Turning, I leaped up the steps three at a time. I tried the door's handle and found it locked, then pulled the caller's knob. A bell jingled somewhere inside.

Ool moved up beside me. I heard him whisper something and glanced over at him. His eyes were closed; his lips moved slowly, mouthing a few magic words. A pale blue light shimmered around his head for a second.

"There are ten guards on this floor," he said abruptly. "I see three in the back room. One will be standing behind the door when it opens. There's one more in the kitchens—"

He fell silent suddenly as the door opened a crack and a tall, dignified, white-haired man dressed all in pale blue looked out.

"Yes?" he said.

"Good evening," I said in my most cultured tones. "I have come to see Aldenius Frago."

He looked doubtful. "Do you have an appointment?"

"He will see me."

"Who should I say is calling?"

"His adopted son."

The servant frowned and looked me over more closely. I knew what he was thinking: Frago had never mentioned a son, adopted or otherwise.

"I think you had better leave, sir," he said. "Come back tomorrow, and I'll see about an appointment. Perhaps later this year, in the winter, the master might—"

Ool cried, "No. Fel, it's a trap—"

But I was already hurtling forward, throwing all my weight against the door. It flew open with the sound of splintering wood, striking the guard who had taken up a position behind it. The servant opened his mouth to shout for help, but as he did so Ool muttered several short, sharp words. The inside of the servant's mouth flickered with blue and yellow light. He screamed, but instead of words, bubbles came out, large pink bubbles covered with an oily sheen. One by one they popped around the old man's head, and as they did, I heard faint whispers of sound: "Help. Guards. To arms. Thieves have—"

A muffled groan came from the guard as I continued to press him between the wall and the door. I heard ribs crack, and a second later a shortsword clattered to the floor. I scooped it up.

Slowly I let the door swing open. Slowly the guard slipped out. He sprawled, unconscious, across the floor.

The servant had given up trying to speak; the air around him was full of oily pink bubbles. As they broke I heard Ool, and all wizards, called things that shouldn't have been in a dutiful servant's vocabulary.

"Calm down," I said. "We're not going to hurt you. Isn't that right, Graff?"

"Who, me?" Graff had been standing in the doorway,

somewhat agog over what had happened. "Whatever you say, Captain." He shut the door behind him and stooped to make sure the guard was unconscious.

"Is Frago upstairs?" I demanded of the servant. "I've come to pay him a social call."

A loud, echoing voice came from somewhere above and to my right: "No, I am not upstairs. And kindly release Deele or my guards will pin you to the wall with crossbow bolts."

It was then that I noticed the tiny slots set at regular intervals around the entryway's ceiling. Through the slots I could see the sharp metal tips of crossbow bolts aimed at Graff, Ool, and me. I swallowed. This was something new since last I'd been in my old master's home.

"I tried to warn you," Ool said with a sigh.

I released Deele and made a show of brushing the dust from his shoulders. Then, smiling, I dropped my sword and raised my hands. I motioned for my first mate and navigator to do the same.

"Come on out, Captain Frago," I said. "Take a good look at me and see if you don't know who I am."

"He sailed with Fel Blackmane!" Graff called.

I glared at him. "Shut up! I'll take care of this."

"Come into the next room—*slowly!*—and we'll talk," Frago ordered. "If you're lying . . ."

A high arched doorway led into the next room, which turned out to be a small antechamber with long wooden benches and hooks along the walls for cloaks and hats. I stood there patiently. A moment later a small door opened and Captain Aldenius Frago swaggered out, a loaded crossbow in each hand. He was flanked by two guards. But I noticed there were plenty more crossbow bolts aimed at us from slots in the ceiling. All of his men were ready.

My old master was a huge, barrel-chested man with an unruly mop of white hair and a short beard that still held touches of red. He moved like a bear, slowly and ponderously, with reserved strength. I'd seen him break a man's back in a street brawl, and I would've bet even money that he could still have done it.

Head cocked to the side, he stared intensely at me. "Who are you?" he demanded. "Why did you force your way into my home?"

"Who am I? I was a poor boy with a dead father and a mother who'd been carried off by traders." I saw recognition slowly dawn in his eyes. "You took me in and treated me like your own son. Eventually, you gave me a ship of my own and retired here. Don't you remember? I certainly do."

"You're dead," he whispered.

"You said," I continued, "that if I ever needed anything, I should come back and see you. Well, I need a new ship and a new crew, so . . . here I am!"

"What trick is this? Are you some ghost come to haunt me? Some demon?"

"Find me a bottle of brandy. I've got a long story to tell you. And, by the gods, I swear it's true." I laughed. "You don't think a little thing like a dragon would stop me, do you?"

"What—how—?"

"How about putting those crossbows away first? Then we'll talk. We've got a lot of catching up to do."

Frago grinned and tossed his crossbows to one of the guards, then stepped forward and gave me a crushing hug. Laughing, we pounded each other on the back until we were both gasping for breath.

"Come on," he said at last. "Let's get some food into you. You're all skin and bones. And your beard and hair—I hardly recognize you now!"

"And my men?"

He motioned to his guards. "Find them rooms and get them whatever they need."

I nodded to myself as he led me down the hall. If things went well, I'd have a new ship to command before the month was out. And then it would be on to Almanthia to find the Master of Dragons!

TWELVE

Frago and I talked through most of the night. We had a lot of catching up to do. After I'd told him all that had happened to me, and all that I planned to do to Alna Savina and her 'Master of Dragons', Frago told me he had some plans of his own.

"This house, this life," he said with a grand gesture, "it's not for me. For months I've dreamed of nothing but the sea. I hear voices in the waves calling to me, whispering my name. Flotsam along the tideline takes on special meaning, like the wreckage of ships I've sunk come to invite me back. I see faces of old friends in the foam of the waves."

"I know what you mean," I said.

"Do you really? I wonder, sometimes, if anyone truly understands. I feel the sea's nearness . . . as though she's a lover calling me."

I nodded slowly. "I've felt it myself . . ."

"Then you do understand." Frago smiled. "It's in our blood, Fel. I'm a rich man, and I thought comfort and luxury were all I ever wanted. I never expected to miss the hard life at sea, the fighting, the blood." He sighed. "Retirement is boring me to death!"

"Call me Dray," I said pointedly. "And what are you getting at?"

"I'm giving up my life ashore. And I'm taking you with me."

He smiled. I'd seen that look of infinite superiority before; it meant he had some plan afoot and he wasn't going to share it—at least, not yet. "Wait and see," was all he'd say, much as I prodded him.

I swallowed uneasily. Retirement hadn't changed Frago a bit; he still had a crafty, dangerous glint in his eye. I loved him like a second father, but I still didn't trust him.

He rang a small crystal bell. "I'll have one of the servants take you to your room."

*   *   *

Someone was shaking me. Abruptly I sat up in bed, squinting into the brightness of a candle. All I could see were fuzzy rings of light. My mouth tasted like old rags, and my head throbbed. The drink Frago had plied me with the night before had taken its toll, and now my thoughts were confused, jumbled.

"Go away," I muttered. I didn't know how long I'd been asleep, but with my head aching so, all I longed to do was crawl into a hole and pull it tight around me.

"Ah, Fel, my boy—" Frago began.

"Name's Dray now."

"—the time's here. Get dressed and come down to the banquet hall. The others are waiting."

"Others?" I groaned. "What others? What are you talking about?" I didn't want to think about anything. Maybe in five or six hours, after I'd had something to eat . . .

Frago set the candle down, then left without another word. Puzzled, still grumbling, I finally slid out from between the featherbed's sheets to stand on the cool stone floor. The clothes I'd been wearing the day before had vanished. New ones, magnificent red silk pantaloons, a white silk shirt, gloves, and various scarves and handkerchiefs, had been laid out for me on a small wooden rack. As I dressed, I noticed another rack in the corner, holding knives and swords. When I'd knotted my last scarf in place I went to examine the weapons.

Each blade had intricate gold and silver designs etched into its steel. After admiring them all, I selected four small throwing knives and tucked them into the sash around my waist, then put on a sword belt and a saber with a basket guard. The sword fit my hand comfortably; Frago hadn't forgotten my taste in fine weapons.

Suitably dressed, I swaggered out into the hall, feeling much like my old self. I could have taken on the world.

"It's about time you woke up, Dray!" Ool scolded me suddenly, laughing. "Indulge a bit too much last night?" I looked up to see him leaning lazily against the door jam of the room across the hall, Graff next to him. Frago had obviously supplied them with new clothing as well. They looked rested and refreshed.

I smiled sheepishly. "When old friends meet again . . ."

"How did it go?" Graff asked eagerly. "Is Frago going to help us?"

I scowled slightly at my new crewman's impertinence. But before I could respond, one of Frago's servants joined us in the hallway.

"Mr. Sorrel, please follow me," he said stiffly, giving Ool and Graff disapproving glances. "The master is waiting for you."

"Frago knows I go nowhere without my men," I said.

The servant shrugged. "As you wish, sir," he said. Turning,

he led us down a maze of hallways to a small stone staircase. "We must hurry," the servant added, "the banquet has already begun."

From below came the muted sound of voices, laughing and talking mingled, and the clink of crystal goblets. I hesitated as the servant started down the steps.

"Banquet? Who's here?" I demanded.

"Some of the master's other . . . shall we say, business acquaintances?"

"City guards? Nobles?"

"It's not my place to comment on the master's choice of friends." There was a hint of a derision in his voice.

That made me feel better; if the servants didn't approve, it could only mean Frago's guests were of a somewhat disreputable nature, just like me. Taking a deep breath, I started down the steps.

As the talk grew louder, I began to recognize voices. Wasn't that Clay . . . and Tristal. . . and old Fets Redeye . . . and even Garan? Yes, I was certain of it. They were crewmen from our days aboard the *Blithe Spirit*, the last ship Frago had commanded.

Hurrying now, I shoved past the servant and almost burst through the door. I stood there gaping in astonishment at the thirty-odd people gathered about a long, wide banquet table covered with plates of rich foods. The men all wore colorful silks, bright scarves, gold earrings; swords dangled jauntily at their sides.

Scanning their faces, I recognized them all. These men were the core of *Spirit's* crew, all the officers, the most skilled crewmen. They had scattered to the corners of the world when Frago went into retirement five years before. Frago must have begun planning his return to the sea long before I arrived, for it would have taken months to gather these men together again. With Clay and Garan and the rest backing him, Frago would have enough men to command a small schooner.

Several of them rose to their feet when they saw me, hands dropping to the hilts of their swords. Their faces creased with distrust. Clearly they'd been discussing something they didn't want outsiders to hear. Disguised as I was, without my long black hair and my jeweled beard, I was a stranger to them. Beside me, I could almost feel Ool and Graff tense defensively, fingers moving toward their weapons as well.

Fets Redeye, the nearest to me, stepped forward and demanded, "Who are you?"

"Dray Sorrel," I answered quickly. "Captain Frago asked me here."

Redeye studied me a moment, scowling, but there was no recognition in his eyes, or in anyone else's. Good, they won't be able to give me away. Pirates had some loyalties and scruples, but I still wouldn't care to trust these men with my life. And I knew the Countess of Fleurin would pay quite well to find out that I was still alive.

"Sit down, Dray," Frago said to me. "Tell your men to relax and eat something. Plans are afoot!"

Frago turned to the others. "He's the last one we've been waiting for, lads, and you can trust him. I do." That seemed to satisfy everyone, for they turned away and studiously ignored me, going on with their meals and private conversations.

I looked for an empty chair. In the old days I'd always had a place at Frago's right hand, but now tall, thin, black-haired Garan sat there in my stead, looking smugly confident of his new position. It seemed he'd been promoted to first mate in my absence, which I thought a grave mistake. I'd always found Garan something of a bully, even though he was a more than competent fighter. I wondered what had possessed Captain Frago to give him such a high position.

Shaking my head, I found a seat at the end of the table, next to Clay Durran and Redeye. The others reluctantly made room for Ool and Graff as well. With a glance, I instructed my friends to sit down and keep silent. I helped myself to sweetmeats and fresh, crusty brown bread, and a servant filled my goblet with wine. I drank thirstily.

"Lads!" Frago shouted suddenly, shoving back his chair and rising. Everyone fell silent and looked at him. He leaned forward, fists on the table, eyes wide and wild. "Tonight our company is complete. Tonight we take our ship!"

Everyone cheered and pounded knife hilts on the table. I cheered with them, though I didn't know the plan and only had the faintest idea as to what was going on. Taking a ship could only mean we were going to seize one of the vessels in Zorvoon's harbor, and that would be a tricky, dangerous business at best. Even so, I knew the chances were good that we'd succeed; like me, Aldenius Frago planned things to the smallest detail.

*   *   *

We left Frago's house at twilight. Our little band of pirates marched through the dark city streets, to all appearances a band of sailors come ashore for a rowdy time of wine, women, and song. Frago had the men singing loudly, and their jokes and laughter drowned out the other sounds of the night. No one gave us a second glance, not the cutthroats lingering in dark alleyways, not the other bands of sailors at ease, not even the few squads of city guards we passed.

Graff kept close to me, obviously ill at ease. Between bawdy verses of drinking songs, we talked.

I elaborated a bit about Dray's life, details I'd concocted during my journey to Zorvoon. I told him I'd commanded a small ship called the *Gray Prince*, out of Almanthia, which had gone pirating and been sunk on the Shark Reefs. I'd sailed with Frago once before and welcomed a chance to do so again, since he was the finest captain ever to turn a crooked hand to pirating.

Graff nodded. "I've heard a lot of stories about him—him and Blackmane, may his bones rest quietly. There's not another man I'd rather serve under—save you, of course, Captain."

"Don't call me that in front of the others." I said. "I'm Dray from now on."

"Yes, sir."

"You won't be navigator on Frago's ship, but when I take my own ship, you'll have a place then. And one more thing—try not to get killed tonight!"

"Yes, Cap—Dray"

I grinned. "Now join the others. I've got some catching up to do with Frago."

Without a second's hesitation, I edged forward, pushing

my way through the other pirates until I came to Captain Frago, who marched at the head of our band, head thrown back, singing at the top of his lungs. He winked at me and sang even louder.

A moment later, rounding a corner, we came into sight of Zorvoon's huge harbor. Three long piers stretched from the docks. Tied to the thick oak pilings were literally hundreds of seagoing craft, ranging from small fishing boats to the single-masted yachts of Zorvoon's wealthier citizens to the King of Zorvoon's warships. And there were merchant ships by the dozens, and freight barges, and even a few pirate ships.

Several vessels already had lanterns hanging in the rigging. Their warm yellow light made the whole scene soft and dreamlike, breathtakingly beautiful. It made me realize how much I missed by living on board a ship. In easier times I might have welcomed a quiet life in this city. I understood how Aldenius Frago had fallen for her siren call.

"There she is," Frago said, touching my arm and pointing to the largest ship in the harbor, an immense galleon painted a pale blue from stem to stern. "That's the *Blue Maiden*, the finest vessel in this part of the world."

"That's the ship you want?" I asked, incredulous. "You expect to steal that with only thirty men?"

"Thirty-five, but who's counting?"

I shook my head, certain he was mad. "Well, what do you know about her?"

He looked at me slyly. "She's currently owned by Black Jordan."

"That monster?" I demanded. "How by all the gods did

he get a ship like that?"

Jordan was more a living fiend than a pirate. When he captured ships, he *did* indeed loot them—but to him treasure was a secondary goal. What he really wanted was to torture people, and captured sailors made excellent victims. I'd heard rumors that when he couldn't find prey on the seas, he'd land and slaughter small, remote villages instead.

His kind gave a bad name to piracy. I welcomed any chance to do him harm. *Take away what he loves best,* that was the way to deal with his kind. I knew he had to love that ship of his. I smiled at the thought.

Frago just shrugged. "How did he get a ship like that? How would I know? Maybe he had her built to his specifications. Maybe he stole her. Who cares? All that matters is that she's there, ripe for the taking."

"We don't have enough men to sail her," I mused, half to myself.

"Neither does he. He recruited in Raltania, and when he put into port here, quite a few of them deserted." He chuckled. "Rumor has it his first mate is off on a drinking binge right now because he doesn't want to tell Black Jordan half the company is gone!"

"Still . . ."

"I'm certain some of Jordan's men will come to our side once we explain ourselves to them."

I nodded. "Once we've taken her, you mean."

"Of course."

I rubbed my chin thoughtfully, gazing at the seamen in the shadows. "If the ship is really that badly undermanned . . ."

"It is."

". . . then you might be right."

"Of course I am!"

Graff had been waving frantically for my attention. When I finally looked directly at him, he motioned me over. I went, keeping a careful eye on Frago.

Graff whispered. "Captain, I've got to speak to you. Now. Alone."

"Why?"

"Not here." He drew me away from the others.

"What is it?" I asked when we could speak privately.

"The *Blue Maiden* is my ship—that is, I was signed on as one of her crew."

"You deserted?" I demanded.

"You would, too, if Jordan was your captain."

I nodded. "How many others deserted—and how many good men could you find in an hour, if you had to?"

"Over one hundred deserted. I know where some went. I might be able to find a dozen or so."

"Are they good men?"

"Some I'd trust to guard my back in a fair fight."

"Go round up the ones you trust," I said. "We'll need more men than we've got if we're to take the *Maiden* safely. You and your friends will be able to get us aboard."

Graff grinned. "Yes, sir!" He sprinted off.

Suddenly, the world exploded in bright lights and sharp pains behind my eyes. I staggered and fell to my knees, gasping in agony. My head felt like it had been split in two.

It took me a second to gather my wits and realize someone had struck me from behind. I heard the hiss of steel leaving a scabbard.

"Get up, traitor!" a familiar voice shouted.

Shaking my head, I scrambled to my feet and stood unsteadily. Garan stood there with sword drawn, hate and anger and bloodlust in his eyes. All the others were looking now. They formed a circle, ringing us.

"What are you talking about?" I demanded, rubbing the back of my head. It was just like him to strike an opponent from behind.

Garan's voice was sharp, taunting. "I saw you whispering to your servant. Where'd you send him, to get the city guard? Or to warn your friend, Jordan?"

"Jordan's no friend of mine!"

Garan stepped forward, sword ready. I drew my saber in response; I wasn't about to stand there and let him run me through.

Frago shoved his way through to the front of his crewmen. "Stop this at once!" he bellowed. "I'll not have you fighting among yourselves!"

"You should never have taken a stranger into your confidence, Frago," Garan sneered. "Your friend here sent someone to warn Jordan."

"I've known Dray longer than I've known you," Frago said. "I trust him with my life. He wouldn't betray us."

He looked at me, clearly waiting for an explanation. "Well?"

"Garan saw me talking to Graff," I said quickly. "Graff is a deserter from the *Maiden*. Now he's working for me—for us.

That much is true. I sent him to round up a few other deserters from Jordan's ship, men who can be trusted. They'll help us get aboard the *Maiden*."

"Liar!" Garan shouted. He lunged.

I parried his thrust and stepped close, engaging his blade. Gritting his teeth, he tried to push me back, but I set my feet and held my place by brute strength.

With a grunt, Garan leapt back and hacked wildly at me. I parried again, then again and again as he thrust at me. Slowly I retreated before his wild, savage attack. Time after time he stabbed at me with his sword. Sweat glistened on his brow, and he panted heavily; he couldn't keep this up much longer without dropping from exhaustion. All I had to do was keep him from hitting me and I'd win the fight.

At last his blows slowed. His face had grown ash-pale and his whole body trembled. He staggered, but somehow managed to keep the tip of his sword pointed at my belly. There was raw hatred in his expression and more than a little pain and frustration.

He leapt forward again in one last attack. This time I knocked his blade aside easily. Feinting to the right, I beat down his sword when he tried to parry. Then, closing, I punched him in the stomach as hard as I could. He doubled over, wheezing, unable to defend himself.

Rather than kill him, I kicked his wrist and sent his weapon spinning into the air. He stared in dismay as it landed ten feet away, outside the ring of onlookers, clattering loudly on the cobblestones.

I put the tip of my saber to his throat. "Yield," I said.

He glared up at me, hardly able to breathe, and for a moment I thought he was going to defy me, but then his shoulders slumped and he looked down. "I—yield," he gasped.

I resheathed my sword. The others were still staring at me, but I frowned at them and they looked away, none daring to meet my gaze.

"I told you the truth," I said to Frago, to them all. "I was about to tell our captain what had happened when Garan attacked me. Graff will be back in an hour with friends. Wait until then and you'll see."

"And if the guards come?" Clay demanded. "What then?"

Aldenius Frago snorted. "Use your head, lad, not your bloodthirsty heart. We're just a group of sailors out for a stroll on the docks, sampling the taverns. We've done nothing illegal . . . yet. Right?"

"Right," I said, thinking back to Grayhaven, how I'd made the law protect me from my fellow cutthroats.

Reluctantly, the others agreed.

"Come on, then," Frago said, starting for the nearest tavern. "If we must wait, we'll wait in comfort."

"I'll wait here for Graff," I said. I settled onto a rain barrel. Ool stood beside me, arms folded, a thoughtful expression on his face. "I'll find you when he gets back."

"An hour," he said, "no more. If Graff isn't here, we start out on our own. Right?"

I smiled. "Of course. And I'll even lead the attack, if you want."

"Agreed!"

*   *   *

Time passed all too slowly. I waited impatiently for Graff to return, looking this way and that, staring up the street every time I heard the slightest noise. Surely an hour had already passed, I kept thinking. Surely Frago and the others would return at any moment. What if Graff really had gone to the city guard—or, worse, to Black Jordan?

"You're not doing yourself any good worrying," Ool said, startling me from my thoughts.

I grinned up at him. "How come you always know what I'm thinking?"

"I've sailed with you for four years. You're predictable. Anyone who knows you can anticipate exactly what you'd do in any situation."

"Is that so?"

"Besides," he said with a wink, "I'm a wizard."

I snorted, then sat up straighter and gazed out across the harbor. The small fishing boats swayed slowly on the low waves. Among them stood two hundred other ships, almost any of which we could have taken without much of a fight. Schooners, small galleons . . . But of course Frago had to take the biggest and the best, just to show off.

At last I heard a light footstep beside me and glanced up to find a very smug-looking Graff. He had three others with him. From their stance and bearing I could see they were seasoned sailors, not raw youths. They wore white cotton shirts and breaches like merchant crewmen, rather than the colorful costumes of pirates, a mark in their favor; they were smart enough to disguise themselves. Gaudily dressed pirates stood out in crowds; plainly clothed, these men would be nearly impossible to spot.

They had the dark good looks of Slekans. Their bare arms bulged with muscle, and they all carried knives. Instantly I agreed with Graff's assessment of them; I wouldn't mind having them at my back in a fight.

They looked me over in return. If Jordan found them talking to another captain, or if he found them at all, I knew he'd kill them. I didn't blame them for being wary.

"It's about time," I said to Graff. "I was beginning to get worried."

"The others are hiding. Word's out that Jordan's ashore and searching the bars for them personally."

"I'd expect that."

"Anyway, these are the best men I could find. Rand, Teigh, and Aranel."

"I'll tell Captain Frago they're here," Ool said.

"Do that." I turned back to the three sailors. "I don't know what Graff's told you, but he says you're to be trusted. I hope for your sakes that's true."

"He said there'd be money in it," Rand said.

"And places in a good ship's crew," added Aranel.

I grinned. "Yes, there's that."

"Which is your ship?" Teigh asked.

"In an hour it'll be the *Blue Maiden*."

Rand swallowed. "What—?"

"There's a group of us who don't like Captain Jordan. It seems a shame to waste such a nice ship on scum like him, so we decided to take the *Maiden* for ourselves. We'll need your help."

"What if we refuse?" Teigh said. "How do we know you're any better than Jordan?"

"Our leader is Captain Frago."

"Frago?" Rand asked with slack-jawed awe. "Aldenius Frago, who used to captain the *Blithe Spirit* with Fel Blackmane?"

"I see you've heard of him."

"Who hasn't? If he thinks he can take Jordan's ship, I'm with him!"

Aranel and Teigh heartily agreed.

Graff had chosen his friends well. I had faith in them already.

A moment later Ool returned with the others. Frago was in the lead, chuckling and looking immensely pleased with himself. Garan and the others grouped behind him.

"Captain," I said to him, "these are the men."

He swaggered up and looked them over, then nodded approvingly.

"Good, good," he said to them. "You're going to get us on board Jordan's ship, and I know just how you're going to do it."

"How?" Teigh asked, his tone skeptical.

Frago smiled. "In a minute," he said. He looked at me. "Dray, my lad, congratulations!"

"For what?" I asked slowly.

"You've been promoted to first mate."

"What about *him?*" I jerked my head at Garan, who pursed his lips and stared out into the harbor. "I thought he was first mate."

Frago chuckled. "We made a bet in the tavern. He thought you were trying to betray us; I knew otherwise. Since he insisted on making a fool of himself, I suggested he bet his place in my crew. He was stupid enough to agree."

"What did you wager?" I asked.

"Why, the *Blue Maiden*, of course."

I swallowed. "You bet the *ship* on me?"

He winked. "I know you, Dray. You're predictable in your loyalty, if nothing else."

I glanced back at Ool, who only shrugged. "Yeah," I said. "So everyone keeps telling me."

Frago looked around at the others, then clapped his hands for attention. "Listen up, lads! I've got two porters who should be here at any moment. They'll have wooden crates. We're going to borrow their carts and make a special delivery to Jordan's ship."

So that was his plan, smuggling a few of us aboard so we could surprise the crew, rather than risk everything in an all-out attack. It might work if we could catch Jordan's men by surprise.

Now Frago said, "Clay, take a walk down to the dockfront and see if you can find those porters. I paid them well; they'll have waited, even after an hour's delay."

"Aye, sir!" Clay turned and raced off.

*   *   *

Half an hour later I found myself crammed into a small wooden crate with Clay and Ool. Frago tapped the lid shut with the hilt of a dagger, then knocked once for luck. I heard him bark orders at the others, getting them settled, getting them loaded onto the carts.

"Garan's furious," Clay whispered to me. "Watch your back during the fight."

"I will," I said, then chuckled. "Why was he stupid enough to bet with Captain Frago? I would've thought he'd know better by now."

"The captain shamed him into it. If I didn't know better, I'd say Frago wanted you for his first mate and got rid of Garan deliberately."

"If you didn't know better," I said.

"Garan had it coming," said Ool.

Clay laughed. "You're a sly one," he said to me, "another Blackmane. But watch your step with Garan."

"Another Blackmane?" I echoed. "You flatter me!"

Ool tried to suppress his laughter but didn't quite succeed. There was a long, puzzled silence from Clay. Fortunately, the cart lurched and we were off before he could say anything else.

We bumped over the cobblestones, then the noise of the wheels became a constant thrum as we rolled across the wooden pier.

Luckily, the bone-jarring ride was short. When we pulled up at the *Blue Maiden* the mate on duty called down a challenge. I strained to follow the talk outside as best I could through the wooden crate.

"It's only us, Dirk!" Teigh called.

"What're you doing here? First mate said you'd deserted. The captain's looking for you—"

"Yeah, I know," Graff said. "He found us. We just had a

little too much to drink, that's all. He told us to take this stuff aboard. Lend a hand and break out the gantry, will you? There's another load yet to come, and I want to get some sleep before the night's over."

"What've you got?"

"Raltanian wine for the captain's table, bundles of silk and spices, and some special items for the captain's pleasure, if you know what I mean—whips, a few branding irons . . ."

That seemed to satisfy Dirk because I heard him shouting orders to his men. I pictured him running rope through the pulleys, and throwing down cargo nets so the boxes could be hoisted aboard.

I shifted uncomfortably as my legs began to cramp. I rubbed them hard, grumbling softly to myself.

"Shouldn't be long now," murmured Ool.

One by one I heard the crates being lifted aboard the *Blue Maiden*—the squeak of rope, the grunts and curses of straining men. Then our turn came. The bottom of our crate swung wildly, and we were airborne.

"Easy," I whispered. "Get ready."

They set us down with a jarring bump. Silently, I put my hand to the wood overhead, ready to push it open at a moment's notice. I listened while two last crates were brought on board, then I heard a piercing whistle, Frago's signal.

I heaved open the top of my crate, seized the edge, and pulled myself out. The deck around me was clear; I had a few seconds until Black Jordan's men caught on to what was happening. I swung my legs clear.

Turning, I pulled Clay up and out of the crate. Behind us

came scuffling sounds and a few startled shouts, the first sharp dang of sword on sword. Someone started screaming an alarm which would bring all the crewmen below decks running for their weapons.

"Get Ool," Clay said as he drew his own sword. "I'll watch your back."

As I reached down for the wizard, though, he shook his head and began to mumble some spell. The air around him rippled and shimmered, and his body took on a faint blue glow. I'd never seen him use a spell quite like this one. I stared in surprise as he began to rise into the air, floating up toward the masts.

Clay called me, sounding a little desperate. I whirled, sword in hand. We'd been set down near one of the hatches; men were swarming up through it three at a time. Some were sleepy-eyed and others half-dressed, but they all carried weapons. They looked shocked and frightened.

Screaming battle cries, they rushed us. I fell back before them, hard pressed to defend myself. It seemed Jordan's ship hadn't been as undermanned as Frago thought. I cursed him under my breath.

THIRTEEN

I retreated quickly before the swordsmen, running for cover. They pressed their attack, trying to circle behind and surround me.

Luck was with me; I made it to the crates we'd used to smuggle ourselves aboard. From there, no more than two men could get at me at once.

A tall, broad man with muscles bulging across his chest forced his way past the others. "He's mine!" he called, looking me over with a sneer. Then he leapt forward, sword swinging in a vicious down stroke.

I parried, parried a second violent swing, then feinted and thrust high to nick him in the shoulder. He stepped back with a curse, pressing one hand against the wound to stanch the flow of blood. He looked at the red on his fingers, then glared at me, savage hatred all too clear in his eyes. I knew then that he wouldn't yield until one of us lay dead.

Screaming ferociously, he raised his sword and charged. I lunged and let him impale himself on my saber. He hardly seemed aware that I'd put two feet of steel through his body. Raising his sword, grinning, bloodlust in his eyes, he prepared to cut me in half.

And then a startled, bewildered expression crossed his face for an instant, and he moaned, a pitiful mew of a sound that tore at my heart. Dropping his weapon, he pawed a bit at his belly, then collapsed when I jerked my own blade free. He lay at my feet, twitching faintly, and then he died.

His companions hesitated a moment, the opportunity I

needed. Drawing one of the throwing knives from my sash, I flipped it underhand. It struck the foremost man in the shoulder and buried itself a good two inches. He screamed and reeled back, reaching for the blade.

Almost before the knife struck, I drew another and held it ready, all the while flicking the point of my saber from left to right and back again, as though daring the next two sailors pushing their way forward to attack.

I heard a shout of warning from above and behind me. "Get down, Dray!" cried Ool.

Instantly I dropped flat on the deck. My attackers laughed and started forward, obviously thinking me easy prey now. But before they reached me, a sizzling, glowing ball of light streaked down into their midst. Magic. I pressed my eyes shut and turned my head away, not quite knowing what to expect.

Even through closed eyelids the intense burst of light reached me, waves of blinding brightness that spread outward like rings in a lake. I heard screams and curses from the sailors. When I opened my eyes, I saw a haze of colorful after-effects and men kneeling on the deck rubbing their eyes or reeling among the crates like drunks.

"Help me!" one of them cried. "I can't see!"

Taking a deep breath, I ran forward and started clubbing them with the hilt of my saber. Blind, unable to defend themselves, they fell before me like wheat to a sickle. In a moment the six who'd chased and cornered me between the crates all lay unconscious on the deck, along with three more who happened to be standing near enough to be affected by Ool's magic.

Beyond them the battle still raged, sword ringing on sword, men cursing, shouting, dying. I couldn't tell which side was winning.

Taking a moment to catch my breath, I looked up and saw Ool floating serenely in the rigging, a halo of blue light surrounding him. I also noticed, with more than a touch of awe, several dozen crossbow bolts hanging suspended in mid-air around him, as though lodged in that glowing shield. The shifting light, the glowing halo, all made him look unearthly, inhuman.

Thirty feet away Clay was slowly retreating in my direction. His opponent, a tall, broad-shouldered crewman with long black hair, pressed his attack like a madman, his sword an almost constant blur of movement.

I ran forward to help my old comrade, but before I could get there the black-haired man ran his sword through Clay's shoulder. Clay stood like a statue for a second, then gasped in pain. The black-haired man jerked his blade down and twisted it cruelly, making the wound larger. When he pulled his sword free. Clay crumpled to the deck, blood spurting from his wound. Roaring, the man raised his sword to finish the job.

I wouldn't make it in time, I realized, a sick, helpless feeling in the pit of my stomach. I yelled my most fearsome war cry. The black-haired man glanced up, startled, and saw me coming. Rather than finish Clay, he set his feet and prepared to meet my charge, massive hands tightening around the hilt of his sword.

I reached him at a dead run, swinging my saber as hard as

I could, putting all my weight behind it. He parried, staggering back as steel rang on steel and sparks flew like fireflies. But he was a strong man, and he danced back a few steps to recover his balance. He watched me cagily, eyes narrowed to slits.

Closing with him, I tried to ram the knife I still held up and into his stomach. His powerful left hand closed around mine and forced it back. Bones grated in my wrist. A sharp pain shot the length of my arm. Cursing, I dropped the knife.

The black-haired man leaned forward and used his weight and muscle to force me back an inch at a time. He was a good deal stronger than I, so strong that I realized it hadn't been a good idea to close with him. I tried to leap back, to disengage, but he followed me, eyes locked with mine, refusing to release my arm or give a hint of weakness.

He began to twist my wrist once more. Little shivers of pain raced through my arm, my side. I looked up into his face and saw his mouth twist back in a sadistic grin. He was enjoying my pain, much like Black Jordan enjoyed the pain of the men he tortured to death. My mouth was suddenly dry. Again I felt bones grating, and I realized he'd break my wrist if I didn't do something fast.

"The battle's over," I hissed to him. "Let me go, and I'll make sure the others let you live."

His laugh was a little purr of sound. "I'll kill them later." A hairline scar along the length of his jaw stood out starkly white against his sun-bronzed skin. "But first I'm going to watch you die!"

Desperate, I threw my weight to the left suddenly, going with his strength instead of against it. I felt my legs start to slide out from under me. Dropping my sword and leaping forward, I tucked my feet to my chest and tumbled into an acrobat's somersault.

Somewhere in the fall, my arm twisted free of his grasp. I landed hard, flat on my back with the hilt of my fallen knife digging painfully into my shoulder. Looking straight up, I saw my opponent's startled expression.

Before he had time to react, I seized his ankles and heaved as hard as I could. Already off balance, he toppled backward with a curse, sword flying to one side.

Rolling over, I found the knife I'd dropped and grabbed it. I didn't need it, though: my opponent had struck his head on the planking. Blood oozed from a deep wound on the side of his head.

I buried my knife to the hilt in his chest. He twitched once, then lay still. I had too many enemies already to let one more live.

Retrieving my saber, I looked around to make sure I wasn't in danger of being attacked again. I realized abruptly that there weren't any other fights going on; all of Jordan's men still on their feet had thrown down their weapons and surrendered.

I hurried to Clay's side and bent to see to him, but the wound was more serious than I'd thought. From the frothy blood around the wound, I knew the crewman's sword had pierced a lung. When I felt Clay's neck for a pulse, I found his skin already cool. He was quite, quite, dead.

Up in the rigging, Graff suddenly shouted, "Captain Aldenius Frago has defeated you. If you hope to escape Jordan's tyranny, you'd better join Frago's crew!"

Jordan's men looked more bewildered than anything else. A sad lot they were, but we'd need most of them if we were to sail the *Maiden*. The best crewmen had either deserted in Zorvoon, like Graff and his friends, or had died in the fighting. Only the dregs remained: the weak, the cowardly, those who had been wounded early in the fight.

Ool floated down from the rigging gracefully, his robes fluttering, his expression aloof. The golden halo of light dissolved, sending the crossbow bolts caught in it tumbling to the deck in a sharp-pointed hail. Men covered their heads and ducked out of harm's way, cursing loudly. Ool smiled beatifically.

"Ho, my lads!" came a shout from the quarterdeck. Turning, I saw Frago leaning on the railing, looking down on us with a smug expression on his face.

"It *is* Frago!" I heard several of Jordan's crewmen murmur in wonder. The whispers spread among them like a sudden rush of wind. They all turned to see what the *Blue Maiden*'s new master had to say.

Frago paced, hands behind back, head down, building suspense, letting the silence and tension grow until the men shifted before him like hungry dogs tied before a banquet table. I watched Black Jordan's surviving crewmen carefully; they looked apprehensive, fearful. Frago had them exactly where he wanted them, his theatrics perfect as they'd always been. I'd studied his style, made it my own, and I'd never regretted it. He was the best of all the pirate captains.

Seeing him like this again, after so many years, made me

realize how gladly I'd served him. He inspired confidence, loyalty, courage.

Even so, I couldn't let my old loyalties tie me down. I had my own life to lead, and my own private mission: to find the Master of Dragons, to avenge the *Pamah Reach*, to return to the Countess of Fleurin and strike anew.

At last Frago called down, "I am, indeed, Captain Aldenius Frago! I trust you have heard of me." He chuckled. "Life ashore has not agreed with me, so I have chosen to return to my life at sea. The *Blue Maiden* will be my flagship and you my new crew.

"Listen well, my lads," he continued. "I need good men to sail the *Maiden*. I've brought quite a few of my own crewmen, but they're not enough. I will welcome those of you who wish to join me. If any of you choose to stay here in Zorvoon with my illustrious comrade-in-piracy, Black Jordan, you may do so, and I will wish you all the luck you will need. Go now."

Pausing, he looked over Black Jordan's crew, meeting each one's gaze. They all shifted uncomfortably before his scrutiny, but not one of them spoke up or moved to leave. Jordan, it seemed, inspired little loyalty in his men. Frago's charisma and enthusiasm had swept up everyone around me, had already bound them to him more surely than threats and violence ever could. Had I been among Jordan's crew, I would have left to serve Frago, gladly, eagerly.

"Very well, then," Aldenius Frago said, "you have made your choice. Now I have just one more thing to say, the same promise I've made to all my men through all the years I've been a captain: We will sail together, fight together, and grow rich together. My word is law. I am a fair man, but I am hard. Serve me well and you will be rewarded accordingly." He pointed to me. "Dray Sorrel is my first mate. He has my full authority and confidence. Obey him as you would me." He nodded. "Give the orders. Dray. We sail as quickly as possible."

Graff leapt forward and shouted, "Three cheers for Captain Frago!"

Thrice they shouted Frago's name, raising their fists in salute. Graff shouted loudest of all. He was a clever man, I knew then. His actions would not go unnoticed by Frago . . . or by me.

"You heard the captain—get a move on!" I bellowed abruptly. "You and you—" I pointed—"see to the wounded. You five, clear the decks. The rest of you see to the sails. Move it!"

They jumped to the tasks. I strode among them, bawling orders, keeping them moving, lending a hand when necessary. Even with Jordan's sailors, the ship was still badly undermanned; we'd need a crew of one hundred fifty to be near full strength, and I estimated our company at just over seventy-five.

Wagons began pulling up on the pier. A dozen brawny dockworkers began unloading huge crates and carrying them aboard. The crates contained provisions for our journey, plus Frago's personal possessions and those of the others he'd brought with him.

Just looking at the ship, I knew she'd been worth the cost. There weren't a dozen vessels her equal in the whole Seren Sea.

*   *   *

A little over an hour later, the hawsers had been hauled back aboard, the gantlines cleared, the hawsers taken from the rigging, and the gangplank pulled back on board and stowed away. A few small sails were raised, and the ship began to drift slowly away from the pier.

Several dozen sailors from other ships and a number of minor port officials had gathered, at first to cheer on the fight (more than a few wagers had been made on the outcome, I was certain), then to watch our frenetic preparations for departure. It became clear that Frago had bought off the magistrates, inspectors, and other port officials: no one had called the city guard, during the fight or made a move to challenge our possession of the *Maiden.* Not that the King of Zorvoon particularly cared who owned the *Maiden*—one pirate was as good as another to him. Rather, he liked to maintain a facade of order, of law and justice, to keep the populace content. With us firmly in control of Jordan's ship and the battle already over, he would leave us alone to carry out our business.

As we slowly moved away, those lined up on the dock began to wave and shout good wishes for the voyage.

"May the gods look favorably on your meals!"

"Let the riches you find bring you wealth!"

"May the wind fill your sails!"

They were laughing. Most of them were quite drunk.

Abruptly a group of men hurried down the pier toward us. As they drew near I recognized the man at their head, a tall, gaunt fellow with a flowing black cape. Black Jordan himself, all hate and fury.

He skidded to a halt directly across from my position at

the rail, shouting curses and vile threats.

"Throw a rope across!" I called to him.

Black Jordan looked around, saw a coil, and grabbed it. Quickly he made a loop in one and threw it to me.

Instead of belaying it to one of the huge brass rings set in the deck. I hauled in the slack, then gave a quick tug that set Black Jordan off balance. He teetered on the edge of the pier, arms flailing wildly.

One of the drunken sailors seemed to stagger a bit and bumped into Jordan, as good as a shove in the small of the back. The *Maiden's* former captain tumbled off the pier. With a garbled cry and a loud splash, he hit the water and vanished from sight.

His former crewmen on board the *Blue Maiden* roared with laughter.

Jordan came up, choking and gasping, and shouted for help. I threw him my end of the rope just as a man on the pier threw him the other. Next to me, Frago laughed so hard the tears coursed down his cheeks.

Leaning over the railing, Frago called down to Black Jordan, "The *Blue Maiden's* my ship now, Jordan. Keep away from her, or I'll have you thrown in irons for trespassing."

Jordan began screaming incoherently—something having to do with ships and hot irons. One of his mates had gotten hold of another rope by then and thrown one end down to him. Together with several others on the pier, he strong-armed Black Jordan back up out of the water.

Once on his feet, Jordan drew his sword and brandished it wildly, swinging at everything around him. His rage was hot and blind, and he cursed and shouted insane, incoherent threats. Everyone on the pier—including his own men—ran for cover.

We were fifty feet from the pier. The mate at the wheel turned the rudder, and I felt the ship shift direction ever so slightly to port, heading out of the harbor and toward the open sea. The men crowded the yardarms with sails, and we gradually picked up speed. The wind was pleasant; I enjoyed the smell of brine, the taste of salt on the air. It was like old times again. If I closed my eyes, I could imagine myself ten years younger, serving a captain at the height of his power and influence.

Yes, this is the life for me.

If I strained, I fancied I could hear Jordan's curses carrying over the water. I smiled to myself. Black Jordan had certainly loved his ship.

*   *   *

For all the commotion and fighting during our capture of the *Blue Maiden*, we spent a quiet night at sea. I retired to my cabin early, knowing I'd need to be rested the following day since Frago showed no sign of going to bed before every last chore had been seen to.

When I woke the next morning, I was stiff and sore. I wandered out on deck, rubbing the kinks from my muscles and the sleep from my eyes.

The sun was bright, the sky cloudless; a steady wind filled our sails. I'd seldom seen a more beautiful day. It was a favorable sign, as if the gods themselves approved of our mischief the night before. Indeed, there was an undercurrent of enthusiasm seldom found among sailors. I knew the crew were happy with Frago as their captain.

We were sailing due north, toward the heart of the sea lanes. Pickings would be good this time of year, with dozens of trade ships from Corwen carrying early harvests to market in Zorvoon and the other southern kingdoms.

I found Frago still on deck, supervising, keeping things running smoothly. He looked haggard from a night without rest, and I could tell he was ready to drop. He nodded a greeting as I joined him by the wheel.

"There's a lot of work still to be done," he said.

I agreed. "Where do you want me to start?"

"Below decks. I need an inventory of the cargo."

"Weren't there manifests?"

He shook his head. "I had Garan go through all of Jordan's papers last night. They were junk, mostly: lists of things taken from ships I know were sunk ten years ago, dozens of different cargo manifests, any one of which could be correct, a lot of promissory notes which I've burned, and a few old ledgers, which I haven't been able to make sense of. Unfortunately it seems Jordan wasn't much of a bookkeeper."

"Have any of his men had a chance to loot the hold?" I asked hesitantly. It was a common problem; men who knew where the valuables were stored often stole them before anyone else learned that they existed.

Frago sighed. "You know me better than that. The cargo hold was sealed when we came on board—I made sure of it. Here." He took a chain with a large iron key from around his neck and handed it to me. "I found this in Black Jordan's cabin. It fits the lock."

I took the key. "I'll need paper and ink, too."

"In my cabin."

"And someone I can trust to do the counting. Graff will do."

Frago cocked his head to the side. "Can he read and write?"

"He can."

"Very well."

"Aye, sir." I turned and looked around for Graff. He was sitting on the foredeck with two other men, yards of canvas gathered around them. They were patching one of the sails.

When I called him, he put his work aside and hurried over. As we headed for Frago's cabin, I told him what we had to do.

"I hope you don't mind my dragging you away from the sails," I said with a grin. Sail mending was painstaking, tedious work.

"Oh, I don't mind, Dray," he said quickly. "Besides, I've always wondered what Jordan kept in the hold."

"You don't know?"

"No, sir. Only he and his two top officers were allowed inside."

Frowning, I said, "What about dock-workers? Surely they went in to load and unload things."

Graff shrugged. "I never saw any go in myself. Twice when Jordan made port he sent us all to our quarters, said he'd string up anyone who so much as poked his head out. Perhaps he was loading and unloading the cargo then. There were plenty of rumors. But you know how things are aboard a ship like Jordan's."

We reached Frago's cabin. Pushing open the door, I stepped inside, into a jumble of crates and sea chests, odd pieces of furniture and piles of clothing.

I found the chart table in a corner, half buried by the contents of several large boxes which had apparently been dumped on top of one another. Maps, leather-bound books, scrolled parchment—it was impossible to sort it all out at a moment's glance. I rummaged through the stacks until I finally found a large ledger with most of the pages still blank. I handed it to Graff, along with a pair of quill pens and a small bottle of ink.

"Come on," I said, heading for the cargo hold.

The hold had been divided into three sections aboard Jordan's ship. The aft section housed the crewmen and the galley; the section amidship held various provisions, ship's stores, and the armory; the forward section held cargo.

The cargo section had its own hatch leading down from the main deck. Pulling the wooden cover aside, I climbed down the ladder into a large square room. It was unfurnished except for an oak bench against one wall. Hanging above the bench on a series of brass hooks were four oil lanterns. Flint and steel sat conveniently on the bench. I lit one of the lanterns, and Graff climbed down to join me.

"I don't like the looks of this place already," he grumbled.

"Nonsense. It's a cargo hold like any other." I held the lantern high and stepped forward to examine the hatch leading into the main compartment. Set flush with the wall, it was a huge slab of dark-stained wood with a brass ring in its center and a small hole for a key at one side.

Taking the key from around my neck, I fitted it into the lock, turned it, and heard bolts sliding on the other side. Then I took the ring with both hands and pulled. The door opened with surprising ease, gliding on well-oiled hinges.

It was dark inside, and the sickly sweet smell of rotting meat issued forth. Gasping, eyes tearing, I turned my head away. Graff, too, was gagging from the smell.

"What the hell is *that*?" I demanded.

"I don't know!" he said. "Gods, it stinks!"

I took a pair of perfumed handkerchiefs from my pocket and handed him one. Pressing mine to my nose and mouth, breathing deeply of the scent of rare Zorvoonian flowers, I lifted the lantern and stepped into a large, empty corridor. There were wide hatchways every fifteen feet or so.

Before I'd taken ten steps, Graff grabbed my arm. "Did you hear that?" he asked.

"What?"

"Shh! Listen!"

Then I heard it, too. From ahead came a low noise, a soft animal like grunting, and the dink of metal striking metal. I tensed, one hand dropping to the hilt of the knife tucked in my sash. Something was alive ahead, and from the looks—and smells—of the place, I didn't particularly want to meet whatever it was. What if Jordan kept wild animals down here to guard his treasure? What if he kept something worse?

Suddenly I didn't feel quite so sure of myself. "Go get a pair of crossbows," I said, "and Ool. I think we'll need his help."

"Aye, sir." As he turned and sprinted off, I retreated to the huge oak door. Again I heard the grunting noise. I couldn't help but shiver. Whatever it was, it didn't sound quite human.

FOURTEEN

A few minutes later, I heard voices behind me. Turning, I saw Ool and Graff climbing down the ladder. Graff held a pair of crossbows and a small bundle of bolts; Ool had nothing but his robes and a slightly amused expression.

"What's this all about?" Ool asked as I took one of the crossbows and loaded it. "You wanted to see me?"

"There's something alive in the cargo hold," I said. "I wanted a crossbow. And you."

"Alive?"

"That's right. And it's not rats."

"We need to see what we're doing."

"That's what the lantern's for," I said impatiently, raising it.

"That's a toy; I could do better in my sleep."

"All right." Shrugging, I retreated. Who was I to argue with a wizard?

When I had gone a safe distance. Ool cupped his hands together, raised them to his lips, and whispered into them. I watched, fascinated, as something in his hands began to glow, becoming brighter and brighter, thin blades of light leaking between his fingers. His hands shone pink with blood, lined with dark shadows of bone. The room seemed to spin ever so slightly, and a deep hum like that of thousands of bees filled the air.

Hearing a startled gasp, I glanced at Graff, who was backing away slowly, mumbling prayers and entreaties to the gods for protection against sorcery. Didn't he realize Ool would be our best defense against anything that tried to kill us?

Ool cast the brightness into the air. It rained down on us like sparks in a smithy, brilliance all around us, swirling yellows and whites and pinks. I couldn't look away. I couldn't move as the light touched my arms, my face, my eyes. But it did not burn. Rather, it melted like warm snow, dissolving into a soft glow like the light of a thousand candles burning in the night. And the darkness around us was gone.

Distantly I was aware of Graff speaking. I forced my attention to him and saw that he knelt on the floor, head bowed, still whispering prayers and making signs of aversion. I understood his fear, his incomprehension of a wizard's powers.

I looked at Ool. He just leaned against the wall, watching Graff with a tolerant smile. He winked at me.

"Anything else, Master Dray?"

Swallowing, I hefted my crossbow once more and said, "Stay close. I may still need you." I extinguished the oil lamp and set it back on its hook.

"Aye, sir," Ool said.

I pulled Graff to his feet and shook him until he looked blearily up at me. "Sir—" he began.

"Save your prayers for when you really need them," I told him.

"But *magic*—"

I shook him again. "Ool doesn't take kindly to superstitious nonsense. You would do well to hide your foolishness in his presence. Magic has saved my life a dozen times over, and I've never regretted it once."

Graff straightened and tried to look more composed, but

I could see he was still as fearful as ever. Shaking my head, I gave up; I had more important things to think about. What sort of creature lay ahead? Why was it here? What could it be guarding?

As we moved forward, I noticed that the glow seemed to follow us—was part of us all. A sphere of light perhaps twenty feet across moved down the corridor around us.

Again I heard the noise. I raised my hand, looking back at Ool.

"Listen! Did you hear it?"

The wizard nodded, then frowned, lines creasing his brow. Did he know something? He seemed to recognize the sound.

"Curious," he murmured.

"That's all you can say?"

"It sounds hungry."

"Great," I said with a bark of a laugh. "That's just what I needed to hear."

Ool chuckled, and Graff joined in, but their voices were too high and nervous. They were just as worried as I.

Easing up to the first hatchway, I peeked around the corner into a storeroom of some kind. It held nothing but a half dozen huge wooden crates stacked against the far wall. The crates were marked with trader symbols, red and white silks from Almanthia, the property of a Paladian merchant named Cornel Thane. Black Jordan must have robbed Thane's ship just before making port in Zorvoon.

I moved on toward the next hatch. The sounds of grunting and growling seemed to be getting distinctly louder, and I heard the tap-tap sound of claws on wood.

I peered into the next room. It held bags of spices, nothing else. I kept going.

The next hatch was closed. Pressing my ear to the wood, I heard the growling noise quite distinctly. The creature lay on the other side.

"This is it," I said, moving back.

"Open the door," Ool told Graff.

"Me?" He gulped.

"Yes, you," I said. "Swing it open, then step to the side as fast as you can."

"Aye, sir," he said reluctantly.

I hefted my crossbow and took aim at the door, at where a man's stomach would be if he—or it—charged out at us.

"Ready?" I asked Ool.

He nodded, then raised his hands and began to trace mystical symbols in the air.

"Open the door," I said.

Graff pushed it open, then leapt to the side, swinging his crossbow up into firing position. He trembled a bit, but I couldn't blame him—I felt the same fear. My finger tightened involuntarily around the crossbow's trigger, but I didn't fire. I just gazed with amazement into the large, dimly lit storeroom.

A pair of bony, half-starved black panthers were chained inside. Hanging upside down over them from the ceiling, bound in irons, was a naked man. It was a scene from a horrible nightmare, but I should not have been surprised, considering Black Jordan's reputation as a cruel sadist.

As I watched, one of the panthers leaped at the prisoner.

He jerked feebly, just managing to arch his back and raise himself a few inches farther above the floor. The panther's claws grazed his skin, and he moaned weakly. A splatter of blood splashed across the room. The panther lay down and began cleaning up the blood, licking its claws with methodical grace.

The fellow turned his head and stared at us with bleary, unfocused eyes. He seemed to be trying to say something, but all that came out was a low whine.

"Easy," I called to him. "We'll have you out of here in no time."

At once I saw the rope which would lower the man to the floor. Unfortunately, I didn't see any way to swing him out of the panthers' reach first.

"What do you suggest?" I asked Ool. I was loathe to shoot the two cats. They'd be beautiful beasts if fattened up, and quite valuable in most civilized lands. I could think of a dozen markets for them.

"Feed them," suggested Ool. "After they gorge themselves, they will sleep. Then you can let the man down."

"And if they wake up?"

"Use drugged meat."

"No!" Graff said with revulsion. "Do the world a favor! Shoot him now, the murderer!"

I raised my eyebrows. "Any particular reason, or are you just feeling bloodthirsty today?"

"I thought Jordan had killed him. We all thought it. That man tried to poison the crew!"

"Oh?"

"Yes," Graff glared at the man. "He used to be our cook."

*   *   *

It took an hour for Frago to find a sleeping draught in his belongings. I poured the white dust onto a ten-pound slab of salted pork, then carried it below and tossed it to the panthers. The two cats, snarling and hissing, gorged themselves. In fifteen minutes they lay quietly, their tails and paws twitching every few seconds. Only then did I undo the rope and lower the cook to the floor.

After I'd struck the chains from his arms, I rolled him onto a litter and, with Graff's unenthusiastic assistance, carried him up onto the deck. All the sailors on duty crowded around, with mingle shock and curiosity. Most seemed to feel some measure of sympathy for the fellow, but Graff and a couple of others kept grumbling to themselves.

"Take him below to one of the empty cabins!" I barked, handing my end of the litter to Pup, one of Jordan's men who'd sworn allegiance to Frago.

"Aye, sir," he said. They carried the cook away.

"The rest of you get back to work! If I see you lolling around deck again, I'll make sure you draw extra duty."

The crew reluctantly returned to their places and took up their various tasks. Satisfied, I followed after Graff and Pup.

Since we didn't have a physician or healer aboard, and I didn't trust any of Jordan's crew not to kill the cook, given the opportunity, I decided to see the man's injuries myself.

After tearing a sheet into bandages, I took a bottle of brandy from the ship's stores and prepared to clean and dress the cook's wounds. It was not a task I looked forward to since I knew It would be excruciatingly painful to the man, but fortunately for him he was now unconscious.

Pup stayed and helped me as best he could. He was young, perhaps fifteen, formerly a cabin boy. When the cook began to moan and thrash, Pup held him down so I could continue bandaging his wounds without fighting off half-hearted blows.

"Tell me about him," I said to Pup.

"His name is Kelmar, and he used to be the ship's cook. Two days before we reached Zorvoon most of the crew became deathly ill, Jordan among them. He blamed the food. That night Kelmar disappeared, and I guess everyone assumed the captain killed him."

"I would imagine so," I said, "knowing Jordan's reputation." Finished, I pulled a sheet up around Kelmar's shoulders. "Stay here and give him water or broth when he wakes."

"Aye, sir." Pup said.

With a sigh, I rose to my feet, rubbing my eyes and stretching my tired muscles. It had been a long day already, and I still had the hold's cargo to catalog.

Pushing open the hatch, I went out into the corridor. It was deserted; the men were either on deck and working or asleep in their quarters. I nodded happily, thinking this was the way things should be. My thoughts turned to manifests and inventories, and I headed for the main deck.

But before I'd taken five steps, I saw movement ahead of me, a subtle change in the darkness, as though someone was concealed in a hatchway further down the hall. It was enough to set my teeth on edge, enough to make my every sense scream *danger!*

Pretending not to have noticed anything out of the ordinary, I continued walking down the corridor at an even pace. Silently I eased a knife from my sash and held it ready. I wouldn't be caught off guard.

I glimpsed the furtive movement again, three hatches down. Someone was certainly trying to hide and doing a pretty good job of it. Still, I continued without pause. I even whistled a bit, a nameless tune I'd heard once in a tavern. If that didn't put my waiting foe at ease, nothing would.

As I passed the hatch, someone lunged at me from the darkness.

Falling back, I parried a knife thrust toward my ribs, then seized the hand wielding it and began to squeeze as hard as I could. I heard a startled, frustrated gasp, then the knife clattered noisily to the deck. Pulling the man into the light, I looked into his face.

It was Garan. I shouldn't have been surprised, I suppose. I had no great respect for him, but I hadn't thought he was the type to be desperate enough to try to kill me on board the ship. He'd be the first one Frago suspected if I suddenly turned up dead. If I'd been him, I would have waited six months, until my humiliation had been forgotten by others, before exacting revenge.

I punched him in the stomach as hard as I could, then knocked his legs out from under him as he doubled over. When he lay on the floor, trying to breathe, gasping like a fish out of water, I knelt on his arms and pinned him to the deck.

"Why, Garan?" I said. With the tip of my knife I drew little lines on his forehead, lacerating the skin. I kept the other hand on his throat. "I've always known you were a bully, but I certainly never thought of you as a backstabbing murderer."

"Who are you?" he gasped. His eyes were bright with pain. "You fight like a demon!"

I tightened my grip on his throat. "Just a sailor like any other."

"You . . . fight like . . . Fel Blackmane—" His eyes widened in sudden recognition. "You are—"

"I'm sorry you recognized me," I said grimly, closing my hand and twisting until I heard his neck snap.

After I'd caught my breath, I dragged the body up on deck. The crewmen were silent as I tied a rope to Garan's foot and hanged him, head down, in the rigging for all to see.

"Discipline will be maintained," I said. "We fight traders, not each other. Remember that."

Someone had called Frago. He thundered out on deck, looked at Garan hanging there by his foot, looked at me. I saw a touch of sadness in his eyes.

"Well?" he said at last.

"Garan was waiting for me below decks. He tried to kill me."

"He was armed?"

"With a knife."

Frago looked at the body again. "I don't see any wounds on his body. Or yours."

"He was clumsy. During the struggle I broke his neck."

There were murmurs of disbelief from some of Frago's old crewmen, people who'd known Garan as long as I had and owed him a measure of loyalty—at least more loyalty than they owed a stranger named Dray Sorrel.

Redeye spoke up first. "I find it hard to believe an un-armed man could kill a man with a knife so easily."

"I had a knife, too," I said.

"I always trust my first officer's word," Frago said, "and I trust Dray with my life. He has no reason to lie, and Garan had every reason to want to kill him. The matter is ended. Leave Garan there until tomorrow, then dump his body overboard. The sharks can have him for breakfast."

With that, he turned and stumped back into his cabin. When the door shut, there was a tense silence.

"Get back about your tasks," I said quietly. "There's more than enough to be done yet."

Grudgingly, it seemed, they obeyed. I could tell that between saving Kelmar and killing Garan I hadn't made a favorable impression on them. Still, I could win their respect in one battle; loyalty would come when I proved I always had the ship's best interests in mind. All it would take was time.

*   *   *

Three hours later, the inventory completed, I went to see Frago in his cabin. I found him bent over his maps and charts, plotting our course.

"I finished the inventory," I said, putting the ledger down on the corner of the table.

"Good." He scarcely looked up. "Briefly, what do we have?"

"A few crates of silks, a few bags of spices, and two black panthers."

"That's all?" He looked up at me, amazed.

"Unfortunately. Jordan must've unloaded everything else

in Zorvoon before we took the ship."

"Damn," he whispered. "I'd counted on a full hold."

"We'll just have to take a trade ship," I said.

"Yes. And soon."

"Where, Captain?" I asked. "How about Almanthia? It's harvest season, and I hear trade's up. There'll be plenty of ships worth taking . . ."

He shook his head. "Freighters, mostly, stuffed full of grain. We'll need silks and spices and shipments of gold—especially shipments of gold. The best place for that these days is Gallistan."

"Gallistan?" I frowned, puzzled. Gallistan was, to the best of my knowledge, a poor country several weeks' sail to the east, full of a petty nobility always bickering among itself. I couldn't imagine why anyone would want to go there, let alone pirates.

I said as much.

"Fel, you really should pay attention to what's going on in the world. Gallistan and Kaldistan have been at war for the last six months, and rumor has it that quite a few of the noble-born are fleeing to neutral lands with their fortunes. The seas are crowded with their ships. It only seems reasonable that they share their wealth with us."

I nodded reluctantly. It didn't fit in with my own plans. Well, I'd just have to bide my time. I'd make it to Almanthia yet, even if it took me the better part of a year.

"Very well," I said. "Gallistan it is. I'll see to the course."

"Do that," he said.

But as soon as possible, I added mentally, we were going

to Almanthia.

*   *   *

The next few days were spent working at fever pitch. Black Jordan had been a sloppy captain; discipline under him had been alternately brutal and lax. It took a long time to get the *Blue Maiden* into shape, and longer still to mold the crew into proper fighting trim. Sails, decks, and rails had to be repaired, and fresh oakum put down to keep the wood from rotting.

When I finished inventorying the ship's armory and galley, I found quite a few things in short supply, especially food. At our current rate of consumption, we'd be on short rations in less than a week.

I talked to Kelmar about it. He was healing nicely and, although weak, could talk.

"Food was always a problem with Jordan," he said. "He never let me take care of supplies. He always took care of procurement himself, and he didn't much care what he got as long as it came cheap."

"Is that what happened when the crew thought you'd poisoned them?"

"Aye." Kelmar nodded slowly. "Jordan brought a haunch of beef on board and had me cook it. I thought there was something wrong with it and said so, but he ordered me to make it into a stew anyway, said it was nothing but my imagination."

"But it wasn't," I said.

"No. The meat was bad. And everyone—Jordan among them—blamed me, though I'd been ship's cook for almost two years with nary a case of food sickness."

"What about supplies? Provisions are running low. Is there a store of food I haven't found yet?"

"No. Jordan liked his crew a little hungry, so there was almost never enough to eat on board—or not enough for long. He took what he needed from coastal towns or ships he captured."

"I see," I said, rising. "Tomorrow you can report to the galley. And I warn you now, we'll be expecting the best meal you've ever cooked!"

"Aye, sir!" he grinned.

I went to Frago's cabin. When I told him about our lack of supplies, he only nodded. "It's to be expected; Jordan probably planned to get provisions for his next voyage while he was in Zorvoon."

I shrugged. "So we must somehow steal provisions. I'll have the men keep a lookout for any likely ships."

"Do that," he said. Rummaging through the papers still stacked on the chart table, he drew out a map of the waters between Zorvoon and Gallistan and smoothed the wrinkles from its parchment. A thick finger traced our course. "Yes," he said, "we should be in the sea lanes between Gallistan and Tázgul any day now. Pickings will be good." He glanced up at me. "See to it, Fel."

"Of course," I said. "And the name's Dray."

*   *   *

Three days later I heard the call: "A sail, portside!"

I ran from my cabin, buttoning up my shirt. Half the crew was already present, clustered against the port railing, straining to see in the growing darkness. I finally picked out a small gray-white speck. Yes, it was most certainly a ship. She was a good way off, though; we'd never catch her before nightfall.

"Back to your stations," I called. "We'll board her in the morning if all goes well."

"Aye, sir," the men said. There was an undercurrent of excitement, of anticipation.

I went back to see the mate at the wheel. We'd alter our course slightly to port so we'd catch up with the other ship early the next day. With the night to cover us, we'd be on her before the crew knew we were coming. I smiled to myself. A fight was certainly what I needed to win the crew's loyalty.

*   *   *

The plan worked perfectly. Our two ships sailed throughout the night, theirs unaware of ours, ours stalking theirs. When dawn came, I was already on deck, watching the waves, looking for our prey.

I spotted her perhaps a half mile ahead, her sails full and billowing, her wake a startling white against the deep azure sea. I felt my breath come quicker, my heart beat faster. We would have her before noon.

Turning, I bellowed orders, sending the men running to put up every yard of sail we had. In minutes the *Blue Maiden* surged ahead, racing across the waves.

As the men took grapples and rope from the ship's stores and prepared their swords and knives for the fight, I stayed by the rail and watched the other ship draw close. At last, when she was a scant fifty yards ahead, I could see her crew scurrying like rats about their tasks. I knew then that we'd take her easily;

the captain was obviously inexperienced with pirates. Rather than preparing to try to fight us off—and it would be clear to any practiced eye that we were under strength—he was hoping to catch a sudden breeze and outrun us.

All the better for us. We'll take them all the more easily.

At last we drew even with the ship. I saw her name, *Camarre Dream*, painted on her bow.

"Hard to port!" I called. The man at the wheel sent us up alongside her.

Grapples were cast and made tight, and the ships were drawn together. Frago moved next to me, sword in hand. I drew my own saber, touched its cold steel, testing its edge.

"Now!" Frago cried when our ships almost touched.

"First blood's mine!" I shouted, leaping across to the *Camarre Dream*.

I landed on top of a short, balding man who tried to raise his sword in defense. He wasn't fast enough. I mashed in his head with the hilt of my saber, then was on my feet and swinging at the men around me. Screaming my war cry, I waded into the thick of the fray.

Everything became a blur of slashing, parrying, lunging. Blood roared in my ears, and I laughed like a madman, feeling stronger than I'd ever felt before, my spirit soaring. This was what I remembered best from my days with Aldenius Frago; this was what I loved most.

It seemed the battle had scarcely begun before the *Camarre Dream*'s captain shouted for his men to lay down their arms. Somewhat disappointed, I let the sailor I'd been fighting disengage and surrender his sword to me.

I became aware of many of my fellow crewmen giving me strange looks. I grinned openly at them as I cleaned my sword on a dead man's cape. Blood covered me from head to heel; I must have appeared almost a demon in battle, since I'd killed some six men and wounded three others.

"He's another Fel Blackmane," I heard Redeye say in awe.

I turned and laughed. "I'm better than Blackmane," I told him. "I'm still alive."

Frago was calling me, and I went to help him sort out the ship's papers. A busy day lay ahead of us.

FIFTEEN

When Alna Savina left the soothsayer's house, she felt curiously relieved and uplifted. Her whole body tingled with the power of the blind woman's visions. She had spoken with the spirits of the night, had entered beautiful realms no mortal eye was ever meant to see, had listened to songs more lovely than any ever played.

Her memories were vague, misty, and she could not remember the answers to her questions about Fel Blackmane. Still, it no longer seemed quite so important as it once had. What did she have to worry about from a dead pirate? After all, hadn't Karnekash slain him and his men?

His kiss . . . She shivered a bit at the memory of Blackmane's lips on hers, at the fire and passion of his touch. No one before Blackmane had ever dared to touch her thusly, as a woman instead of a countess.

Praemir opened the carriage door and offered her a gloved hand. She accepted it, and he helped her up the two small steps into the cushioned interior of her carriage. She barely noticed him, her thoughts were so far away.

She looked out at the soothsayer's small house. The translucent, white windowpanes flickered with more than light from a lantern. What magic was the soothsayer working?

An image came to Alna Savina of a beautiful, pale woman with long black hair and haunting gray eyes. She wore a funeral gown which some unfelt wind billowed out and around her like waves in the sea. She seemed to be calling Blackmane's name, reaching out like a long-dead lover welcoming him into the next world.

In the blink of an eye the vision was gone. Alna Savina shuddered uncontrollably and sketched a character in the air which, her tutors had assured her as a child, would ward off any evil spirits.

Perhaps the old soothsayer had summoned the ghostly image when trying to answer her questions. If he could summon such spirits, then what else might he be able to do? He was more powerful than she liked. Idly, she made a note to have him killed; he had set up his magic shop too close to Bar Altibb for her liking. She could have tolerated him if he'd stayed in the wilderness, living like a hermit, but *here* . . .

She only wished she could remember what he'd said about Blackmane! Other prophecies she'd heard over the last two months came to her, drifting up into her thoughts like water bubbling from a spring. She had gone to see every oracle and fortune-teller and soothsayer she could find, asking them about the pirate. And each had given her a different answer.

The first was a woman who claimed to be possessed by two spirits: one proclaimed, "Fel Blackmane lives!" and the other proclaimed, "Fel Blackmane is no more!" Next was the tall, muscular sorcerer who said he saw into the next world, and told her Blackmane's spirit had not yet arrived there. "But if he died by violence, he could be haunting the place of his death. . . ."

Last came the strangely beautiful child, who spoke as no other human spoke, whose eyes were bright with the mysteries of the gods, who said merely:

"Rats and cabbages and flies all die. But who shall favor

the sea? Vain ladies cross lands of gold. Where angels bless the wicked. Beware the doom of a friend."

Every one of them had unsettled her, especially the child and her riddle. Or was it a riddle? It seemed nonsense (and that was what her advisers deemed it), but still she wondered. What if she were just too stupid to figure it out? What if the answer lay there, somehow twisted and trapped in the words?

She hated puzzles. She had never enjoyed games, even as a child, except those which allowed her to dress up and show off her beauty.

Never again, she swore to herself, would she let a prophet trick her. No wonder her people thought her obsession growing toward madness, if she let every minor magician upset her.

But even as she swore off them, she knew she was lying to herself. How could she live without knowing, once and for all, whether Fel Blackmane was dead?

She frowned, thinking of Caneel and Ril and how the wizard had killed them so casually, as though it meant nothing to him. She didn't like losing friends; she had too few.

SIXTEEN

Over the next two months, we robbed three ships heading out from Gallistan. Two numbered among their passengers rich noblemen fleeing their country's war, and each had kindly brought his personal fortune with him. The third ship yielded a small cache of valuable gems and Zorvoonian gold.

I led Frago's men in each attack, as I had in the old days, and I found my deeds did not go unnoticed—with Frago, with the crew, with the sailors we fought. Frago praised my bravery and gave me first choice among our loot. More importantly, to me at least, Frago's old crew proclaimed me the new Fel Blackmane and drank toasts to my name when we celebrated our good fortune. That meant they had accepted me, that they now held a measure of respect for my battle prowess.

Word had also begun to spread about me among the traders. Each time I boarded a ship the sailors shrank away from me and cried out in surrender—whether their captain gave the order or not. Were it not for my sworn quest, I might have been content to follow my old master for the rest of his years. As it was, I managed to postpone thoughts of vengeance, by throwing myself into my work, and spending long hours guiding the men, keeping the *Blue Maiden* running at peak efficiency.

So it was that, nearly nine months after I'd lost the *Pamah Reach* and my crew, we sailed into the small northern harbor of Janjor and disembarked to celebrate the voyage.

*   *   *

In a small tavern called The Slaughtered Goat, I drank

and toasted our success with Frago and the *Maiden*'s other officers. The wine and silver flowed freely, and good humor kept the place ringing with laughter until well into the night. As dawn approached, the men began to fall asleep one by one, putting their heads on the tables and snoring softly. The few of us still awake sat quietly, sated with rich food and wine, lost in introspection, or just telling tall tales of adventures we'd had only in our dreams.

As I mumbled some deeply philosophical remark to a sleepy serving maid, I grew aware of Ool bending over me. Blearily I looked up at him.

"Dray," he whispered.

"What is it, man? Speak up!"

"I have some private errands to run," he said softly. "I will be back before the *Maiden* sails."

"Oh?"

He smiled. "I have friends in Janjor whom I haven't seen in many years. It's only proper that I stop by and pay them my respects, now that morning has come. Besides, they may have news of the wizard you seek."

I caught my breath, barely able to contain my excitement. "Then go, and good luck to you!"

He stood and angled toward the door. I watched him go with a measure of interest, then took another drink. Not long after that, I must have passed out, for it was approaching noon when someone finally shook me awake. My head throbbed and my eyes burned; I felt sick and feverish. Groaning feebly, I put my head back down on my arms.

Then someone had the ill manners to shake me again.

"Dray, get up," I heard Ool say. "I have some news for you."

I groaned and covered my head, but Ool wouldn't go away. Finally I gave up and looked at him. He now wore splendid wine-colored robes with a white sash about his middle: his friends had given him new clothes, ones more suitable to a wizard of his stature. From head to heel he looked the epitome of fashion . . . at least among wizards in a backwater port like Janjor.

"You have news?" I mumbled.

He nodded excitedly. "Yes," he said again. "The Master of Dragons is nearby."

"What?" I demanded, suddenly wide awake, my hangover all but forgotten. "Where?"

"Lystia. One of my friends met him not three weeks ago. It seems he goes by the name Karnekash, and the stories he tells of defeating Fel Blackmane have made him popular in certain courts. Anyone with enough gold can buy his services."

"Lystia." I sank back, rubbing my eyes. It was a small kingdom not too far from Janjor—perhaps two weeks' journey. Since it, too, was a minor seaport, perhaps I could persuade Frago to head there next. I had to try.

"Dray?" Ool said. "What do you want to do?"

I smiled happily, my thoughts full of bloodlust and vengeance. "Make him pay for all the pain he's caused me. How I've waited for this!" Standing a bit unsteadily,

I looked across the table. There were only six of us left in the tavern; Frago was gone. "Let's get back to the ship. The sooner I see the captain, the sooner we'll be off to Lystia."

On the way out the door, Ool whispered a spell and

touched the center of my forehead, almost as an afterthought. I felt a burst of pain, like little needles pricking behind each eye, and the docks before me wavered sickeningly. Then I blinked and my vision cleared. I felt better—much better, as though I hadn't spent the last twenty-four hours drinking myself into a stupor.

Straightening, I smoothed the wrinkles from my shirt and tightened my swordbelt. "Thanks," I said. Then, taking a deep breath, I shambled out into the bright morning sunshine.

Janjor sprawled across half a mountain, a small city with narrow, winding streets and numerous dead-end alleys. The red-tiled roofs, the whitewashed walls, all spoke of an orderly nature which, on closer examination, didn't really exist. The laws were vague and scarcely enforced; pirates such as ourselves were safe here.

I swaggered across the stone to the narrow wooden docks, where a couple of small boats from the *Blue Maiden* had been tied up for the night. Our ship lay at anchor three hundred yards out; Janjor's harbor didn't run deep enough to accommodate her keel.

I looked around for men to row us out, but the place was deserted. Everyone was either still drunk in taverns or had returned to the *Maiden* long ago. Not even fishermen moved about—they had left with the tide long before dawn, eager to cast their nets and see what the day's catch would be.

Reluctantly Ool and I climbed down into the smaller boat. Ool folded his arms imperiously, so I unshipped the oars myself. After locking them in place, I rowed myself and my wizard mate out to the *Maiden*.

*   *   *

Returning to the galleon, I went at once to Frago's cabin. He let me in, looking concerned.

He said, "Something's bothering you, Fel my lad. What is it?"

"I want to go to Lystia. The wizard who destroyed my ship is there."

"I can't go sailing off on a sudden hunch or whim! How do you know he's there?"

"Ool told me. He spoke to friends of his in Janjor who had spoken with Karnekash in Lystia not three weeks ago—and that's enough proof for me. Will you set the course?"

"No," Frago said, "it's not possible. I have better plans for us than chasing phantoms—we're off to Iazgul. The spices should be harvested by now, and we'll arrive in time to steal shipments heading for Zorvoon and the other southern kingdoms. There's a fortune to be had, if we're quick. I don't intend to let it slip away."

"That wizard *murdered my* crew—"

He laughed. "I understand more than you think, Fel, my boy. The years away from me have softened your brain. Once you cared only for gold. Now look at you! Such a small bit of revenge has turned you into a feeble old man who must go begging to his former master for crumbs of justice. Justice!" He spat. "A pirate deserves only what is taken by force!"

"Is that all you have to say?" I demanded, hot and angry, my cheeks burning.

"It's enough. For now at least. Go sleep off last night and

forget about Lystia and that wizard. I've got more important work for you, work that will make us rich."

Turning, I stalked from his cabin, slamming the hatch behind me. Even through the thick wood I could hear him laughing.

Damn him. Nine whole months had passed since the Countess of Fleurin destroyed my ship, my crew, and my life. What had I done in all that time? Nothing. I'd worked to help an old man regain his place at sea, but that didn't help me now. What had I done for myself? And what had Frago done for me?

I cursed my own stupidity, my own lethargy.

Ool was waiting for me. He must have seen the anger and frustration on my face, for he wisely said nothing.

I said, "He won't go to Lystia."

"I didn't think he would. He's done nothing to help you yet in your quest. Rather, he's done everything he could to bind you to him, to make it difficult for you to leave."

I scowled. "What? He gave me money and weapons in Zorvoon."

"So you could help him steal a ship."

"He made me his first mate—"

"So you would work for him on the *Maiden*."

"But—"

"But nothing!" Ool said. "He has been using you, Master, and you are just too blind and too trusting to see it. Why do you think he would not go to Almanthia when Karnekash was there? Why do you think he will not go to Lystia? Because he does not want to lose you. Even as Dray Sorrel you're worth more to him than all his other men combined."

I frowned. I didn't like what he'd said, but I had to admit it made a kind of sense. Perhaps Frago *had* been using me—was still using me. It certainly sounded like that the way Ool put it. Whatever, the time had come for me to leave.

"Let's go back ashore," I said, "and find Graff. We've got some planning to do."

*   *   *

The three of us met in The Slaughtered Goat, at a back table, and sipped sweet brandy as we talked. I felt like a traitor involved in some great conspiracy, but it had to be done. At least I could make sure Frago came out of it looking as good as possible—it would never do to make him lose face among his men.

"I don't want a mutiny," I said slowly. "Frago can keep the *Maiden* and all those who owe him their loyalty. What I want is a small ship to command and enough men to sail her. I know I can count on Ool's support and yours, Graff. But what about the others? You're closer to them than we are—you hear their talk. Would any of them leave Frago to come with me?"

Graff took a long swallow, then set his goblet down and wiped his lips thoughtfully. At last he said, "Not everyone is happy with the way Frago runs things. Oh, the pay's good, but some say he should show less mercy to those we capture, that we should kill the passengers and sink the ships. That way there won't be any witnesses. . . ."

I nodded. "Go on."

"And—well, you lead the men into battle, and they respect you for that. It's more than Frago does."

"He's an old man."

"Aye," Graff said. "People were figuring to follow you after he dies. You're the natural choice for his successor."

I smiled. "That's all I needed to know."

*   *   *

The next day, we set sail from Janjor. The winds were favorable, and the sky was clear; we made quick progress toward Tázguli shipping lanes.

On our eighth day out, we spotted a small ship heading in our general direction. I gave the orders—without telling Frago—to alter course, and we headed straight for her.

She was a small two-master out of Tázgul, I saw as I studied her through a spyglass. Her sails were trim and she was running light—probably on some diplomatic errand. She had clean lines and a good cut to her sails . . . much like the *Pamah Reach*. Instantly I wanted her for my own. I had to have her, whatever the cost.

Eagerly I sought out Ool. "This is it," I told him. "That's the ship I want."

He nodded, studying her with a practiced eye. "A good choice, I think. She's fast."

Laughing, I said, "Nothing but the best will do." I headed for Frago's cabin to tell him I'd given orders to intercept the schooner. I knew I had to seize this opportunity. I'd let myself become too soft, too attached to him and the *Maiden*.

When I told Frago what I'd done, he fumed in silence for a moment. "You should've left that ship alone, Fel, my lad—that's the first mistake you've made in a long time." He paced up and down before me, frowning, hands clenched behind his back. At last he sighed. "We don't need to capture some imperial courier. They're more trouble than they're worth. Do you even know what nationality the ship is?"

"Tázguli, from the cut of the sails."

"Tázguli? Tázguli? Don't you realize how powerful the king of Tázgul's new navy is? Suppose he takes offense and orders us captured and the *Maiden* sunk? What then?"

I laughed, though I didn't feel very humorous. "You worry too much. Navies have been after us before."

"I know, I know, and somehow we've always eluded them. But I didn't have them after me by choice, and I had a better crew in those days. Look at the sorry lot we have now!"

"There are enough good men to keep you alive."

He frowned, studying me. "A curious turn of phrase."

"I'm in a curious mood."

"I'll grant you that. But still—a Tázguli ship!" He shook his head.

"But we'll take the ship," I said.

He grimaced. "Of course. We have to now. The men are interested, and it's not good to get their hopes up for a fight, then disappoint them. But it had better be worth the effort, Fel."

"Oh, it will be," I said, with conviction. "I'm certain."

*   *   *

The schooner tried to steer past us, but I hadn't spent twenty years at sea for nothing. I swung the *Blue Maiden* around, catching the wind, robbing the schooner's sails. I watched as she lay there, all but dead in the water, and we coasted up next to her. Her name was *Breen Wind*.

Frago's men scurried in preparation to board, swinging ropes with grapples, throwing them across to catch the *Breen Wind*'s railing, lashing the ships together so tightly that they could not be separated easily.

On board the *Wind* I saw several squads of soldiers rushing into formation. I knew, then, that the battle would be over quickly: these were men used to the land, not the sea, for what experienced sailor would wear armor on board ship? If they fell overboard . . .

Drawing my sword, I prepared to leap across. Ool put his hand on my arm. "Stay back," he said. "Let the men fight this time. Direct them from here, as Frago would do."

"I'm no coward or cripple!"

"You must live through this battle. Dray, if you're to see Karnekash in Lystia."

"I'll live," I said, shrugging off his hand. "But I'd rather be dead than left alone on deck while others fight my battles. If you want to protect me so much, put a spell on me—make me invincible!"

"That's impossible, and you know it. I am bound by the limits of magic just as you are bound by the limits of your strength."

"Then stay out of my way." Leaping the *Blue Maiden*'s railing, I cried, "Death to the Tázguli!" Then I jumped across to the *Breen Wind*'s deck. "Take no prisoners!"

Cheering, the men followed me across.

*   *   *

It was a short battle, and very bloody. My old master had, I distantly noticed, tried to restrain his men during the battle, shouting for them to spare the schooner's crew when they tried to surrender. But my cheers and cries for blood had drowned out Frago's voice, and the men heard only me during the fight.

Frago glared as he crossed to the *Wind*. I calmly wiped my saber clean, studying the new nicks and scratches in its blade. I would have to polish them out.

"Have you gone completely mad?" he demanded. "Or just deaf?"

"No," I said calmly. "I'm following your advice."

He stared at me incredulously. "To murder innocent people?"

"To take what I want. This is my ship now, Captain, and I intend to sail her to Lystia."

"Mutiny—that's what it is!" His hand dropped to his sword.

"I wouldn't do that if I were you," I said softly, so the others couldn't hear. "Ool doesn't take kindly to people trying to kill me. He's been known to turn them into little white mice. Or worse."

"If you leave me," he snarled, "you'll sail this ship alone." His hand drifted away from his sword, I noticed—a promising sign.

I smiled, sheathing my own saber as I stood. "Come now. Captain, surely you wouldn't begrudge me my first mate and navigator? They were my men long before they were yours."

"Take them, then."

"And perhaps a few others, if they come of their own free will?"

He quivered with rage. "You'd never make it a day without me."

"I lived five years without you." My voice was hard. "I have my own life to lead. Captain, and some old scores to settle. You've wasted eight months of my life, and I've run out of patience. If you won't help, then you're standing in my way."

Frago stepped back, spat, then turned and stomped off. He swung over to his own ship, then bellowed, "All hands return to your posts. We're casting off. Move your lazy asses!"

"Wait!" I cried, and the men turned to hear what I had to say. "You know me. We've lived together, worked together, and fought together for the last eight months. I can offer you nothing that Captain Frago hasn't already given you—except a chance to fight at my side, to seize your fortunes and hold them tight. Within three months, I promise you a prize none has had since Fel Blackmane—we will take Bar Altibb!"

There were shocked expressions on the sailors' faces, and I thought for a moment I'd overplayed my hand. But then a number of them began to cheer and rally around me, raising their swords in salute and shouting my name.

I grinned across at Frago. "I have my crew," I said. "Now let us part with friendship between us, as we parted the last time. I offer you my hand. Will you take it?"

"Bah," he said, and he turned and strode angrily to his cabin. In the hatchway he paused and looked back. "Take the men. Dray—I owe you that much. But now I consider whatever debt I might have owed you gone, and whatever debt you owed me canceled. There is nothing to bind us together any more. I wish you all luck and speed, and may the gods grant you all you deserve."

Silently, those men who chose to remain with him filed back to the *Blue Maiden*, and cast off. As they raised their sails, it seemed a strangely grim scene. I felt as though I'd betrayed my only friend and ally, but Frago had given me no choice.

I moved to the foredeck to address my new crew. I saw Kelmar and Pup and twenty-odd others I knew I could count on. It felt strange to be standing before them as captain. Nevertheless I took a deep breath and decided to tell them everything. I would need their help and loyalty and understanding in the next few months, and I owed them an explanation.

I said: "Some of you know who I really am. My name is not Dray Sorrel, but Fel Blackmane."

There were startled mutters from the crew. Ool was nodding, and so was Graff—he must have suspected who I was since the day we'd gone to Frago's house in Zorvoon. I waited for the excited talk to die down before continuing.

"I escaped the Countess of Fleurin's attack on me with the aid of my first mate, Ool. I have planned to avenge myself on the Countess of Fleurin and the wizard she hired, and you're going to help me. I took Fleurin once, and I can take it again!"

The men cheered and began shouting my name—my true name this time, Fel Blackmane. I knew they would follow me to the ends of the earth. They were as loyal as any crew I'd ever had, hardy men all.

"Captain," Graff said, sounding eager, "shall I set the course for Lystia?"

"Do it!" I said. "And Ool, see to the cleanup. I want the

decks cleared as soon as possible." Turning, I headed toward the captain's cabin.

Behind me, I heard my first mate bellowing orders, sending the men running to their places. If I closed my eyes, I could imagine myself aboard the *Pamah Reach*. I began to smile, and a bit of my old jauntiness returned to my step. Our next task, I promised myself, would be renaming my new ship the *Pamah Reach II*. I liked the sound of it.

SEVENTEEN

"My Lady," the spy said, bowing low. He was a nondescript man, so ordinary you could have passed him a thousand times in the street and never given him more than a cursory glance. In fact, the Countess of Fleurin mused, the only thing extraordinary about Ralli was that he'd been in her service so long and with so much success; most of her spies lasted only a few months before being discovered and exiled—or executed.

Ralli was a master of his trade. He had served her almost as long as she could remember. That he'd returned to Fleurin and asked for an audience meant he carried information of great import. He'd never disappointed her before.

"What is it?" she asked with interest, leaning forward in her low throne. Except for Praemir and the other bodyguards, the room was deserted.

Ralli bowed once more. "Rumors, my lady, which I knew would interest you."

"Tell me, then—what are they?"

"There is a pirate, a madman some say, and certainly a demon in battle."

"So? Why would this disturb me?"

"His name is Dray Sorrel. Everyone in the world is calling him the new Fel Blackmane. I know of your interest in Blackmane, so I thought you would be interested in this man who pretends to his name."

"Dray Sorrel, you say? Why have I never heard of him before?"

The spy shrugged. "His past is a mystery. No one knows

where he came from—he just appeared one day in Zorvoon. A few months ago he was known to be sailing with Aldenius Frago, Blackmane's old master. Now word has come from Tázgul, from a man who never before failed me, that Sorrel has seized two merchant ships. And the name of his vessel is the *Pamah Reach II*."

"The *Pamah Reach II*?" The Countess of Fleurin sat up as if an electric shock had hit her. "Blackmane's ship was named the *Pamah Reach*."

"Yes, Lady."

Alna Savina bit her lip. *One who is dead shall attend your wedding.* That's what the madwoman had said. She was suddenly, obscurely, terrified.

"Send out my assassins," she said. Best to take swift, decisive action. "Kill this Dray Sorrel, whoever he is."

Fel Blackmane come again! It was enough to give her nightmares. And she knew she wouldn't sleep well until her men reported the pirate dead.

EIGHTEEN

"There it is," I said to no one in particular, as I gazed out across the sparkling blue-green sea at Lystia. It was a small but magnificent little port city, full of gleaming silver spires, polished white marble, and glittering brass domes. In the fading light of the sun it shone like a beacon, like the land of faery in ancient legends.

Even so, it was the work of man—one man in particular. As far away as Zorvoon stories were told of King Rafanel of Lystia, who had long been a member of the Order of Aesthetes. His love of things elegant and beautiful had made his city one of the most strikingly picturesque places in the world. Architects had been known to travel thousands of miles for the privilege of basking in its beauty.

"Did you know," Ool said, "that there are more wizards in Lystia than in all of Zorvoon?"

"So many?" I said. "I knew some great magic protected the city from siege or invasion, but I'm surprised that more than one or two wizards live this far from Zorvoon and the other great cities of the world."

"A wizard who has mastered teleportation can well afford to live here and travel to Zorvoon at will."

I turned to him. "Like you?"

He laughed easily. "I'm happier at sea, just as you are. And anyway, have you ever seen me try to teleport?"

"No."

"It drove my old teachers to tears of frustration, watching me try. I know my own abilities, and teleportation is well beyond them."

"Too bad," I said. "I can think of quite a few times it would have come in handy." Like when we were being attacked by the dragon. I looked again at that magnificent city and thought of Karnekash living there, surrounded by splendor. Something hardened inside me. "Enough of this talk," I said, turning away. "Now we have work to do. Tell the men to drop anchor here and prepare to spend the night aboard ship. This evening you and I will take a small boat ashore."

"They won't be happy without leave of some sort."

"Have the cook give them all extra measures of rum. They can drink here as well as on land. And I want the ship ready to sail at a moment's notice."

"Aye, sir." Frowning, he turned and gave the orders. If I killed a wizard, I'd need to leave Lystia by the fastest means possible. I didn't need four or five more wizards chasing me through the streets, trying to turn me into a pig or a goat or whatever they did to their enemies. And I couldn't let the men go ashore because I didn't want to spend three or four hours hauling them out of taverns and brothels when I was ready to leave.

I watched as my crew set about lowering the sails and stowing them away. Soon . . .

Letting one hand drop to caress the hilt of my saber, soon. I could almost feel my hands tightening around Karnekash's throat.

* * *

Black was the color of night, the color of shadows, the color of murder. I dressed in silence in my cabin: black leather pants, a black silk shirt, and a black cape with ermine trim. When I drew the hood up over my head and gazed into the looking glass, my pale image seemed almost a portrait of death itself. Lastly I buckled on my sword belt, checked my saber, and tucked a half-dozen knives into my sash.

When at last I strode out on deck, I heard the soft sounds of a lute. One of my men played and sang a sad old ballad, a tale of love lost and lovers killed. The rest of the crew sat in a semicircle, sipping their rum, listening to the music, watching the bright moon shimmer off Lystia's silver rooftops. There was an air of melancholy about them that depressed me. I felt uneasy—a premonition, perhaps, that this evening would not go as I hoped.

"Captain."

I jumped, startled. I hadn't heard Ool approach.

"A boat's been lowered for us."

"Good." I climbed down the rope ladder after him. After he had unshipped the oars, I fitted them into the locks and bent to the task of rowing. As usual, Ool was not going to exert himself at manual labor, and besides, I was a good deal stronger than my first mate.

At last we reached the docks. Ool climbed up the marble ladder and tied the mooring rope to a thick brass ring while I stowed everything away. At last, eager, I joined him and got my first close look at the fabled city of Lystia.

Sailors, laughing and talking, drifted between the docks and a row of taverns, but even without them the place would have had a festive air. The warm breeze carried the sweet, heady perfume of flower gardens, rather than the stench of open sewage so common in most other cities; and beyond the taverns rose tall, spired buildings, all brightly lit to show off their magnificent architecture. Even the streets were illuminated: tall wrought-iron poles stood at every corner, and from each hung a large oil lamp in the shape of a bird.

I stood and looked and listened and breathed the sweet air until Ool touched my arm. Turning, I said, "Which way?"

"Over here, I believe," he said confidently, starting to the left.

The people we passed wore bright colors and laughed cheerfully; I refused to get caught up in their gay mood, however, and concentrated on thoughts of retribution. At last we came to a small marble building with a small green door.

Ool stepped up to it and knocked once, sharply. A second later it swung open, revealing a small, pale man dressed all in gray. He looked my first mate over once, then nodded and stepped back.

Ool turned to me. "This is the wizards' guild," he said. "Say nothing, and speak to no one but me. Further, do not act surprised by anything you see, for some wizards like to play tricks on those who venture inside unsuspecting."

"Perhaps I'd better wait out here," I said, a bit uneasy. I didn't like the idea of mages and transmutationists and other wizards playing tricks on me.

"That would be worse," he said, "for that would only draw attention to you." He entered the building. I had no choice but to follow.

I found myself following my first mate down a wide, heavily carpeted hallway. Doors to my left and right stood open, and though I heard tantalizing sounds from each, a thousand sweet voices whispering songs, the lap of waves, the shrieks and cries of strange animals, I didn't look into any of them.

At last the little man who'd let us in stopped suddenly by a doorway. I almost bumped into Ool.

"The records are kept in here," he said softly. "Good luck finding your brother."

"Thank you," Ool said. He nodded once, then went in. I followed him.

It was a small, musty room filled with huge ledgers on stands. Several other men were already inside, seemingly absorbed in their reading. A faint smile on his face, Ool went to the newest ledger, opened it, and began leafing through in search of Karnekash's whereabouts.

As I stood there looking over his shoulder, my arms began to itch. Absently I tried to scratch them, but found my hands thick and rubbery. I glanced down. From elbow to fingertip I now had two gray flippers. And, as I watched, the gray rippled along my body faster and faster, changing clothing and flesh alike to something alien, unnatural. Suddenly I began to gasp like a fish out of water, finding it hard to breathe. The world wavered in front of me.

I tried to tap Ool on the shoulder, but ended up bludgeoning him with my fin. He staggered a bit, then turned with a low oath. But when he saw me he just shook his head sadly.

"Must you do that?" he asked.

He seemed to be addressing me, but I knew he really spoke to the other wizards in the room, I looked at each in turn, but they all seemed completely absorbed in their reading, ignoring us. Somehow I wasn't surprised. When I tried to speak, all that came out were low, animal grunts.

"Very well," Ool said, and he spread his hands. A ball of swirling silver light appeared between them. "I have no choice but to disintegrate you all, and everything else in this room."

One of the wizards looked up and sighed. "Oh, very well, if you have no sense of humor." And suddenly I was back to normal once more.

Ool clapped his hands together and the glowing ball of light dissipated. Then he bent over the ledger and went on with his reading as though nothing had happened. A moment later he muttered, "Aha!" and turned to me. "I've found it. Let's go."

I went out into the hallway and turned back the way we'd come, but the passage now dead-ended ten feet away. Ool took my arm and pulled me in the other direction. We walked perfectly straight for what seemed far too long for any one building, then turned left, then left, then left again. I lost all sense of direction.

Just as I was about to ask if he knew where we were, I saw the green door ahead of us. It seemed to be sliding along the wall like a piece of wood drifting on the ocean. Even so, Ool put his hand on it, pushed, and we were suddenly back on the street. I shook my head, disoriented, but didn't pursue the matter. Wizards were notorious for their strangeness; houses with moving doors, walls, and impossibly long passages were probably all too common in their circles.

"Karnekash lives about three blocks from here," Ool said,

turning at the corner. "We should find him in."

"Good," I said firmly. "It's about time something went right for us." Then I caught movement from the corner of my eye and glanced back.

Three grim-faced men dressed in drab gray shirts and pants were all studying something in a merchant's window with a little too much interest. Amid the crowd of laughing, celebrating people they stood out like hawks among chickens: members of the assassins' guild. I let my gaze wander past them, then put all my attention to the street ahead of us, looking for a likely place to make a stand against him.

"You've noticed them, too, then," Ool said cheerfully.

"Yes. And you needn't sound so happy about it!"

"That alley?"

I agreed.

We turned into the small, dimly lit alley. At once I pulled up my hood and drew my saber, doing my best to lose myself in the shadows. Ool whispered something, and darkness gathered about him like a robe; in seconds I could no longer see him.

Two of the three assassins appeared in the mouth of the alley. The light from the street silhouetted them nicely; if I'd had a crossbow, I couldn't have wished for a better shot. They started forward, drawing knives, separating.

The one covering my side of the alley was almost on top of me before I did anything. Silently I lashed out, kicking him in the stomach. The breath whooshed from his lungs, but he made no sound. Rather, he used the impetus of my kick and rolled backward, throwing both his knives as he did.

Fortunately I was off balance and falling backward; both blades spun past my head and landed further down the alley. In a moment I'd recovered myself, though, and leaped forward, sword swinging.

He tried to backpedal, but my saber caught him in the neck. He died without a sound.

Tense, I faded back into the shadows. I could hear Ool scuffling with the other assassin, but I had little doubt as to who would win. In a moment I heard three soft thumps, then a bit of dirt sifted down from somewhere overhead. I jerked back, then looked up. I saw a shadow move against the tapestry of stars. The third man was climbing down.

Light flared behind me. Ool! He didn't see the third assassin. I whirled, a warning on my lips.

But the light was something special, something magical. It uncoiled like a rope, snaking upward. The assassin slashed at it with his knife, but the blade did no damage. Slowly, taking its time, the rope wound itself around the man's arms, legs, throat. Gently it pulled him from the wall and lowered him to the ground.

I pried the knives from the assassin's hands. He stared at me, bewildered, obviously terrified. The rope tightened for a moment, and his eyes bulged. Then it relaxed and he could breathe again—barely.

Ool edged forward. By the glowing rope's light, my first mate looked distinctly sinister: his eyes were dark, his cheeks hollowed, his lips thin and hard set.

"Kill me," the assassin gasped. "Get it over with."

"Who sent you?" I demanded.

He remained silent, looking at the far wall.

Ool said, "The rope can tighten around any part of your body. Imagine it breaking one bone at a time, moving from your legs toward your head. How many times would you scream? How long would you live . . . and what if we left you here alive? Think of what you would spare yourself."

"I have sworn an oath before the gods," he said. "Whatever you do to me, I will not speak."

I asked suddenly, "Was it Aldenius Frago?"

The bewildered expression that crossed his face for a second made me sure it was not.

"Karnekash? The Countess of Fleurin?"

He jerked a bit when I mentioned her name.

"Ah!" I said. "The lovely Countess. But how did she find out? Frago was the only one who knew."

"He would never tell her," Ool said, "no matter how you angered him."

I looked at the assassin. "What's the name of the man you were sent to kill?" I demanded.

"Dray Sorrel," he whispered, "the pirate."

"Thanks," I said, and I nodded to my first mate.

As we headed for the mouth of the alley, I heard a muffled scream, then the dry crack of breaking bones as the ropes tightened one last time. Alna Savina didn't know, but she must have suspected something was wrong to have sent assassins after me. I smiled. The jaws of vengeance were closing. She would be next.

*   *   *

"This is it," Ool said.

I rapped loudly on the rambling old house's front door, then looked up, studying the glass-paned windows. Light shone in a few of them, so I knew people were still up and about inside.

At last I heard bolts sliding and the door opened a crack. An eye peered out suspiciously at us.

"What do you want?" its owner demanded.

"To see the wizard Karnekash."

"He's busy. Come back later." The door started to close.

Grinning, I threw my shoulder against the wood as hard as I could. The door burst open and the man tumbled backward—Karnekash! I recognized him from the crystal ball of the Seer in Zorvoon. Fortune smiled upon me.

As the wizard caught his balance against a small table, I drew my saber and charged him, screaming a battle cry. This would be for my lost crew. This would be for my proud *Pamah Reach*.

Rather than flee, he raised one hand and shouted a single harsh, guttural word. Instantly something dove down from the ceiling, striking me in the chest. I reeled backward, stunned, and then the air filled with dozens of beating wings and glowing red eyes. Small flames stung my hands and face, and I swung my blade wildly back and forth, trying to ward off whatever beasts the wizard had set upon me.

Abruptly, calm came. Light glowed all around me, a wall of energy that moved as I moved. Hovering just beyond its edge were dozens of small gray-green dragons, each no longer than my arm from nose to tail. They beat the air with powerful, leathery wings, hovering and hissing. Every now and then they shot small blasts of flame at me, but fire did not penetrate Ool's magical shield.

I glanced at the table, but Karnekash had vanished. I cursed my luck.

"Out the back door," Ool said. He had a wall of light surrounding him, too. "Hurry!"

Maybe we could still catch the wizard. I sprinted through the house and burst out into a narrow, cobbled alley. There I caught a glimpse of Karnekash as, robes billowing, he fled around the far corner of the next building. Quickly I followed, Ool at my heels.

It wasn't a road to which Karnekash ran, but a building under construction. The workers had long since retired for the night, so we were alone amidst tall piles of stone and sand and wood. I prowled through the place. Finally I heard a scrabbling sound from behind a stack of marble slabs.

I motioned Ool around the left side. He could attack from the rear. When he nodded, I raised my sword and rounded the marble slabs, treading heavily so Karnekash knew I was coming.

The wizard waited patiently. He straightened his robes, arched his back, and glared down his nose at me.

"Before I kill you," he said imperiously, "tell me who sent you. I bear a long grudge and will see that your master dies a thousand painful deaths."

I tried not to laugh. Such theatrics might frighten common assassins, but I was Fel Blackmane, and I feared no man.

I said: "Blame the Countess of Fleurin, then." Let him think she had sent me. If Karnekash managed to escape, he could seek his own revenge against her.

The wizard smiled, and it was a look of supreme superiority, as if I were some insect about to be squashed. "Put down your sword and run away. For that news I feel merciful; I will spare your life. Here!" He tossed something, and I heard a coin clink at my feet. "A gold kaled for your trouble."

"Keep your money." I drew my knife as well as my sword.

"As you wish," he said sadly, like a father who had tried to do an ungrateful boy a great favor. "I seldom show such mercy, and you have thrown it away. So be it!"

Raising his hands, he clawed at the air in front of him. At his fingertips appeared little jags of blue light that shimmered with opalescence, with magic.

I stepped forward, hate raging through me, my thoughts on death and blood and vengeance. This was for the *Pamah Reach* and all the men I'd lost. This was for me. I leaped forward to run him through.

His hands rose again, then clove the darkness. Thunder roared. Blue lightning flickered around him, then leaped out and struck me. Magic! Blinded for a second, I reeled back. Again thunder crashed, and a blast of hot wind hit me in the face, knocking me off my feet. I climbed unsteadily to my knees. Then I could see again, and the blue light flickered all over Karnekash, dancing across his face, his arms, his robes.

His head cracked and split, and an oily darkness poured up and out, shadows that seemed to shift and move with a life of their own. His empty skin flopped to the ground like a discarded garment.

I screamed in terror and tried to look away, but could not.

It hurt to gaze upon him, hurt my eyes and my head. I could not move, could not breathe.

He rose higher, spreading arms that were not arms. Reddish scales rippled. Flesh unfolded. Leathery wings stretched. Those glowing red eyes! The sight of them sent a convulsion through me. Against my will, I shook all over.

He loomed over me, a dragon now, standing ten or fifteen feet tall at the shoulder—rising and rising—

With a screech more terrible than any sound I had ever heard before, he opened jaws as long as my forearm and lunged at me.

NINETEEN

I tried to leap back, to scramble for cover, but even as I did a sinking feeling told me I'd never make it. Three feet from my face, Karnekash let loose a blast of fire from deep in his belly. I closed my eyes and raised my arms to protect my face as an inferno surrounded me. And then it was gone—and piles of wood behind me blazed like bonfires.

Ool's spell—it had protected me against the dragonlings in the wizard's house. Apparently it protected against larger dragons, too—or at least against their breath.

Light from the fires rippled across the dragon's body, glinting on the hard scales of his belly and the glistening leather of his wings.

Movement caught my eye. The huge stack of marble slabs to the left of the flying beast teetered.

"Karnekash!" I shouted.

The dragon's head turned. Mouth open, eyes narrowing, he hissed at me.

Slowly I set my sword and knife down, then motioned the head toward me. Cautiously he advanced.

"Perhaps we can make a deal after all," I said, letting a tremble of fear enter my voice. "I have one more piece of news. It's worth a great deal to you."

The head came down to my eye level. We were only a foot apart, human nose to reptilian nose.

Then the stack of marble slabs fell over onto him with a grinding, grating sound that set my teeth on edge. Then another pile fell, and another, all on top of the wizard-dragon. In a second he lay completely buried beneath a ton of stone.

Panting, I picked up my sword and knife. Ool joined me, then helped me stand. From head to heel, I ached.

"Gods!" I said at last. "Did you see that?"

He nodded. "I should have guessed he was a shape-shifter. Fortunately there are limitations to what a human can do with his body. Had he been much larger, the stones would not have stopped him."

I nodded my thanks. After another minute I forced myself upright and staggered over to the pile of stones. "Help me dig," I said as I began pulling first one, then another, from the pile, tossing them behind me.

Ool moved forward. "Stand back," he said. "I will move them."

I did as instructed. He stood there a moment, eyes closed, gathering the remainder of his strength. At last he began to speak in the curious sing-song language of magic. A soft glow spread over him, then leaped from his fingertips to the pile of stones. I found myself leaning forward, watching avidly, as one by one the marble slabs rose by themselves and drifted off to the side.

In minutes the job was done, and the dragon lay uncovered. Wings scarred and ripped, scales scratched and broken, the wizard's breath came in little puffs. It didn't move—didn't seem conscious of anything. Suddenly it shimmered with an odd blue light. The body writhed and reformed, and then Karnekash lay unconscious before me, body covered with cuts, scrapes, and slowly discoloring bruises.

I hefted my sword and moved forward, grimly determined to finish the job. Ool, though, stepped in front of me.

"Wait, Captain," he said. "He cannot hurt us now, and if we bind his hands he will not be able to work his magic."

I stared at him incredulously. "After all I've gone through, you expect me to spare his life?"

"Not if you truly wish to kill him. But consider this: he was but a tradesman hired by the Countess of Fleurin to perform a service. Left alone, he never would have bothered you. Alna Savina is the one at whom your anger should be directed."

"I'll see to her next." A dangerous edge crept into my voice.

"Perhaps Karnekash could be persuaded to aid you as well."

"Not if he has an ounce of sense," I said. "Not only did he fail to kill me for the Countess of Fleurin, but I've just tried to kill him!"

"He is a wizard, and on top of that, he is a shape-shifter. I have heard tales of his kind. He has spent too much time as a dragon, and now he shares their cunning and avarice. He hungers for the coolness of gold, and he would gladly serve any man who adds to his hoard—even you. And, with his help, think what could be done to Fleurin . . ."

I hesitated, torn. A dragon—a real dragon—could devastate an island, even one as strongly built as Bar Altibb.

"You can always kill him later," said Ool, "if he refuses to help. And such a death would be at your leisure, drawn out as you see fit."

At last I nodded. "You'd better be right."

*   *   *

We sailed for Zelloque with the morning tide. Karnekash went straight to the small, dark brig, securely bound in irons.

Ool himself cared for the wizard, sewing shut and bandaging his wounds. Over the next two weeks, Karnekash pulled back from the edge of death and began to recover his strength and his wits. He knew he had been saved by me, and yet he did not know my name—my *true* name—as yet. I planned to surprise him with that information the next time we met.

When Ool judged the wizard recovered enough to see me, I sent Pup and Graff to fetch him. They hauled Karnekash into my chart room—his arms bound behind him, his legs in shackles—and forced him to kneel. Then they took up positions to either side, crossbows pointed at his head. Ool watched secretly from the next room, where he could work his magic unseen, if necessary.

Karnekash still looked a mess. Yellowed bruises covered his face, and a long jagged scar creased the line of his jaw. Even so, he tried to glare at me with such mingled anger and superiority and disdain that I almost felt sorry for him. It seemed he hadn't learned much from his brush with death.

"Do you recognize me?" I asked folding my arms and leaning back against the chart table almost casually.

"No," he sneered.

"You should. You tried to murder me. My name is Fel Blackmane."

"Blackmane—" He gaped.

"I escaped your attack at the Grayhaven Fair. But that's not important now. I've dreamed of killing you for the last nine months of my life. At times, it was the only thing that kept me going."

He paled. "Then kill me," he said at last, almost choking on the words. "Be done with it."

I forced myself to speak quietly, calmly. "I don't want to kill you—I have come up with a better plan. I would like to hire your services."

"Hire—me . . . ?"

"That's why you're here, rather than dead in Lystia."

"You have a strange way of recruiting men to your cause," he said. He smiled thinly, the smugness beginning to return. And why not? I had just said I needed him, after all.

My face hardened. "This is the deal: You will help me capture Bar Altibb. In return, I will spare your life."

His face quivered, and for an instant I thought he was going to refuse. But then he looked down and finally nodded. "I will agree to those terms."

"Not so fast. There are a few more things. First, the attack on Bar Altibb must involve a dragon."

"Poetic justice," he said quickly. "Agreed."

"Second," I continued, "you must swear never again to attack me or my crew, or be a party to any other attacks. My first mate, who knows something of wizardry, says to trust you only if you swear by Faramigon."

Karnekash climbed to his feet, chains jingling. Graff and Pup shifted uneasily but kept him covered with their crossbows.

"I swear by Faramigon and all that I hold dear in this world and the next," Karnekash said, "that I will live by the terms of our agreement, so long as you honor your end."

Faintly, from behind me, I heard Ool whisper, "That will bind him, Captain."

"Excellent," I said. I drew the key to his irons from my pouch and tossed it to Pup. "Set him free."

"Captain . . ." he said. "Are you sure?"

"Yes." I studied Karnekash. Ool had vouched for his pledge. I would trust him to carry out his part of the bargain.

*   *   *

Even under better circumstances, Karnekash would never have been my choice for a dinner companion. He was too smooth in his talk, too vaguely reassuring and yet at the same time threatening for me to be comfortable around him. Things being what they were, however, I bade him welcome and invited him to dine at the captain's table with Ool and the other mates.

"How soon," Karnekash asked as the last course's dishes had been removed, "until we get off this wretched little ship?"

We had been almost a month at sea since leaving Lystia, and we had encountered not so much as a single trade ship in all that time. I did not mind terribly much; we were searching for Frago and the *Blue Maiden*, not treasure. That Karnekash had no great affection for sea travel was obvious from the way he complained at every possible opportunity.

With a sigh, I said, "Four weeks after we find Aldenius Frago's ship, we will be in Fleurin." I wanted my old master's help in taking Bar Altibb. He had more men than I did, and I wanted the insurance of their numbers.

Washing down his food with a cup of wine, Karnekash glared at me, rose, and left. After the door swung shut. Ool said, "I almost wish I'd let you kill him."

I only smiled. It was worth tolerating Karnekash. Or so I hoped.

*   *   *

The next morning I was awakened by shouts from the deck. "A dragon!" somebody screamed. "To arms! A dragon!"

In a second I was on my feet, pulling on clothes. I raced out on deck to find a dozen men stringing bows. Scanning the sky, I soon saw it—a small black dragon rapidly approaching.

It looked familiar, somehow. Then I realized it had to be Karnekash.

"Belay that!" I shouted to the archers as they notched arrows. "It's the wizard, Karnekash. Give him room to land."

Grudgingly, it seemed, they moved back and cleared a space on deck. The dragon set down neatly, waddling to a stop, then folded its wings and sat on its haunches. Around me I heard my men muttering to themselves and shifting uneasily. I couldn't blame them for their fear—I felt it myself.

Finally the dragon's skin shimmered and rippled, then seemed to pull into itself, reforming. In a second, Karnekash stood there, fully human. Ool brought him a robe, which he shrugged on easily.

Only after Karnekash had knotted a sash around his waist did he move. He headed for my cabin, Ool at his side. I met them at the door.

"What's all this about?" I demanded, looking from one to the other and back again.

"Inside," Ool said.

I pushed open the door. Only after we were seated around

the chart table did I repeat my question.

"I went looking for that ship," Karnekash said, "the *Blue Maiden*. The sooner this voyage is over, the better."

"It was my idea," Ool said merrily.

"Yes, yes," I said quickly. "But what about the *Maiden*? Did you find her?"

"She's in Janjor," Karnekash said, "buying provisions."

I grabbed up the chart and measured the distance to Janjor. Three days' journey, I estimated, if the winds were favorable. We might be able to catch her yet!

*   *   *

Two days later we sighted Frago's ship. Now I'd be able to get the help I'd need to conquer Fleurin. Aldenius Frago was the only man I trusted enough to make a partner in my plan. But would he trust me once more?

We drew near the *Maiden* and signaled our desire to talk. A bit to my surprise Frago readily agreed. The ships drew close, hawsers were let out, and our vessels were lashed together. Then, dressed, in all my finery, I crossed over to see my old master.

Smiling, he stepped up—and punched me in the face with all his might.

I hadn't seen it coming, and for a moment there was blackness. My face throbbed. And when I opened my eyes, I was lying on the deck with Frago leaning over me.

"Drink this, Fel, my boy," he said, unperturbed, holding a goblet of wine to my lips.

I sipped as I studied his face. He seemed his kindly old self again.

"Why?" I asked when he lowered the goblet. It didn't make sense.

"You had it coming, you know," he said. "Had any other man led a mutiny against me . . . But I'll forgive you for old times' sake." He offered his hand; I took it and he pulled me to my feet. "But do it again and I'll do more than knock you senseless!"

"For old times' sake," I said, "I'll forget you hit me." I owed him that much. And, after all, right now I needed him more than he needed me.

We embraced briefly, he pounded my back, and the episode was forgotten. He had always been that way.

"Come, my boy!" He strode toward his cabin. "We must celebrate our second reunion!"

I was a bit bewildered, but I followed him anyway. Only after we both had goblets of fine Varanian wine did I ask him:

"Why are you so happy to see me? After that reception, I thought you'd sworn off our friendship."

He set his goblet down. "Let's put the past behind us, Fel, my lad. There is no friend like an old friend—or an old enemy, for that matter." He laughed heartily and added with a wink, "Besides, it was very nicely done—stealing my own crew out from under me!"

"Then I have a deal I wish to propose to you," I said.

"Aha!" he said. "I knew it! And I imagine it involves that wizard you were chasing. You want my help killing him, right?"

"Not exactly. I found him already." And then I launched into my tale of how Karnekash was now in my employ.

"So," I said, "you see my problem. I want to capture Bar Altibb again, and to do it I'm going to need more men."

"My men," Frago said.

"Exactly."

"Very well. But half the treasure is mine."

"Certainly."

He grinned, then raised his goblet in salute. "You have a deal."

"Onward," I cried, "to Fleurin!"

TWENTY

The voyage to Fleurin took a little over a month, due to inclement weather. It was a hectic trip for me; I found my hands full between keeping Frago happy, working on our plan to capture Bar Altibb, and pretending interest in Karnekash's moans and complaints about shipboard life. Fortunately Ool knew his duties and saw to daily tasks.

In my few free moments I thought about Alna Savina, wondered what I could take away from her. She'd already lost her beauty. That left her power, her wealth, and her life. Which did she value most?

To make things worse, high above our ships I sometimes spotted a black dot that moved far too quickly to be a bird. I finally cornered Karnekash and demanded to know what it was.

"I called a dragon to keep us company. After all, there are pirates in these waters."

And there was Frago. He spent most of his time on my ship reminiscing about old times. It almost seemed as though he'd rather be with me than sailing with his own crew. From the stories I overheard some of his sailors telling mine, it seemed things had taken a sharp downward turn since I'd left the *Maiden*.

I made up my mind that, once Fleurin belonged to me, I'd make sure Frago settled down to a comfortable retirement ashore. I owed him that much at least.

My beard grew out, and my hair became long once more. I was going to return to Fleurin as the Fel Blackmane of old.

*   *   *

The days passed until finally we neared Fleurin. When Graff told me we were three days away, I crossed to the *Blue Maiden* with Karnekash and met with Frago.

"The first problem," I said, "is going to be Alna Savina's navy."

Frago nodded. "Twelve ships, the last I heard, all fast and well-armed, with orders to stop and search anything that enters Fleurinian waters."

"That's partly why I brought Karnekash," I said. "His dragon can take care of anything we meet."

The wizard smiled. "She will do what I tell her."

A call came from the rigging. "Ship ahead, port side!"

The three of us hurried to the railing. Far off, misty in the distance, I thought I saw a sail. Frago drew a spyglass from his pocket and raised it to his eye, squinting.

"A warship," he said after a minute's study. "And it's flying Fleurin's colors."

I looked at Karnekash. "Send your dragon," I said. "Scare them off."

"As you wish, my captain," he said. Raising one hand into the air, he spoke a couple of low words. If it was magic, I saw no sign of it.

Nevertheless, the results became dear a moment later when a few of Frago's men shouted warnings. I looked up into the sky, following their pointed fingers.

The dragon trailing us had begun to descend. It spiraled down from the sky in ever-widening circles, growing nearer and nearer. Soon I saw it distinctly: a huge black monster with a wingspan larger than my ship was long. It roared as it approached, a horrible, grating noise which set my teeth on edge. In seconds it passed overhead, its huge body blotting out the sun.

I looked at Karnekash and found him laughing. For an instant I thought he'd betrayed us, set his dragon to attack our ships rather than Fleurin's, but then the creature banked to the right and glided toward its target.

The sight held a kind of morbid fascination for me, like watching a spider wrap its prey in strand after strand of silk. I couldn't look away as the dragon passed over the other ship. One wingtip brushed a mast, which broke and fell in a flurry of white canvas. Then the dragon circled up and around, toying with the ship.

The warship drew steadily nearer. I could see the crew scrambling valiantly to make a last, desperate defense. When the dragon passed a second time, the crew fired crossbows at its underbelly—all to no avail. If anything, the dragon roared all the more loudly, as though angered by the puny attempts to slay it.

On the third pass it slowed, rearing up, beating the air with its powerful wings. Throwing back its head, it seemed to swell as it inhaled. Men were already diving off the warship and into the safety of the water. Then the dragon snapped its head forward, shooting gouts of flame across the deck, the broken mast, the sails.

Under the heat and fire, everything ignited at once. Flames climbed the rigging, shooting fifty feet into the air. From the distance we heard the horrible screams of men trapped below, those drowning and others dying from the dragon-fire.

Karnekash had deliberately betrayed my orders! I turned to him and said angrily, "I wanted them frightened off, not destroyed."

"The result is the same," he said placidly. "There are enough men in the world that these won't be missed."

"How can you be so . . . *unfeeling?*"

"Unfeeling?" he asked. "Unfeeling? For centuries men have hunted dragons and slain them, driving them to the corners of the earth. Who felt for the dragons? Men? I think not. Do not speak to dragons of compassion. Mine will kill men at every opportunity. Be satisfied that she does not slay you as well."

Minutes passed as the warship burned; the fire engulfed everything. The ship began to settle lower into the water. A thick black pillar of smoke rose into the clear blue sky, marking the place like a gravestone.

Frago said impatiently, "What's done is done. We've got ourselves to worry about. The smoke will draw the rest of Alna Savina's fleet here, so I trust your dragon will take care of them when necessary."

Karnekash smiled, showing unnaturally sharp teeth. "Of course."

*   *   *

Later that afternoon we came across two more warships. Both tried to fight off the dragon. Both burned like floating torches. And Karnekash . . .

The wizard seemed to be enjoying himself, taking pleasure from the deaths and annihilation. His eyes glowed red from more than reflections of flame as he watched the ships turn to embers and sink beneath the waves. He had truly become more dragon than man.

The night passed uneventfully. I managed to doze in my cabin for a few hours. My muscles were knotting from pent-up energy, though, and I found myself pacing, as I'd paced so many times before while waiting to mount an attack.

At last I could bear it no longer. Rising, I dressed in my brightest silk shirt and fanciest silk pantaloons, put on rings that sparkled with diamonds and rubies, and finally buckled on my sword belt. Then I went out on deck to wait for the dawn.

Frago stood in the bow, gazing out across the water. Ahead, I saw muted lights: Bar Altibb.

"It won't be much longer," my partner said, "and all that will be ours!"

"It won't be soon enough." As I watched the harbor lights, I saw a sudden flash of fire, and then flames leaped high into the air. I ran to the rail.

Behind me Frago snarled, "That bastard wizard didn't wait for us!"

The dragon, I saw, was attacking the warships in the harbor, burning and sinking them. I felt rage growing within me. Now all of Fleurin's guardsmen would be stirred up, ready to fight when we arrived. I cursed Karnekash and wished for the thousandth time that I'd killed him. I would have strangled him then and there if it hadn't been for his dragon—I feared what it would do to my ship if I murdered its master.

"Tell the men," I said, "we attack immediately."

*   *   *

Alna Savina stood on her balcony watching her ships burn in Fleurin's harbor. She could smell the smoke on the wind, but it was no more bitter than the feelings within her. A dragon had done it. That's what the survivors had said. It could only mean one thing: Karnekash had returned to collect the second half of his money.

But why had he attacked her ships, rather than coming to collect in person? Did he suspect a trap?

She summoned a messenger.

"Lady?" he asked, appearing in the doorway.

"Have extra men stationed on the walls, call the townspeople inside, then close the gates," she said. "We've withstood sieges before."

"Yes, Lady."

He raced off. But she felt no confidence.

Alna Savina bit her lip as she turned back to her balcony. Her ships still burned, but the fires were dying. *A dragon.* She shivered as she thought of what such a creature might do to her fortress.

*   *   *

The rowers strained; our little boats made slow but steady progress toward the docks. Two hundred of us were going ashore. Frago was leading his men to the northern gate; I was bringing mine to the docks.

Our force would be more than enough to capture the whole island. Only one thing made me uneasy: Bar Altibb, which loomed over the docks like a watchful giant. I could already see men along the walls, preparing for our assault. What tricks would Alna Savina have? How many men would we lose before victory?

I looked to the harbor itself. Not a sign remained of the ships Karnekash's dragon had sunk.

"Don't forget," I told Ool, "we'll be attacked by archers when we reach the docks."

He just laughed. "Have I ever failed you?"

At last we reached the docks, where the boats were quickly tied up. The men swarmed ashore, then stood there uneasily, waiting for instructions.

Oddly, the place was deserted. Crates lay scattered here and there, some broken where they had been dropped, others neatly stacked and waiting for transport to warehouses. It was an eerie sight, as though someone had snatched all the people away.

Overhead, the dragon circled. I looked at Ool, but he was busy mumbling some spell to himself.

I started forward, drawing my saber. "Be ready to fight," I called to the men, "and fear nothing, for Fleurin will be ours before the day is through!"

Cheering and brandishing their swords, they fell in step behind me. Together we marched toward the huge doors leading into Bar Altibb. Guards suddenly appeared on the fortress's walls, each armed with a crossbow. They shot a hundred bolts toward us in the first volley, then began to reload. A couple of my men gasped and dove for cover, but the bolts slowed halfway toward us, then drifted up into the sky and out of sight.

I set my feet and shouted up to the men cringing on the

walls: "My name is Fel Blackmane, and I've returned from the dead for revenge. Tell that to your mistress. And tell her I will rule Fleurin before nightfall!"

My men cheered. The guards on the wall scowled and raised their crossbows, but they didn't fire again. I saw their commander hurrying away.

I only laughed.

*   *   *

"Fel Blackmane?" Alna Savina said, paling. "You're certain it's him? If you're mistaken—"

"I'm not mistaken, Lady," said Larran, the commander of her military. "It was Blackmane."

She rose a bit unsteadily. It all seemed so impossible, her worst nightmare come to life. How could he have escaped Karnekash's dragon? How could he have raised an army without her hearing about it?

Blackmane never lost a battle, it was said.

"Lady?" Larran asked. "What are your orders?"

"Hold the walls," she said. "Kill Blackmane if you can."

"That's it?"

She just looked at him. "Do you have a better plan?"

He shook his head. "No, Lady." Saluting, he turned and hurried from the room.

The Countess of Fleurin stood slowly, regally, then headed for her throne room. Until Blackmane actually broke through the walls and put a sword to her throat, she would continue as usual, ruling her land and people.

*   *   *

As Frago's men brought up a battering ram and started working on the door. Morning turned to afternoon. It looked to be a long, tedious siege. I stood apart from the men with Ool, Karnekash, and Frago, and asked for their ideas.

"Let the dragon destroy the fortress," said Frago.

Karnekash said, "Gladly! I'll tell her—"

"No," I said quickly. "That won't do. Fleurin is worthless without Bar Altibb. Besides, I want the Countess alive—for the moment."

"It's a pity there isn't another way into the fortress," Ool said, "some passage that isn't well-defended. We'd only need a few minutes to get the gates down."

I laughed. "The way things are going, we're more likely to grow wings and fly." And then I realized what I'd said, and a mad, impossible, daring plan came to me. "That's it!" I shouted. "We'll fly!"

"How?" Karnekash demanded, frowning.

"On your dragon."

"No!"

"Yes!" I said. "If a few of us penetrate the interior, we can capture the countess and end the siege. The sooner we take Bar Altibb, the sooner you'll be paid."

Grumbling, he finally agreed. "But only you may ride her, and when that's done, my debt to you is over."

"Agreed," I said.

He didn't give me a chance to reconsider. Raising his arms, he called his dragon down from the sky.

TWENTY-ONE

The dragon made a low humming sound deep in her chest as she crouched, her wings tucked up close to her body. Karnekash stroked her forehead and whispered lovingly into her ear.

Sweat trickled down my back. My hands shook. I pressed them together so no one would notice.

At last Karnekash turned to me. "She knows what to do," he said. "She will bring you into the fortress, near the gates, and leave you there. Do not expect her to stay and help you fight—she has a fear of closed-in places . . ."

"Uh, yes," I said. "Anything you say."

He smiled, and I saw the fire in his eyes, mirroring the eyes of his pet. "Climb onto her back," he said. "She will be careful to make sure you don't fall as she flies."

I took a deep breath, then forced myself toward the dragon. Feeling distinctly nauseated, I stepped onto one of her scales, grabbed the edge of a wing, and pulled myself up onto the monster's neck, directly behind her head. The scales felt cool, hard, slightly damp to my touch. They also made my skin crawl. Nevertheless I forced an encouraging nod in the direction of the wizard.

The dragon began to move. I leaned forward and hugged her neck tightly, feeling serpentine scales ripple beneath my arms. She waddled forward, then beat the air with her powerful wings. I could tell she was laboring. Slowly she rose above the buildings facing the square, twenty feet, then thirty feet, then higher.

She turned and headed for Bar Altibb, still gaining height. We were fifty feet above the ground now. Wind drove tears from my eyes, but I refused to close them.

We cleared the walls of the fortress. I watched the dragon's shadow ripple smoothly over the battlements. She let loose an earth-shaking roar, and the guards turned and fled their positions with cries of fear.

Spreading her wings, she glided down into the courtyard directly in front of the main gates. The men on duty there cowered back, covering their heads in terror.

Quickly I slid down from the dragon's neck, drawing my sword. Now I could hear a muted banging sound—the noise of a battering ram outside. Ool and Frago were leading the charge.

At a glance I took in the workings of the mechanism which held the gate closed. Running forward, I unpinned the wheel that would raise the huge beam barring the doors and threw all my weight against it. A moment later I was rewarded when—slowly, reluctantly—it began to turn. The oak beam rose easily as counterweights fell.

A hard gust of wind hit me from behind, making me stagger, and then a shadow crossed over me. I knew the dragon had left.

The battering ram struck again, knocking the gates open a half foot. That was what the men outside had been waiting for. With savage battle cries, they drew their swords and pushed forward.

Their momentum through the gates carried them into the courtyard, Frago at their head. He raised his saber and shouted, "Victory! To the throne room!"

"Take prisoner any guard who wants to surrender," I called. "Kill the rest. Onward!"

Cheering, they swarmed toward the doors to the various buildings inside Bar Altibb. I led the way toward the throne room. Ool at my side.

*　　*　　*

The corridors were familiar. I threaded my way through them easily, as I'd done a thousand times in my dreams since I'd lost the *Pamah Reach*. I disposed of the first two guards we came to, scarcely slowing.

At last we reached the huge ivory doors leading to the throne room. I raised my hand and the men behind me stopped, their voices dropping to whispers.

Two guards stood on duty outside the door, swords raised. These were no Fleurinians, I saw, but trained swordsmen—perhaps even assassins—hired to guard Alna Savina.

"We can take them," Frago whispered. "The one on the right is mine."

I was about to agree when a woman's low voice called, "Let them in, my champions. Offer no resistance."

I glanced at Frago. He shrugged, then bowed and said, "After you, Fel, my boy. She's your problem."

"Wait and see," I said. I strode between the two assassins, shoved the door open, and stepped into the throne room.

It had changed little since the last time I'd been here.

Alna Savina sat on her throne surrounded by her serving maids. She held her scepter in one hand, and on her head she wore the crown of Fleurin. Her eyes were bright with tears.

Softly, elegantly, she rose. Her white gown shimmered faintly in the dim light of oil lamps. Even in defeat she held her head high, and there was a pained dignity to her manner.

I lowered my sword. "Do you remember me?" I asked her.

She stopped three feet away, looking me straight in the eye. I saw the fine whiteness of her brow, her silky black hair just starting to silver, the firm curves of chin and cheeks.

"Yes," she said, "I know you, Fel Blackmane."

"I am also Dray Sorrel. . . ."

"You have won, pirate," she said. "I expect no mercy from you, and I will not give you the pleasure of seeing me beg for my life. Only tell me . . . how—?"

"How did I escape? It matters little." I stepped closer, pulling her to me, feeling her warmth against mine. I looked deep into her eyes, then kissed her passionately, as I had done the last time we'd met.

Her body was stiff, awkward at first, uncomprehending, but then she yielded to me and answered my kiss with another. At last I drew away from her.

"Is there a priest in Bar Altibb?" I asked.

"Yes," she whispered.

"Summon him. Tell him to prepare for a marriage ceremony. Then call your maids and have them prepare you—that is, if you're willing to marry?"

A shocked expression on her face, she whispered, "Yes." Then she smiled and it was a look of pure joy—that she would live, that she would yet be able to rule, that she was loved by Fel Blackmane.

"Then hurry!" I said coolly. I laughed as she turned away

and began calling to her servants, summoning them to her, then sending them running for the things she would need.

Her defeat could be turned into a celebration, I knew. The night would ring with cheers and blessings rather than screams and laments of a conquered people.

I rather liked the idea. I began to smile a bit at myself. Yes, I certainly hadn't lost my touch.

TWENTY-TWO

"You look splendid!" I said as I looked my old master over. He was dressed all in gold and silver robes, with a red sash about his waist which matched the ruby in the pommel of his ceremonial sword.

"Of course I do," he said, puffing out his chest and walking with a bit more swagger. "Nothing less would do, for a wedding like this."

"Yes, yes," I said, laughing. "And Ool, too!"

The wizard grinned and nodded.

Then the priest appeared with several novices, and they moved about the small reception room set aside for the marriage ceremony, setting up small shrines to various gods.

All of Fleurin was in surrender. With Alna Savina captured, all her men had laid down their arms and surrendered. When word spread that the Countess of Fleurin would wed one of the conquerors, the people had (contrary to my expectations) rejoiced. It seemed they had long wanted their queen to marry and provide Fleurin with an heir. That the heir would come from pirate blood seemed to concern them little, if at all.

At last the priest signaled his readiness. The shrines had all been set up and a red carpet laid down upon the floor. As if on cue, Alna Savina entered, dressed in a gown of white silk and lace. She looked strikingly beautiful, more beautiful than I'd ever seen a woman look, and when she smiled at me it was with pure contentment. All the fire and hatred seemed to have gone from her heart.

A child of perhaps eight walked through the room, strewing rose petals everywhere, and the air filled immediately with their sweet scent. Somehow, it all seemed perfect, almost too perfect.

Frago and I approached the priest. Alna Savina smiled at me a bit distantly, a bit dreamily, and I smiled back and winked.

The priest began the ceremony, sprinkling holy water on everyone present, calling for the gods to bless the ceremony. "And now," he said, "will those to be married please step before me, so that they can be blessed in the name and spirit of the gods?"

I smiled at the Countess of Fleurin. Even this close, where I could see the fine wrinkles around her eyes and mouth, she was so lovely I could scarcely imagine what she must have been like in her youth.

I couldn't resist. Pulling her to me, I caressed her cheek and kissed her passionately.

She kissed me back, hard, and when we finally parted lips she whispered, "I know I will love you."

I took the gold pendant from around her neck. "Jewelry is dulled by your beauty," I said. "Let me see only you, the loveliest woman a man could cherish."

"Step forward," the priest said again.

Alna Savina took a deep breath, lowered her veil, then moved in front of him.

Nudging Frago, I motioned for him to take my place.

He stared back at me, bewildered. Then he understood, bared his teeth in a complicit grin, and stepped forward. The priest began to drone his way through the ritual.

I grabbed Ool's arm and we began to back away, padding as quietly as a pair of cats. He was grinning madly, and I was too; both of us were free and dear with all the world left to conquer.

We had almost reached the hall when the ceremony ended and Alna Savina turned to kiss her new husband. She took one look at Frago and her face became a fright-mask of shock and horror. Then she turned and pointed her finger at me.

"Fel Blackmane, I'm going to strangle you!" she screamed.

Frago shook with laughter, then caught her and pulled her tight; he raised her veil and kissed her forcibly. She was still struggling with him as I headed for the docks and the *Pamah Reach II*.

Hefting Alna Savina's gold necklace, I smiled. I had one last errand to run . . . a present deliver to a little girl who had dared to love a hawk.

THE END

TALES FROM
SLAB'S TAVERN

INTRODUCTION

There is a long tradition of bar stories in fantasy and science fiction literature. Just think about it for a minute and I'm sure plenty will spring to mind. Pratt & de Camp's "Gavagan's Bar." Spider Robinson's "Callahan's Place." Thieves' World's "Vulgar Unicorn." Arthur C. Clarke's *Tales of the White Hart.* You even get bars in fantasy classics, like Lord Dunsany's "Jorkens" stories. Isaac Asimov? "The Black Widowers" (though they're mysteries). And, of course, there are scattered stories by the likes of Avram Davidson, Gardner Dozois, Robert A. Heinlein, Henry Kuttner, Larry Niven, Robert Silverberg, and so many more that they can't possibly be listed here. . . . It seems *everyone* likes to write about bars. (Maybe SF and fantasy writers like beer a little *too* much! Hmm . . . gives me an idea for a story!)

As for me . . . I'm guilty of writing bar stories, too. A whole series of them, in fact, set in Zelloque, the greatest city the world has ever known. Slab's Tavern is a sword & sorcery-style bar, near the docks of Zelloque, and it's frequented by pirates and other lowlifes, haunted by ghosts and other uncanny beings, and owned (or so he likes to think) by a rather canny tradesman named Ulander Rasym.

And, by a strange coincidence, Fel Blackmane makes a cameo appearance in one. Most of my fantasy work is set in this Zelloque universe, after all.

So, without further ado . . . here are five of the best Slab's Tavern stories. Enjoy.

1.

On the Rocks at Slab's

The Oracle rode alone through the gates of Zelloque. Around him crackled an almost visible aura of power and authority. The city guard fell in behind him as he headed, intent on his mission, straight for the steps of the palace.

*   *   *

I was watching two disembodied heads sing drunken songs when the trouble started. A couple of city guards sauntered in, glanced around with disdain, then headed toward my private table. They looked splendid in full uniform, with their red capes flapping boldly behind them. Quite a few of my tavern's patrons made a hasty retreat through the back door. The floating heads vanished in puffs of ethereal gasses. I had nothing to hide—nothing much, anyway—so I waited.

"Ulander," the guard on the right said, "I have a message for you." Only then did I recognize him beneath his red-plumed helm: Nim Bisnar, an old city guard who'd worked off and on for me during the last ten years.

"What is it?" I demanded. "You know you're supposed to use the back entrance. You'll give my place a bad reputation!"

He ignored my protests. "Captain Yoonlag sent us. An Oracle from Ni Treshel—that's right, the Ni Treshel, where the bones of Shon Atasha are kept—came to the Great Lord's palace yesterday. He's looking for more splinters of his god's bones. Somehow he'd heard tales about Slab's Tavern. Now he's persuaded the Great Lord to let him search your place!"

I jolted to my feet, startled and alarmed. "What? When?"

"In an hour, maybe two."

Calling to Lur, my doorman and bodyguard, I dug a handful of silver royals from my pouch and poured them into Nim's hands. "Half are Yoonlag's. Split the other half between you."

"Thank you, sir!" they both said, then turned to go . . . through the back door, this time.

Lur lumbered over to my side. He was a large man, about seven feet tall, with broad shoulders and muscles enough to make him look twice as large. I'd always found those characteristics ideal for my purposes.

"Master?"

"Throw everybody out," I said, "except the servants."

"Sir?" he said, bewildered.

"You heard me. Do it!"

The tavern was large and dark, its dim light concealing the crumbling plaster and footworn paving stones. Wooden columns hewn from the hearts of ancient oaks supported the high ceiling. Weird shadows stretched everywhere. There were numerous secluded spots, and off at the curtained booths along the edge of the room, illegal transactions were taking place.

I marked the pirates at their tables, with their rich, colorful, jewel-encrusted clothes that mimicked but never equaled nobles' dress, and nodded to the ones I knew: Griel Teq, Hilan Lammiat, Fel Blackmane, a few others. In return for protecting his city's ships, the Great Lord of Zelloque had made his city an open port ten years earlier. In one dark corner a couple of black-robed slavers threw dice; in another, two dock hands threatened each other with knives. With little patience or gentleness, various barkeeps persuaded them to take their squabble to a nearby alley. But mostly the people drank and talked and sang too loudly, the room ringing with boisterous shouts as they swore, laughed and argued.

Lur moved among them, bending now and then to whisper something in various ears. Usually the men would turn pale, then tremble, then bolt for the door. Even the pirates left without a fight; Lur's imposing bulk was just too much for them, I guessed. Within minutes the place was deserted.

For a long minute, I just stood there are pondered the guard's words. An Oracle, coming to search my tavern for a splinter of a god's bone ...

More than ghostly, disembodied heads that sang drunken songs, my tavern had quite a reputation for strange, magical happenings ... it had helped keep away all but the least bloodthirsty clientele. Slab's was the sort of place anything could happen. Rumor said that, late at night, drunks sometimes inexplicably became sober, the furniture rearranged itself (always when nobody was looking) and people sometimes vanished, never to be seen again. Of course, that was only rumor ... but I did know that against the far wall stood a table where chilled wine tasted like warm blood, and there was a certain spot (which moved every night) where Slab Vethiq himself, the man who'd founded my noble drinking establishment, was known to appear from time to time—or at least, his spirit was. And even if Slab didn't come, chances were someone—or something—else would . . . if you stepped too close.

The two drunken, singing heads suddenly appeared over a table. They both wore the colorful silk scarves and earrings of sailors; only the mistiness of their necks and lack of bodies marked them as other than human. One of the barmaids seized a broom and swatted at them until they disappeared.

If the Oracle saw them or anything else magical he'd tear the building down in search of his bone.

I barred the doors and shuttered the windows. At once the barmaids lit tallow candles and set them in various niches. The place filled with a warm, somewhat hazy light. Everyone stared at me, wondering (I could tell) if I had gone completely mad. It was then that I told them, in short, blunt, angry words, what Nim had told me, and what I planned to do about it.

*   *   *

The Oracle moved through the streets of Zelloque like a hot knife cutting through fat. He wore gold and blue silk pantaloons and a gold silk shirt, slippers of soft, white klindu fur, and he carried a golden wheel in his arms. His wheel glittered brightly, red and blue from rubies and sapphires, gold and silver from the dying sun's light. Behind him, in perfect formation, marched twenty members of the city guard.

He held his divine purpose firmly in mind: to gather all the bones of Shon Atasha the Creator together into one place, to use their magic to summon His spirit back to Earth.

The noise of a hundred tramping feet echoed loudly through the deserted streets.

*   *   *

Trying to reason with ghosts seldom succeeds. Like with Slab.

I stood before him, as I'd stood before him a thousand times when I worked as his servant, and stared into his pale blue eyes. He wore his finest green robes, the ones embroidered with gold and silver thread, almost as if he expected the Oracle and had dressed for the occasion.

"Bones!" he mocked. "Bones!" And then he trailed off in laughter.

I stepped back and he slowly disappeared, disintegrating in wisps of green fog.

"Well," I told him, "at least I'm not going to die by trying to swallow fifty blue-backed crabs—alive!" But gloating wouldn't help; he didn't have to worry about having his livelihood demolished. He could always go haunt someplace else.

I should've known better than to try and persuade him and all the other ghosts not to appear during the Oracle's visit. Now I had a terrible suspicion they'd be certain to show up, if anyone stepped close to their special spot (which, fortunately, was off in one dark corner tonight).

I stood back and surveyed everyone else's work, then gave the signal for the doors to be unbolted and the shutters thrown open. Afternoon sunlight flooded in.

Most of my dozen-or-so employees now sat at various tables, with bottles and goblets of wine before them, looking like the tavern's regulars. I'd stationed them in all the places where I knew odd things occurred; they each had orders to prevent anything unusual from happening at any cost. Only Lur and a couple of the barmaids kept to their regular duties, moving from table to table as usual. For the thousandth time, I thanked my good fortune in having the loyalest servants money could buy. None would give my secrets away.

"Master?" Lur said, looming over me. I took a quick step back and he still loomed over me. "I hear them coming."

Straining, I heard them, too: the tramp-tramp of many booted feet somewhere close at hand. Then they marched outside and halted there. One of the guards, silhouetted in the door, stood for a second and surveyed the place before entering. Then I recognized him: Tayn Lastoq, the Captain of all the city guard, who (unfortunately) was also one of the few city officials I'd never been able to bribe. Behind him came another figure, the Oracle.

Like all the Rashendi, this one wore gaudy, brilliantly colored silk clothing. He carried his future-telling wheel in front of him like a holy relic, which of course it was.

"This is the place?" he asked, with obvious disdain. He sniffed.

"Yes, Oracle," Tayn said.

"So be it. Find what I seek."

I stepped forward. "Wait a minute—"

"Be quiet, Ulander!" Tayn snapped. I could see the Oracle had begun to annoy him and he was taking it out on me. "I know you better than you think. You know why we're here! Now let us get on with our business."

"I have friends in high places!"

He whirled around, his sword suddenly in his hand. Its point touched my chest just below my heart. "Narmon Ri himself ordered the search. You have no choice. Do you understand?"

Lur tensed beside me, growling softly, ready to attack Tayn. I restrained him with a quick look, then turned back to the captain of the guard. "I understand," I told him, smiling faintly. "But if anything's broken, I'm sending Lord Ri the bill."

He laughed, then, and resheathed his sword. "You have a quick wit, Ulander. I'll tell the men to keep the damage to a minimum."

He turned and sauntered out, leaving the Oracle there alone. Through the open door, I heard Tayn instructing his men.

"Who are you?" the Rashendi asked me.

"Ulander Rasym, owner of this establishment."

He stared at me a moment, eyes strange and dark.

I went on, "Perhaps if you told me more about this god's bone, I might be able to help. What does it look like? Where would it be?"

"It may take any form," the Rashendi said softly, "a piece of marble, a building stone. They try to remain hidden. For years I have I located bones for the shrine in Ni Treshel. Each splinter has been different—and yet the same. They have an odd feel, an uncertain look as if their shape is untrue. With my wheel I can perceive a splinter's reality, if it is put before me." He nodded wisely. "So it has always been. I will find one here, I feel."

Then he turned and wandered toward the curtained booths.

Off to one side, I saw wisps of fog beginning to gather

above a table. I gestured wildly to one of the barmaids. With a gasp, she seized her broom and stepped forward, swinging madly at the two disembodied heads that had begun to appear. They'd started to sing—

> *Vimister Groll was a merry old soul*
> *Who loved his wine and women—*

but dissipated just before the Oracle turned to look back. The barmaid pretended to chase cobwebs from the ceiling with her broom while two of the barkeeps took turns continuing the song, mimicking the ghosts' high, drunken voices:

> *He picked a brew and drank up to*
> *The point his nose fell brim-in—*

It rapidly became obvious they'd never heard the tune before and were making it up as they went along. Fortunately, they soon became stumped at a rhyme for sausage and grew silent.

Tayn Lastoq and his men entered and spread through the tavern. For once, everything seemed to be going well; they found nothing but dust beneath the tables and under the booths. I followed Tayn around, looking over his shoulder, trying my best to bother him.

"You see?" I said again and again. "There's nothing here."

Then I turned around and noticed Slab Vethiq sitting at one of the tables, as solid looking as he'd ever been in life. He grinned at me, then turned back to his wine. As I stared, other people began appearing at the vacant tables in twos and threes. I recognized one, then another, then another. They were all patrons who had died! Fortunately, they brought their own wine.

Nobody else seemed to notice.

The Oracle now stood in the middle of the room as the men searched, ignoring the people seated at tables. He looked mildly annoyed at not having found his bone (though I had repeatedly said it wasn't here in front of him). At last he shouted for Tayn. The captain of the guard hurried over.

"Yes, Oracle?"

"Tear out the counter, then have your men start on the booths in the back. I want it found if it takes all night!"

With a sigh, Tayn turned to obey. I threw myself in front of him before he could speak. "There must be another way!" I said. "You can't just tear up my tavern!"

"I'm sorry, Ulander, but—"

Just then, one of his men chose to step too close to that certain spot in the corner. With a roaring sound, a giant mouth appeared, filling the whole ten feet between floor and ceiling. Its lips were thick and bloodless white; its teeth were sharp, jagged spikes; its tongue lolled out like some immense gray carpet. Gazing down its gullet, I saw only blackness.

This seemed to be what Slab was waiting for. With an insane cry, he rose and seemed to flow rather than walk to the Oracle. Seizing the Rashendi by the hair, he dragged him forward and into the mouth, vanishing down its throat. The other ghosts of patrons long dead grabbed all the guards, Tayn included, and spirited them off as well.

The mouth closed with a snap, the tongue flickered over the lips, and it vanished with a slight sucking sound.

Too stunned to do more than stare at the now empty corner, I just stood there. Then one of the barmaids began to scream. I heard a slapping sound and she shut up.

I retreated to my booth and sat down heavily. I was ruined, I knew. The Great Lord would have me executed for killing his favorite captain and twenty of his guards. His assassins
would track me down wherever I went. Well, I figured, at least I
could get drunk, ease the pain of my death. That was the only
advantage left in owning a haunted tavern.

Hearing singing, I looked up. The two disembodied
heads had appeared over my table. Slowly they drifted away.
Sounds from outside told me a number of pirates had entered.
Business went on as usual.

As the day wore on and I got progressively drunker, I began to hear strange rumors . . . tales of how twenty-one of Lord
Ri's guards had been plucked from the harbor by slavers—and
Lord Ri had declined to buy them back . . . tales of how their
leader, Tayn Lastoq, had gone mad and led his men and an Oracle off to fight sea-monsters . . . tales of how the Oracle had
disappeared, never to be seen again.

That night, Slab's haunted spot moved into my private
booth. I first became aware of it when I looked up and found
Slab sitting in front of me, casually sipping a bottle of my best
Coranian brandy. He raised it in salute, gave me a knowing
wink, then slowly faded away.

I shuddered a bit. That wink had always disturbed me
back in the days when Slab still lived and I'd been his right-
hand man, with only as much power as he let me have. That
wink had been a private sign, one last reminder that he owned
the place and I never would . . . or so he'd thought.

But I'd saved my money, made sure I knew all the right

people, and finally taken over when he'd died. But for all the documents that said I owned the place, something deep inside me called me a fool, and cursed, and somehow I knew the truth.

I drank more wine and tried not to think. My pains eased; somehow everything no longer seemed quite so grim. Slab, they'd said when he was alive, always takes care of his own. Secure with that thought, I drifted toward sleep.

2.

Well Bottled at Slab's

A young man dressed all in blue pushed his way into Slab's Tavern. He had the thin good looks and light brown hair of a native Zelloquan, I saw, and his robes were of good material, well cut.

Glancing around, he swallowed nervously, then started for my table. As he neared I looked him over. He couldn't have been more than sixteen, I thought, and nobody that young had much business here.

My tavern catered to the most bloodthirsty of clientele. Slab's had a certain reputation (well nurtured over the years) of being the toughest, roughest bar in all of Zelloque. I ought to know: I'd spread many of those rumors myself. When I took a quick glance around the main serving room, I saw pirates talking angrily in one corner, slavers throwing dice in another, and all manner of cutthroats bellied up to the bar for wine.

They didn't seem to discourage the boy, though. Ignoring all else, he slid into the seat opposite mine.

"Ulander Rasym, I presume?" he said.

"Perhaps." I studied him: pale lips, a paler complexion, the watery eyes of someone who read too much. Indeed, far from my normal run of customers. Something extraordinary had to have brought him here. I demanded, "Who are you?"

"My name is Vriss Arantine. I'm one of Pondrane's students. Perhaps you've heard of him?"

"He's a wizard. So? What do you want?"

"Your tavern has ghosts."

"Of course. Everyone knows that." It was true: among the various magical happenings in Slab's over the years, ghosts often appeared. They were patrons who had died, mostly. And there was a table where chilled wine tasted like warm blood, and a spot (which moved around from night to night) where, if you stepped too close, monsters sometimes appeared.

"Good," Vriss said. "I had to make sure. I need to study them."

"*What?*"

"Yes." He nodded. "I'm writing a book called *Manifestations of the Dead*. It will prove conclusively that ghosts are no more than mental projections of latent magical talents."

He said it with such sincerity that I was left speechless for a moment . . . a very rare occurrence, I assure you. Unfortunately, I wasn't the only one who'd heard that preposterous statement. Slowly, behind the boy's back, a luminous white mist had begun to gather.

Ignoring the ghost, I said, "So what do you want?"

"I need permission to sit at a table in the back of your tavern for a month. To watch for such phenomena, of course."

The mist grew thicker, began to swirl up into a human form. "What do I care," I said, watching it, "so long as you pay for your wine?"

"Ah," he said eagerly, "you have put your finger on precisely the problem. I have developed a rigid scientific method for studying such phenomena—"

"Ghosts, you mean."

"—and I cannot drink anything but water while I am here,

since it might cloud my judgment."

The luminous fog coalesced into a short, broad man in a flowing cape. I recognized him at once: Slab Vethiq himself, my tavern's founder and former owner, whom I'd served for twenty-odd years. After his untimely death I'd taken over his establishment and run it myself. Even dead, though, Slab wouldn't surrender his property. He had a tendency to show up at the most inopportune times to try to run things . . . like now, when I was about to have this would-be scholar thrown out.

I just sighed. Such were the problems of owning a haunted tavern.

Slab nodded to me and winked knowingly. "Let him stay," he said in a way only I could hear. "He amuses me."

"But—"

Slab shook his head in warning. Then he was gone.

I sighed again. There would be trouble, I knew, if I didn't cooperate . . . walls dripping blood, loud, mysterious groans, clanking chains: petty annoyances which had a habit of scaring people away. Why did Slab always have to make things difficult?

Knowing it was a mistake, knowing I'd regret my decision, I turned to the lad and said, "Very well. But stay out of the way, and I don't want you bothering any of the paying customers!"

"Thank you!" Vriss said, beaming. "I'll start tonight!" Rising, he went to a small, empty table, sat down, and drew a small parchment from some hidden pocket in his cloak. Next to the parchment he set a small jar of ink and a quill pen. Then he began eyeing the various areas of the tavern and taking copious notes. He stood out like a hungry boar at a palace banquet.

I motioned to Lur, my doorman and bodyguard, and he lumbered over. Lur was a large man, about seven feet tall, with broad shoulders and muscles enough to intimidate all but the most suicidal of drunks.

"What?" he asked, with his usual eloquence.

I nodded toward Vriss. "See to it he's not disturbed. Let the word get around that he's a . . . a nephew of mine. That should take care of it."

"Yes, master." He lumbered off.

As I studied my patrons with a dispassionate eye, I noticed half the men at the bar giving young Vriss Arantine the once-over. I knew what they were thinking: he'd be an easy mark, some nobleman's son out slumming, or just a lad who'd walked into the wrong bar in the wrong side of town.

But then Lur wandered among them, bending to whisper into an ear here, inserting a terse word or two into a conversation there. I don't know what he said, but it seemed to do the trick. The cutthroats tended to pale very suddenly, then turn back to their drinks, making almost painful efforts not to even glance in Vriss's direction. Even so, I couldn't lose the feeling that the boy would be trouble.

*   *   *

It started out simply enough: I felt a chill breeze, then a beautiful glowing woman with long, glistening silver hair emerged from the thick stone wall to my right. I jumped a bit as her gown brushed my foot, sending little knives of cold shooting the length of my leg, but it was nothing unusual; I'd seen her kind of ghost every now and then.

Ignoring everyone else, she walked straight to Vriss, curtsied a bit, then held out her hand as though asking him to dance. He scarcely glanced up from his note-taking.

Finally the ghost-woman walked on, moving through his table, through the stack of parchments he'd already filled with his tiny, cribbed writing. As she vanished into the wall, I saw a look of puzzlement blended with frustration on her face.

Interesting, indeed! Something was going on, and I didn't like it, not at all. I vowed then and there to see it stopped. But how? Why would ghosts bother Vriss Arantine? And why would Slab Vethiq, who was never a man (or ghost) known for his generosity, take an interest in the lad?

I had to find out more about young Arantine. Rising, I fetched my cloak from the storeroom. A visit to Vriss's master, the wizard Pondrane, seemed in order.

*   *   *

The wizard lived in the better part of town, in a tall, rambling old house surrounded by a high stone wall. I walked up to the gate, Lur at my side, and rang a little silver bell. Instantly, it seemed, a gray-bearded servant appeared from the shadows. He unlocked the gate, pulled it open, and bowed humbly to me.

"This way, Ulander Rasym," he said.

I didn't move. "How do you know me?" I demanded.

"The master is expecting you." Turning, he started up an overgrown path toward the house.

I glanced around once and, seeing nothing to alarm me,

followed. Lur fell in step behind, mace at his side.

The servant led us through a series of dimly lit rooms that stank of mold and decay. Books and scrolls and bizarre objects of all sorts had been piled on every available surface. I recognized human bones among the jumble and wondered if they were the wizard's former servants.

Finally we came to a steep, narrow staircase. Boards creaking ominously underfoot, we climbed, the stench of decay growing stronger around us. At the top of the stairs was a hall, and at the end of the hall a dark, overcrowded little workroom. The servant ushered us in, then turned and shuffled off. Tables lined the walls. On them sat still more books and scrolls, plus bottles and tubes and all manner of jars filled with what looked like magical ingredients. Scattered here and there were trophies from fifty years of wizardry: mummified animals, polished bones, teeth, and strangely shaped pebbles. Lur moved awkwardly here, like an animal in a room full of glass, fearful of breaking something. I didn't blame him; wizards were a difficult lot at best, and there was no telling what Pondrane would do if either of us damaged his possessions, accidentally or not.

I heard a low cough behind me. A board shifted and groaned under my feet when I turned, but I saw no one in the shadows. "Who's there?" I called. "Is that you, wizard?"

Light suddenly flickered around us, jags of gold and silver dancing through the air like fireflies. Then the sparks coalesced into a glowing sphere that drifted up to the ceiling and stationed itself there. By its light I could see an old man sitting on a chair in the corner: Crollion Pondrane.

He was a small man, and old beyond measure. His face had been wrinkled and creased by years spent outdoors, but now his skin was pallid as a slug's belly, his cheeks hollowed, his eyes dark and deep as stagnant pools of water. His hands shook as he raised himself to his feet and took a step forward. The smell of decay seemed to radiate from him, thick and damp.

"Your servant said you were expecting me," I said. It was half a challenge, half a question.

"You are Ulander Rasym, owner of Slab Vethiq's tavern, yes?"

I frowned. "Yes. I am here to ask about one of your students . . ."

He hardly seemed to hear. "Good, good," he murmured to himself. Slowly he circled me, examining my face, my clothes in great detail.

"About Vriss—" I began.

"I have a proposition," he said. "It's worth five thousand gold royals to you."

That caught my interest. "I'm listening," I said.

"I knew Beren Vethiq, *Slab* Vethiq to you. When we were young we played together, travelled together, drank and whored together. We were the best of friends until one sad summer day in Pavania, when we both fell in love with the same girl. That night Beren drugged me, sold me into slavery, and sent me off to Harandel with a trader caravan. I ended up in that despicable city for ten years. I blamed him for all my troubles, swore vengeance. It was hatred that kept me going.

"I pursued him across half the world and finally cornered

him in Frissa. We fought, I with my magic, he with sword and wits. He won again by a fluke, and again he sold me into slavery. It took me fifteen years to get away that time. When I escaped, again I pursued him, but he had already died when I reached Zelloque. Only a few months ago did I learn of his ghost."

"So?" I said cautiously.

"I shall trap his spirit, put him in a tiny bottle where no one can ever find him." He cackled with glee. "That will be my revenge: an eternity of solitude, an eternity of punishment for what he did to me so long ago!"

It seemed to me Slab had once mentioned a wizard he'd known in Pavania, something about the wizard trying to kill him . . . My forehead wrinkled as I tried to remember. And finally it came to me.

"Slab mentioned you," I said slowly. "It was *you* who tried to kill him over the girl!"

"That's not the way it happened."

"I remember now! He said a princess of the Fourth House fell in love with him, and a wizard became jealous. The wizard set fire to the inn in which they were staying, and the princess rushed into the building to try and save her jewels, and the roof collapsed on top of her—"

"No!"

"That's what he said."

He shrugged a bit. "It was a long time ago. Who can remember the exact details? I will have my old friend's ghost, and I will pay you not to interfere."

I swallowed, my mouth dry. "And Vriss?"

"My apprentice. He is the instrument which will capture

Beren Vethiq."

Lur began to growl ever so faintly, like an angered dog, and I knew I had to but give the word and he'd strangle the wizard. Or, more likely, die trying. His loyalty to a dead man was touching. But what did I owe Slab? It might be worth it to sit back and let Vriss capture him. The thought of those five thousand royals jingling in my pouch made my fingers itch.

But then I remembered all Slab had done for me. Sure, he'd made my life miserable at times. But he'd also done his best to keep Slab's Tavern open and running, even when an Oracle tried to tear the place apart in search of a splinter from one of his god's bones, even when One-eyed Seth tried to muscle in on business, and even when the Great Lord of Zelloque's chief counsellor decided I was a menace and ordered my assassination.

I owed him my life many times over. The thought of Slab spending eternity alone, with Crollion Pondrane torturing him, made me distinctly uncomfortable.

Abruptly, I started for the door, before my morals took second place to my greed. Over my shoulder I called, "We have nothing to discuss. And if your apprentice dares set foot in my tavern again, I'll sell him into slavery myself, just like Slab would have done!"

"Fool!" Pondrane shouted after me, and then he began to laugh again, voice high and warbling. It made me realize how much I hated him.

*   *   *

When we came in sight of my tavern, I saw a large crowd had gathered in front, all of them looking in through doors and windows, all of them shouting and passing bets back and forth. At once I realized a brawl must have broken out, and without Lur to break it up, things had gotten out of hand.

"Come on!" I shouted, and raced down the street, Lur thundering after me.

I forced my way through the mass of people around the door, entered the musty pleasantness of my tavern. Instantly I found myself surrounded by a whirling, screaming, shrieking storm of ghosts. Spectral figures stalked between the tables. Severed heads floated over the bar, bellowing snatches of song. Skeletons sipped wine in the booths. In every corner something writhed or slithered or chortled.

At the center of it all, still scribbling notes furiously, sat Pondrane's apprentice. Vriss seemed oblivious to the apparitions around him. Now, however, I knew the truth. He was waiting for Slab Vethiq to show himself.

With a roar of sheer rage—at Slab for sending these ghosts, at Pondrane for sending his apprentice, at all the money they both had cost me by frightening off my customers—I ran into the room and seized Vriss by the collar. Hauling him to his feet, I shook him as hard as I could. His teeth rattled; he trembled all over.

"Get out!" I snarled. "If I ever see you or your master again, I'll beat you both to bloody pulp!"

I cuffed his ear, and with a yelp he went sprawling across the floor. Lur dragged him to his feet and propelled him forcibly toward the door. The crowd there scattered.

It was then that I became aware of the deathly silence around us. All the various ghosts had vanished, gone back to whatever nightmare they had crawled from. I began to breathe a bit easier, confident that my troubles had ended.

However, as soon as I turned, I noticed Lur had stopped. He still held Vriss by collar and belt, dangling the lad half a foot above the floor, but his attention seemed focused on something else. Then I noticed Slab slowly materializing in front of them, blocking their way. Slab's arms were crossed and he looked more than a bit peeved. I saw it all, then, and knew he'd wanted to frighten a boy who didn't believe in ghosts. He wouldn't let Vriss leave yet; his fun wasn't over.

"No!" I shouted to him, a sinking feeling inside, knowing it was too late. "It's a trap—"

Vriss had whipped a small bottle from some hidden pocket. He popped the cork, pointed its mouth at Slab, and shouted a magic word with such sadistic glee I knew inside his innocence had all been an act, that he would grow up to be exactly like his master.

I heard a sucking sound, felt a rush of wind all around me, and then Slab was gone. The wizard had won after all, it seemed. I felt positively sick.

Lur turned Vriss Arantine upside down and begun shaking him by one leg. Bits of parchment, several small coins, and various pouches flew in all directions. At last the bottle dropped free.

Flinging Vriss to one side, Lur grabbed it up and uncorked it. He began shaking it, trying to release Slab. Nothing happened. And, I noticed, Lur had begun to growl again, a sure sign of his anger.

Vriss had, meanwhile, climbed from the wreckage of two

chairs and a table. He seemed dazed, unsure as to where he was and what he was doing. Then he saw Lur and seemed to remember, for he lunged after the bottle.

Lur held it well out of reach, raising the hole to one eye. Peering inside, he said, "Slab?"

Again Vriss shouted that magic word, and again I heard the sucking noise. In the blink of an eye my bodyguard had vanished.

The bottle clattered loudly on the floor. Vriss grabbed it up and bolted, but I tackled him before he'd taken three steps.

As I sat on his chest, pinning his arms, I stuffed my bulging money purse in his mouth to keep him quiet. Only then did I pry the bottle from his clenched fist.

After corking it securely, I held it up to the light, turning it this way and that, looking for some way to release its contents. The thing wasn't made of glass, I thought; the texture felt wrong. It seemed more like ivory or bone of some kind.

Finally, giving up, I decided to have Vriss reverse the magic. I could live without Lur, I was certain; hired muscle could be found anywhere. But I certainly needed Slab. He'd always watched out for me, always made sure the tavern turned a profit. And, beyond that, he'd become almost as much a fixture in the place as the huge block of marble that served as the bar, or the old tapestries on the walls, or the huge brick fireplace where toasts were made and glasses thrown on cold winter nights. Slab's Tavern without its patron ghost would be just another bar. I could never let that happen.

Pulling the makeshift gag from Vriss's mouth, I let him gasp and take large gulps of air until he could talk again.

"All right," I said angrily, "how do I get them out?"

"I don't know."

"I don't believe you." I let one hand tighten around his throat for a second. His eyes bulged.

When I released him, he coughed and wheezed for several minutes. "It's true!" he managed to gasp. "My master did all the magic. I just had to say the word!"

Jal and Ferrin, two of my least timid servants, had dared to venture back inside by then. They tended the bar and sometimes helped out at the door when things got to busy for Lur to handle alone.

Now I glared at them. "It's about time!"

"Yes, Ulander," Jal said, wiping his hands on his apron. He didn't meet my gaze. "It's just that—"

"Never mind. Hold him while I get up."

They seized Vriss with ill-concealed pleasure. The boy struggled a bit when I stood, but Jal bent one of his arms back until he cried for mercy.

"Mercy?" I said, mocking him. "What mercy did you show my friends?" I waved the bottle under his nose. "How the hell am I supposed to get them out of here?"

He just stared at me, gritting his teeth as Jal continued to twist his arm. I finally decided he really didn't know.

Perhaps, I decided, smashing the bottle would do the trick. I fetched a hammer from the back room, set the bottle on the stone floor, and struck it as hard as I could. The hammer bounced off with a ringing sound. Again and again I pounded on it, but to no effect. It wouldn't break.

Sighing, I rose to my feet. If nothing else I'd always prided myself on my inventiveness. If I couldn't get them out, I'd get someone else to do it for me. The wizard Pondrane would certainly know how. All I had to do was persuade him.

I looked at his apprentice and smiled. "Tell me," I said, "the magic word that makes the bottle work."

He thrashed his arms and tried to break free, but Jal and Ferrin held him securely. After I'd hit him a few times, he stopped struggling and began to whimper.

"Stop that sniveling," I said. "You brought it on yourself. I made a perfectly sensible request. Now, answer me!"

"You're going to put me in there!"

"Of course," I said. "That will make sure Pondrane empties the bottle."

Vriss bit his lip and shook his head, but I saw the fear in his eyes. I knew then that he'd tell.

"Save yourself a lot of pain," I said. "What's the word?"

Slowly, grudgingly, he told me. When he'd done so, I drew out the bottle, uncorked it, and pointed the opening at him. He closed his eyes and turned his head away. Then I said the magic word and, in a split second, he vanished.

Unfortunately, Jal and Ferrin vanished with him. It seemed the thing sucked up whoever stood in front of it.

Shaking my head, I tucked the bottle into my pocket, closed up shop, and headed for the wizard Pondrane's house.

* * *

The same servant who'd met Lur and me earlier that night brought me back to Pondrane's damp, dank workshop. The wizard was bent over several small jars, carefully measuring ingredients into each. He looked up when I came in, then set aside his instruments.

His voice held a hint of a sneer when he said, "So, you've changed your mind, have you? Come crawling back for the money?"

I smiled. "No. Rather, I've got a present for you."

"Oh? What?"

I produced the bottle. "Your apprentice."

Frowning, Pondrane demanded, "What's he doing in there?"

"He was a bit careless. After putting my bodyguard inside, he managed to do the same to himself. Needless to say, I want Lur back, and I imagine you'd like Vriss."

He carried the bottle over to one of his tables, set it down, and rummaged through a stack of papers. Finding the one he wanted, he pulled it out and read it aloud. The bottle began to shimmer with a weird, pulsing light. Pondrane held it up and squinted.

"You told the truth," he admitted a bit sadly. "From the aura, there *are* living humans in there."

"You would doubt my word?" I smiled.

"I had hoped you were lying. There is a slight problem with getting them out."

"What?"

"The bottle is not supposed to hold people. It was designed for a ghost, something ethereal. I don't know what will happen if I try to release its contents. The strain might prove too great and shatter them."

"The people or the bottle?"

"Both. Either. It took me months to make this cage, and I

can't go wasting it, can I?"

I made a mental note not to mention Jal or Ferrin. If two people inside the bottle worried him, four might well frighten him off. Rather, I changed tactics and said,

"Don't you have more time than that invested in your apprentice?"

Slowly, almost reluctantly, he nodded. "I suppose so. Very well, then, I will let them out. Stand back."

I retreated into the hall. As I watched through the doorway, he removed the cork, set the bottle in the middle of the floor, then took two steps back and stretched out his arms. His eyes closed; he seemed to be concentrating deeply.

Finally he began to speak, the words strange, slurred, heavy. The air around us took on an odd, liquid quality, as though I gazed at him through a great depth of water. I noticed a blue mist rising around the bottle, tendrils circling, twining upward, then coursing down into the bottle's open mouth. The room grew chill; I felt a cold sweat trickle down the small of my back.

Pondrane shouted a word, then came a blinding flash of light and an explosion that knocked me off my feet. Dust roiled around me, smothering, and I choked and gasped for breath. When the air cleared, I gathered my wits enough to stagger into the wizard's workroom.

Everything lay in shambles, the glass bottles broken, the furniture smashed, debris all over. Pondrane himself sprawled across one of his tables, a mummified cat pillowing his head.

Lur and Jal and Ferrin lay in a jumble on the floor. I heard one of them groan and begin to stir so I knew they were still alive. I didn't see Vriss at first, but then I spotted his foot sticking out from under Lur. Fortunately he'd broken my bodyguard's fall, as well as Jal's and Ferrin's.

Slab stood off to one side, looking faintly amused by the whole mess. I frowned.

"At least you could show a little gratitude!" I said.

He laughed at me, then slowly faded away. His lack of grace in being saved hurt a bit, but he was a ghost and allowances had to be made. When all I'd done for him had sunk in, I knew he'd be grateful.

Meanwhile, I had more important things to think about, like my men. Pulling them off of Vriss, I slapped their faces and called their names until they opened their eyes and looked blearily at me. After that I breathed easier. Their skulls were hard; they didn't seem hurt by their ordeal. In fact, it took surprisingly little to get them on their feet and moving.

On my way out I spotted the magic bottle lying on the floor, cork beside it. Smiling, I picked it up.

Then I crossed to the wizard Pondrane, pointed it at him, and spoke the magic word. With a sucking sound and a gust of wind, he vanished.

Grinning happily, I tamped the cork back into place. Then I put the bottle on the workbench, in plain sight, next to fifty-odd other bottles that looked exactly the same. It would take Vriss months to notice it . . . if he ever did.

Smiling, I followed after my men. It felt good to have saved Slab. Dead or alive, a fellow had to look out for his friends.

I just hoped Slab felt that way, too.

3.

On the Scent at Slab's

The common room smelled, but not of spilled wine or drunken men. I sniffed suspiciously. No, I thought, it wasn't perfume, exactly, but something else light and sweet. More than anything it reminded me of wildflowers.

Such a scent didn't didn't belong in a dive like Slab's Tavern. I ought to know. I, Ulander Rasym, owner of Slab's, took great pride in nurturing my bar's less-than-savory reputation.

Surreptitiously I glanced around at the evening crowd. Pirates dressed in brightly hued silks and bedecked with glittering jewels lounged in secluded booths along the back wall, haggling with local merchant-princes over the disposition of ill-gotten cargos. Since the Great Lord of Zelloque had declared his city a free port, pirates had become common here. To my left, against the far wall, a dozen Coranian slavers in hooded gray cloaks threw eight-sided dice while stamping their feet and shouting with bravado. Meanwhile, at the bar, a motley assortment of thieves and cutthroats engaged in a boisterous drinking game—Queen's Ransom, I realized as their tankards slammed together in the Heroes' Toast. Even the solitary few nursing cups of wine at tables in the center of the room looked ready for a fight.

No, of all the lowlifes who patronized Slab's, none would reek of such a dainty scent. Nor were there any new women about, just my usual crew of barmaids and serving girls, and out of self preservation none of them would dare perfume themselves—they were black and blue already from too many unwanted pinches, pokes, and outright grabs from customers.

That only left one other possible source for the sweet offending smell: Slab Vethiq himself, the founder of my ignoble drinking establishment. Slab had died nearly a decade before, but that hadn't stopped him from taking an active interest in the bar; his ghost had caused more than a bit of trouble over the years.

Perhaps, I mused, things had been too quiet in recent weeks. Of course the bar had its usual nightly show of spirits—earlier this evening the severed heads of two dead sailors had appeared over the bar singing bawdy drinking songs until one of the barmaids chased them away with a broom—but there hadn't been any real trouble in more than a month. It was about time for Slab to put in an unwanted appearance to stir things up . . .

Nodding and smiling to patrons as if I hadn't a concern in the world, I strolled toward the back of the tavern where I kept my private booth. If Slab had indeed returned to interfere in my affairs again, I'd let him think his game didn't concern me. Then perhaps he'd grow bored, show himself, and make his latest demands so I could get on with my affairs.

Sure enough, as I slipped through the curtain into my booth, a ghostly hand appeared before me holding a bottle of my best Merindian wine. It seemed proof enough that I'd done right in feigning a lack of concern: Slab seldom appeared so quickly when he wanted something.

Next a ghostly goblet appeared, and Slab poured me a generous drink. The smell of wildflowers grew stronger.

"What do you want this time?" I asked him.

"A toast to your good health, Ulander!" said his gravely voice.

"That's one thing I'll always drink to." I took a hesitant sip. As I'd half expected, the wine tasted like warm blood; it took all my strength of will to swallow rather than spray it out across the table. I wouldn't give Slab the satisfaction of knowing he'd begun to bother me this time.

As I smacked my lips with pretend satisfaction, the rest of Slab materialized: the piercing gray eyes, the jagged dueling scar on his left cheek, the bearded chin, the one gold earring. As always, he wore splendid clothes: tonight, red silk breeches and shirt, with huge ruby rings on his fingers. As he conjured another goblet and poured himself a drink, the flowery smell grew cloying. I had to cover my nose with a handkerchief.

"Slab," I said, "you're going to ruin business with this stench."

He leaned forward, elbows on the table. "I have come for your good advice," he said, "friend Ulander."

Slab had never called me 'friend' even when he was alive and I'd been his loyal right-hand man. More than anything else he'd yet said or done tonight, that worried me. And he'd never bothered to ask—let alone take—my counsel in the nearly twenty-five years I'd known him.

"Advice?" I asked. I could only give him a blank, bewildered stare.

He smiled. I'd always found his smiles dangerous in the past, but this one looked merely silly. And just as suddenly I knew what had happened.

"You're in love," I whispered, awed in spite of myself.

"She's a most wonderful creature," he said softly. "What should I do?"

"See her, by all means," I said quickly. This could be the answer to all my prayers, I thought. It was hard to imagine Slab finding a friend, let alone a lover, but I would be the last to dampen the flames of such a romance. If some spectral woman would have him, then have him she would. Perhaps this was all he needed. Perhaps now he would now content himself to move on to the underworld and leave me and my tavern alone.

"Tell her," he mused. "What a marvelous idea. You will arrange it, of course."

I stopped short. "You don't mean—she's among the living?"

"Of course."

"How—" I began, at a loss for words. "Who—"

"She is called," he said with the softest of sighs, "Deana Caltonos qua Salian Ri."

A chill ran through me as he spoke her name.

"I must talk with her, Ulander," he continued, more forcefully now. It sounded almost a threat. "Bring her here. To-morrow."

"But she's—" I began.

He shook his head in warning. Then he faded away.

I pressed my eyes shut and took another sip from my goblet, which Slab had had the good sense to leave behind. Its contents tasted a lot more like wine now, and I certainly felt the need to get drunk.

Deana Ri. Of course I knew of her; she was the Great Lord of Zelloque's younger sister . . . and after him, the last of the Ri bloodline, since the Great Lord had yet to marry and produce an heir. Should anything happen to His Eminence Narmon Ri, Deana would ascend the emerald throne to rule Zelloque.

Slab might as well have asked me to bring the Great Lord himself. Besides, I thought, struggling to recall what little court gossip I knew, wasn't she already betrothed to a Coranian prince? What interest could she possibly have in the ghost of a dead barkeeper?

No, Slab had once again demanded the impossible. Only I knew he'd make me suffer if I didn't at least try to carry out his whims. What could I possibly do?

I had to find out more about the Coranian prince, I thought. Ludicrous as I found the whole idea of Slab courting Deana Ri, I had to take it seriously. I knew Slab would make me suffer mightily if I didn't at least try.

I parted the curtain to my booth and gestured to Lur, my bodyguard and doorman. He lumbered over, all seven feet of him, and bent his bald head to hear what I wanted.

"Have any of the Coranian slavers finished with their game?" I asked. I couldn't tell if any of them had joined the crowd at the bar.

Lur grunted once, which I took to mean no.

"I want to talk to one of them. Bring their leader here when he's done."

When Lur nodded, I closed the curtain to a slit, through which I continued to watch. Lur turned at once and strode toward the dice game. I sighed. He was without doubt the best bouncer and bodyguard I'd ever had, but his reasoning abilities left something to be desired. I should have realized my instructions would be too complicated for him—he'd get one of the slavers for me now.

I watched Lur look over the men, select one—the tallest, of course—then bend and whisper a few words into the man's ear. The slaver glanced toward my booth and frowned, but nodded. Passing the dice, he scooped up a few coins, tucked them into his pouch, and he headed toward me with a swagger.

I leaned back and waited until he swept the certain aside.

"Please, join me," I said, and when he did, I asked, "Wine?"

He nodded solemnly, and I gestured to one of the serving girls. When she'd set a goblet before him, I pulled the curtain closed again.

"You are, of course," I said, "familiar with the upcoming marriage between Deana Caltonos qua Salian Ri, the sister of our beloved Great Lord, and one of your Coranian princes."

"Prince Destabo na Laolos of the noble House of Kempon," he said off-handedly. "What of it?"

"Then the wedding is still to be held?"

He regarded me strangely. "The wedding is in thirty-five days!"

"What?" I cried. "Where?"

"Here, you idiot!" He drained his goblet and slammed it down. "Don't you listen to news-criers? Have you heard none of your own Great Lord's proclamations? A month of festivities begins next week in honor of the wedding!"

"Ah," I said. I chewed my lip, recognizing now that Slab's

sudden interest in Deana Ri came at a curiously inopportune time. Normally I would have known about the upcoming festivities—by habit as well as preference I kept myself well versed in the city's affairs—but as Slab surely knew, I'd faced one dire emergency after another for the last few weeks, capped by a pestilence of giant flesh-eating rats in the cellars (and serving girls who refused to fetch wine unless accompanied by well-armed escorts). As a result I'd barely stirred from my tavern in all that time.

"A little more than a month away," I mused. "Then Prince Destabo will have already left Coran."

"I'm not privy to the prince's schedule. But yes, I would imagine his ship sailed last week."

I nodded to the slaver. "Thank you for your help. Your next bottle of wine is on the house."

He grinned with sudden good will. "My thanks, sir, and may the great god Derethigon bring fortune to you." He slipped from my booth.

"And to you," I murmured. My thoughts were already far away.

I suddenly knew with an amazing certainty that Prince Destabo was dead. Perhaps his ship had been attacked by pirates; perhaps it had fallen victim to a whirlpool or a sea monster; perhaps some storm or plague or other natural disaster had overtaken him. It didn't matter. Somehow he had perished on his journey to Zelloque. For Slab to have developed such a sudden interest in Deana Ri, I knew he must have spoken to the dead prince's spirit. Being dead himself gave him a certain advantage in that area.

But why would he want to meet with Deana Ri? Why this whole charade of being in love? For I knew it now it must be a charade. Had Slab gone to such lengths merely to annoy me—always a possibility—or did he have more devious motives? Or could he really have fallen in love with Deana Ri based on the dead prince's description of her?

And at that moment I realized I'd made a singular mistake. Slab had never actually said he was in love. I had assumed it from the way he was acting. And once I'm made that assumption, he had never bothered to deny it. When would I learn never to trust my former employer? He could be a master of deception and subterfuge when he chose.

He probably had a message for Deana Ri from her betrothed, and he undoubtedly hoped to use that message in some way for his personal gain. Now, if I could only find a way to turn it to my advantage rather than his . . . and get that awful flowery smell out of my tavern in the bargain . . .

*   *   *

Later, in the small hours of the morning after I'd seen the last drunk rousted and the my tavern's doors securely barred for the night, I ventured forth to see my good friend Captain Lastoq, who was in charge of the city guard. I always kept my bribes to him paid up, and he owed me at least one favor for certain magical potions of a highly illegal—and highly amorous—nature which I had procured for him at great personal expense. If not that debt, then the pouch of gold royals I carried and Lur's hulking presence beside me guaranteed that Lastoq would see me at once.

As Lur and I strolled through the darkened streets, I

noticed great changes happening throughout the city. These had to be preparations for Deana Ri's wedding, I thought. Despite the lateness of the hour, the city bustled with activity. Thrice we passed long lines of creaking wooden drays pulled by six-legged xylopods. Their reptilian heads and shaggy, doglike bodies strained with sinewy strength, and every so often their broad nostrils flared as they caught scent of the sides of salted meats, bushels of grain, and other foodstuffs they hauled. Still more impressive than that, the streets had been swept, the paving stones scrubbed, and decades of grime seemingly stripped away from the buildings so that everything gleamed in the starlight as though newly built. The air itself smelled sweet—almost a miracle, considering it was a warm summer night in June. Truly, the Great Lord had spared no expense in preparing for his sister's wedding.

Captain Lastoq lived in one of the better sections of the city, but his twenty-room house seemed almost modest in comparison to the walled estates of the merchant princes around him. A single downy-cheeked guard, his silver breastplate and his helmet gleaming with a mirrorlike polish, stood late duty at Lastoq's front gate. As I approached, the young man snapped to attention, throwing out his chest and smacking the butt of his silver-tipped spear on the pavement in challenge.

"Who goes there?" he demanded.

I heard Lur grunt and sensed him reaching for his mace, but I calmed him with a gesture.

"I have come on urgent business to see your captain," I said. I pressed a gold half royal coin into the young man's hand. It was undoubtedly more than he expected or even required, but I felt the need for haste, which such an extravagant bribe would certainly elicit.

"Your name?" he asked more cordially.

"Ulander Rasym. It is a matter of utmost importance."

"Wait here, sir."

He slipped through the gate. I shifted uneasily from foot to foot, studying a fourth line of drays now passing, then watching Lur finger the handle of his mace as though he longed to use it, then gazing up at the stars in the nighttime sky.

At last the young guard returned. "Captain Lastoq says for you to come back after the noon hour. He has just retired from a long day's honest labor and will see nobody."

"Did you tell him my name?" I demanded.

"Yes."

"Tell him," I said in a soft, dangerous voice, "that I bear news of the gravest import, and if he doesn't see me now, I will go over his head to one of the Great Lord's ministers, and he will probably be executed as a result."

"He told me you would say something to that effect, and that if I let you in I would be patrolling the docks to the last minute of the last hour of the last day of my service. You may not pass."

"Did he also warn you about Lur?"

"What's a Lur?"

I turned to my bodyguard. "Show him."

The mace rose and fell with astonishing speed. The guard crumpled, a new dent in his shiny silver helm. I bent to make certain he was merely unconscious—luckily, he was—then pushed the gate open and entered the courtyard. Lur stooped, then followed, dragging the young man along by his heel. Once we were inside, I shut the gate with a soft clang, then recovered my coin from his pouch. There was no sense in rewarding stupidity and incompetence, after all.

By the light of the lone torch that burned by the front door, I noted that Captain Lastoq had redone the garden since I had last visited. Pale, night-blooming flowers sweetened the air, their scent quite delicious compared to the cloying reek in my tavern. Sniffing happily, I strolled up the pebble walkway toward the front door.

"Attacking a city guardsman," said a soft voice from the shadows to my left, "is still a crime, even in these degenerate days in this degenerate city."

"So is the possession of certain magical love potions," I said. "Besides, that pup slipped on a paving stone and hit his head. We were merely helping him inside."

"Of course you were." Tayn Lastoq stepped from the shadows. He wore a loose black robe rather than his uniform and carried no weapons that I could see. "You have done me a favor, actually," he said. "Young Barsil there is from a wealthy family with close ties to the Great Lord. He parents will doubtlessly buy many promotions for him over the next few years, and I expect he will rapidly become one of my most influential officers. Despite that, he shows promise. I needed to know how unquestioning his loyalty to me would be, and he passed the test admirably. He could easily have taken you to see one of the Great Lord's advisors himself."

"He did seem promising," I allowed. "I am pleased to have rendered you yet another service."

"That still doesn't change the fact that your man attacked a member of the city guard."

"As I told you, the boy slipped and hit his head."

"Then I can't possibly owe you a debt of any kind . . . if, as you say, he slipped and hit his head."

"We did bring him inside for you."

"Surely that falls under common courtesy."

I laughed. "You have me, Tayn."

Laughing too, he turned and entered the house through a side door, and I followed. Lur, still dragging young Barsil, brought up the rear. We went straight to Captain Lastoq's study, where a tray of sweetmeats and goblets of fruit nectar had already been set out for us. We sat and sampled them.

"Now," he finally said, after the required first few minutes of polite conversation, "what is it that brings you out of your tavern to see me at such an hour, Ulander?"

"Bad news, I'm afraid." I told him of all Slab had done, then gave voice to my suspicion that Prince Destabo had died in passage to Zelloque.

Lastoq sipped his nectar thoughtfully for a second. "You have no actual proof," he said slowly. "Nothing you have told me would convince the Great Lord's counselors to permit Deana Ri to visit your tavern—let alone halt preparations for the wedding. But if we could get proof of some kind, surely it would be worth a lot for both of us."

"True," I admitted. "I believe Slab can be tricked into giving us the proof we need."

"How is this possible?"

"From years of experience I have come to believe that Slab is somehow bound to my tavern. He sees all that happens within, yet remains blissfully ignorant of all that happens without. In cases such as this one, when he has given me explicit instructions, he must rely on me to do as told—and I have always followed such instructions in the past. He will believe me if I tell him Deana Ri is coming to my tavern to see him."

"But she must come in disguise," he said, catching on. "No one must know she has visited a place such as Slab's."

"Veils and concealing robes will do the trick," I said.

"And I will have the tavern surrounded by half a hundred men," he said. "Security is as important as secrecy."

I gestured grandly. "It must appear that she is there with all due precautions. Make it a hundred men!"

"But who will play the part of Deana Ri?" he wondered.

At that moment young Barsil groaned and stirred. Captain Lastoq and I glanced at him and then at each other. Then we both smiled.

* * *

It took another hour to finalize our plans, then we shook hands in agreement. Dawn had just begun to color the east with pale fingers of pink and yellow when I made it home. Of course I could not afford a grand estate like Captain Lastoq, who collected bribes from half the merchants in Zelloque and extorted protection money from the rest. I lived in a modest three-story house near the city's west gate, with only two servants and Lur to keep things in order.

I knew it would take many hours for someone to arrange even a clandestine visit from Deana Ri, and I intended to spend those hours sleeping, as did Captain Lastoq. I normally opened my tavern's doors around three o'clock in the afternoon, but today we would open late. Lastoq and I had agreed upon a twilight visit, and only after we had wrung whatever news we could from Slab would the tavern be opened as usual to customers.

I went at once to my bedroom and shuttered the windows; already the first sounds of traffic had begun to rise from the street. Far off, a crier proclaimed the morning's news, but I could not make out the words. No doubt it had something to do with Deana Ri's wedding celebration, I thought.

Exhaustion claimed me. As soon as I had changed into my night clothes, I climbed into my large canopied bed, snuggled into the down-filled mattress, and slept a deep and dreamless sleep.

*   *   *

Marina, my elderly housekeeper, awakened me at one o'clock in the afternoon by throwing open the shutters, as usual. Mumbling and groaning, I sat up and squinted at her. She wore her ash colored hair in a tight bun, in the style of Pavonian matriarchs, and bustled about the room with efficient speed. She laid out my clothes, poured fresh water into a basin by the window, and then returned to the kitchens to prepare my breakfast, all without a word.

I rose, splashed lime-scented water on my face from the basin, and studied my reflection in a looking glass. Slab had aged me, I thought. Dark circles lined my eyes; new wrinkles had appeared around my eyes and mouth. If I didn't get rid of him, I knew I'd be an old man long before my time.

Quickly I dressed and descended to the dining room. Marina served a light meal of toasted oat cakes in honey, and I ate in silence, wondering if I had done the right thing. Slab could be vengeful. If anything went wrong and he discovered our plot, I might well come to regret it. But what else could I do?

No, I had made the right decision, of that I was sure. I would have to rely on my own wits and skills to make sure everything turned out as anticipated.

Finishing my oat cakes, I dipped my fingers in a rinsing bowl, wiped them clean on a soft white cloth, felt for my pouch to make sure I hadn't forgotten it, and bellowed, "Lur!" It was time to get going. All else would depend on Captain Lastoq, I knew.

Lur ducked through the doorway into the dining room. "Master?" he said in his low, rumbly voice. He already held his mace.

"It's time," I told him.

*   *   *

The walk to my tavern took a little more than fifteen minutes, primarily because I chose the longer route through Storyteller's Square. Here preparations for Deana Ri's wedding continued at a great pace. We passed piles of lumber intended for platforms and food booths, groups of jugglers and tumblers practicing their arts, and more lines of xylopod drays heading for the Great Lord's warehouses. Old women were busy scrubbing down the flagstones; younger boys and girls painted fresh coats of whitewash on walls facing the square.

The whole city had taken on a festive gleam.

Little had changed in the dockside section of Zelloque, however. The drab stone and brick buildings, the ships bobbing slowly at the piers, the fishy reek hanging over it all. Yes, I thought, you'd never know preparations for the wedding of a lifetime had begun a few blocks away, judging from this section of the city.

My tavern sat one block in from the docks, on Serpent's Row. Several Coranian smugglers I recognized as loyal patrons lounged on the wooden bench by my door; they struggled to their feet and threw back their gray hoods as I approached.

"We're closed this afternoon," I called. "Preparations for the wedding."

They groaned. "Just a few drinks, Ulander," Old Sherton called, squinting at me with his one good eye. "Fer ol' times."

"Not today. Try Slaughter's." I nodded across the street at my nearest competitor, who had already opened.

Grumbling, they meandered away. I didn't blame them: when you find a tavern like Slab's, it's hard to settle for second best. Sarri Slaughter watered his drinks too much, or so I'd heard, and he employed some of the ugliest barmaids this side of Pavonia.

I sat on the bench they had vacated. Lur stood beside me, one hand resting on the handle of his mace. In silence, we waited.

Several times I heard odd thumps from within the tavern, and once came the sound of a wine bottle shattering on the floor. I winced. Hopefully it was just the giant flesh-eating rats at play. But I had the strangest feeling Slab and his ghostly friends were hard at work in preparation for Deana Ri's visit.

Finally from up the street I heard the sounds of marching boots, and seconds later a squad of city guardsmen marching three abreast turned the corner. Captain Lastoq, looking splendid in his gold and red dress uniform with a plentitude of medals pinned on his chest, rode at their head on a magnificent black stallion.

Lastoq stopped in front of me and dismounted, giving the horse's reins to one of his men. Then he clapped his hands, and his guards broke ranks and surrounded my tavern. They drew their short slightly curved swords and assumed a watchful stance, facing outwards.

Sarri Slaughter wandered from his tavern to look everything over. He smiled, showing cracked yellow teeth, then scratched at the fleas nesting in his long, scraggly red hair.

"Trouble, Ulander?" he called. He probably thought the Great Lord had sent Captain Lastoq to arrest me, I decided.

"A few rats in the cellar," I called back. "The city guard is going to exterminate them for me."

"Oh," he said, looking disappointed. Then he ducked back inside his own establishment.

Except for the guards, the street had become completely deserted. The Great Lord's guardsmen often had that effect, I'd found, when they arrived in large numbers.

Lastoq said, "Shall we wait inside?"

"Everything's ready?" I asked him.

"Yes. Her ladyship will be here any time now."

"Good." I turned and rapped twice on the door. "It's Ulander Rasym," I called. "Open up."

I heard the patter of bare feet as the boy I kept to watch the place at night hurried to obey. He shifted the heavy bar out of position, then I heard it thud to the floor. I pushed the door open and went in.

Young Kel—he was about nine or ten years old, with a tangle of unruly blond hair and a mischievous grin—tried to dart past me. I grabbed his tunic and hauled him back. He started to kick, so I passed him to Lur, who held him upside down by the ankle before me.

"What's wrong in there?" I demanded. "Why were you trying to run away?"

"G-ghosts!" he said. "Everywhere! Hundreds of 'em!"

I peered in. "I don't see anything unusual."

"They've went away," he said a little apologetically.

"If they went away, they can't hurt you."

He thought that over for a second. "Maybe."

"Let him go," I said to Lur, who immediately released him. Kel tumbled head over heels and bobbed to his feet with catlike grace. "Kel," I told him, "go home and see your poor widowed mother. Be back by nightfall. We'll take care of the ghosts."

"Thank you, Ulander!" he said and dashed away up the street.

Shaking my head, I turned to Lastoq. "After you," I said.

He gave a nervous laugh, glanced at his men, then ducked through the doorway. I followed.

The place had changed. All the furniture had been moved around to clear a straight path to my private booth. At least the ghosts had done some good, I thought: the floor had been swept and the tables scrubbed. Although the scent of wild-flowers lingered in the air, it had become a subtle, almost appealing smell. Everything seemed altogether too perfect, I decided.

"Slab?" I asked.

I heard nothing, not a whisper, not a creak from the floor-boards, not a rustle from the rats in the cellar. The bar seemed completely deserted. I hesitated, my stomach feeling jumpy and nervous. More than ever, it felt like a trap.

Lastoq called to four of his men. They ran inside, swords drawn, and saluted smartly.

"Check the winecellar," he told them.

"There's a lantern by the door," I called. "Watch out for the rats!"

They gave me puzzled glances, but kept their swords out. One of them lit the lantern, and then they proceeded down the steps with exaggerated caution.

Shaking my head, I led Lastoq to the bar and pulled a bottle of Coranian brandy from my private store. I poured us both large drinks.

Then, as if from a great distance, I heard Slab's voice call, "Ulander."

I glanced at Lastoq, who had abruptly paled. He had heard it, too. Quickly he downed his drink.

With a sigh, I went into my private booth and pulled the curtain. Instantly Slab was there. I stared at the magnificent gold-and-emerald robe he wore, the ornately carved emerald rings on his fingers, the sparkling emerald pendant around his neck. He was dressed like a prince . . . a Coranian prince, I thought.

"Well?" he demanded, leaning forward and putting his elbows on the table.

"She will be here," I promised. "It cost me a fortune—"

"What do I care of money now?"

"It keeps the roof fixed," I pointed out, "and the cellars stocked."

"Bah. This is love, Ulander. When will she be here?"

"Twilight. A lady of her standing cannot parade through the streets like a common barmaid. And especially not in this section of the city. She is coming in disguise."

"What of the guards?"

I gave a dismissive wave. "The Great Lord's councelors insisted. Slab . . . I had to tell them a lie to get her here."

"What lie?" he demanded, eyes narrowing suspiciously.

"That the ghost of her mother had appeared to me and asked for her. It's well known my tavern is haunted; why shouldn't Deana Ri's mother come here, too? It was the only thing I could think of at the time. And it worked."

"Twilight . . ." he said softly. Then he smiled. And then he slowly faded from view.

*   *   *

Lastoq joined me in my private booth, and for the next few hours we drank and waited together in silence. Several times we heard cries of pain from the wine cellar, followed by cursing and the clank of swords on stone. I could imagine his men fighting off hordes of giant flesh-eating rats, but it could just as easily have been some of Slab's ghostly friends playing tricks.

Eventually the four guardsmen clambered up the steps and marched over to Lastoq. They had what looked like numerous bite marks on their hands and faces, and blood smeared their uniforms.

"The rats," announced said the one on the left, "are all dead."

"Excellent," I said, rubbing my hands together. They had saved me a lot of aggravation. "Then we will all be safe tonight."

Lastoq nodded. "Help yourself to a few bottles from behind the counter," he said to his men. "When you're done, return to barracks and have the company physician dress your wounds. The wine will ease your pains tonight."

I gave him a mildly displeased look because it was expected of me, but said nothing. His men had rid me of my rat problem, and a few bottles of wine were a small enough price to pay.

His men took their leave with happy grins, cheerful salutes, and six bottles of my finest Merindian wine. It was no wonder, I thought, that Captain Lastoq remained so popular among his troops.

The barmaids and other serving girls arrived as expected. I set some of them to cleaning up the mess in the winecellar and dispatched others outside with cool lime-scented water for Lastoq's men. There followed calls of thanks from outside.

At last twilight began to fall, so I sent all my servants outside to wait. In case anything unfortunate happened, I didn't want anything to happen to them. Good help is hard to find.

Right on schedule, I heard a horse's hooves and the rattle

of carriage wheels drawing to a stop in front of my tavern.

"This is it," Lastoq muttered unnecessarily, rising and hurrying to the door.

I followed. We got there in time to see young Barsil step down from the carriage. He was dressed in a noblewoman's rich concealing robes, with a veil of purple silk hiding all but his eyes and his freshly—and quite neatly—plucked eyebrows. He hesitated for a second, looking at Lastoq and me, then stepped forward with slow, mincing steps.

Captain Lastoq bowed to him, and I bowed too. That's what we would have done with the real Deana Ri, after all.

Barsil waved us back up with casual indifference. He had taken his role to heart, I could tell.

"This way, Great Lady," Lastoq said, escorting Barsil inside. They headed toward my private booth.

"Your mother will be joining us shortly," I said. "May I offer you any refreshments? Wine, perhaps?"

Slowly Barsil shook his head. He was trying not to speak, I realized. I decided not to ask him any more direct questions. Slab might get suspicious if he discovered our so-called Deana Ri spoke with a male voice.

The room's temperature dropped abruptly. Giant phantom rats appeared, scurrying over the walls, and then Slab himself materialized before us . . . and beside Slab stood another ghost, this one dressed in tattered silks, with strings of seaweed draped from his shoulders and a gaping would in his left cheek. I swallowed. This had to be Prince Destabo.

"I see you have not failed us, Ulander," Slab said in a booming voice that shook the walls. He turned to the prince.

"All is as I promised," he said.

"Truly," Destabo whispered, his voice a horrible gurgle. He took a step toward young Barsil, raising one hand. The flesh had come off it, leaving bare bones, but I could see a huge diamond ring upon one white knuckle. "Come, my love . . ."

Barsil shrank back in fear. I found I didn't blame him.

"Slab!" I cried, "you can't do this!"

"It's worth it, Ulander," he told me.

"But the Great Lord—"

Slab laughed. "He's welcome to join us!"

Lastoq drew his sword. "Begone, foul creature!" he said to the thing that had been Prince Destabo. "You have no claim upon the living!"

Destabo raised his fleshless hand. "By this ring, she gave herself to me . . . and I will have her!"

"Then behold your betrothed!" I cried, snatching away young Barsil's veil.

Barsil understood and quickly ripped away his concealing purple robes, letting them fall to the floor. Then, standing there in nothing but a white loincloth, with a fierce, determined look on his face, he was unmistakably a man.

Prince Destabo howled in anger and frustration. I thought he was going to strike Barsil, but instead he whirled to face Slab.

"What—" Slab began. "But—" For the first time in my life, I saw him speechless. For once I had outsmarted him, I thought with some satisfaction. It felt good.

Destabo didn't give Slab a chance to explain. "Liar!" he cried. "You betrayed me!"

Seizing Slab around the neck, Prince Destabo threw him to the floor. The two began to roll around, screaming, cursing, trying to best each other. Unfortunately they were both already dead, so they couldn't do any real harm, not even when Slab ripped off one of Destabo's arms and began to bludgeon him with it. The moment he let go, the arm reattached itself.

The phantom rats were all squealing and circling the battle.

"Help me!" I cried to Barsil and Lastoq.

I ran to the windows and began throwing open the shutters. The last dying rays of the sun streamed in, and where the light touched the ghosts, they grew pale and insubstantial as mist. The giant phantom rats, hissing and gnashing their teeth, slunk away to the corners.

At last the two figures broke apart. I could barely see them now. Destabo continued to glare at Slab.

"Be warned," he said in his horrible, gurgling voice, "you have made an enemy this day. I will not rest until I see you destroyed!"

"Make no threats you cannot fulfill," Slab said.

He gave a quick nod, and that seemed to be the signal the rats had been waiting for. Dozens of them swarmed onto Prince Destabo, fixing their ghostly teeth and nails into him. He shrieked and tried to flee—but they dug in their feet and began to drag him away, toward the winecellar.

Lastoq, Barsil, and I stood well back, watching with mingled horror and revulsion. The rats bore Prince Destabo into the darkness. I thought I heard him scream, then came a drawn-out cry of, *"No-o-o-o-o—"*

I shuddered. The rats, I realized, must have been under Slab's control all along. They must have carried Prince Destabo to the underworld, from which no ghost could ever return.

Slab turned and glared.

"Ulander—you've cost me a fortune!" he snarled. "He agreed to give me half the treasure aboard his sunken ship!"

"But you've made a fortune for me," I told him. "Captain Lastoq and I have successfully foiled a murder attempt against Deana Ri, for which service the Great Lord will doubtless shower riches upon us, and we can also report that Prince Destabo na Laolos of the noble House of Kempon is dead, for which we can expect similar rewards."

"A fortune indeed . . ." he mused.

"*My* fortune," I pointed out.

"Half of a fortune," Captain Lastoq said to both of us.

"I am of a generous nature," Slab said. "A third of a fortune will suit me. Just throw it into the cellar when it arrives, Ulander, and I'll take care of the rest. And you can thank me for being such a forgiving fellow . . ."

He slowly faded from view.

I looked at Lastoq. "Don't expect any of his share to come from my half," the captain of the guard said. "I have my own expenses to take care of."

"Such as . . . ?" I prompted.

"Young Barsil here . . . he needs to be rewarded, and promotions are expensive. And then there's the matter of paying the men who rid you of those rats. And all the other men we borrowed for this little adventure. And the carriage rental, and the robes which Barsil tore in his haste to reveal himself . . ."

"I see," I said, frowning. "Very well—part of a fortune is still better than nothing."

Just take care," he whispered, leaning close so only I could hear him, "that Slab doesn't end up with all your share."

I forced a hearty laugh. "I have no intention of letting that happen."

He nodded once, turned, and strode out the front door, calling to his men. In quick order he had them back in formation and marching off toward their barracks.

Sighing, I turned and looked over my tavern. "Well," I said to my barmaids as they ventured back inside, "let's get this place back in shape. It's business as usual tonight."

I noticed one of the barmaids had a handkerchief over her nose. That's when I thought to sniff the air—really sniff it. The flowery smell was gone. But now, replacing it, was a stench like that of rotting meat . . . and it seemed to be coming from the wine cellar.

"Slab?" I said. "Slab?"

Far off, I heard a ghostly chuckle. And I knew, suddenly, that it would cost the rest of that fortune to get rid of the phantom stench of rotting meat.

4.

The Brothers Lammiat

I: Hilan Lammiat

I jingled the jewels in my beard with one meaty hand. The diamonds and rubies sparkled like the sun at noon, despite the tavern's dimness, and brought a quiet gasp of awe from the scantily-clad serving girl behind the counter. I leered at her. The jewels weren't real, of course—not even I, Hilan Lammiat the Pirate, would wear my valuables into a dive like Slab's Tavern.

"So, my pretty," I said, louder than the bedlam of swearing, dicing, fighting and general mayhem behind me. "Let's slip out back for a bit and—"

"Hey, Hilan!" The greeting was immediately followed by a hearty clap on the back that sent the breath whooshing from my lungs. I am not a small man, nor a patient one. Few people—very few—would've dared to pound me on the back.

I choked, gasped once, then turned with a low growl—to face my brother. "I see you found me after all," I said.

Nollin stood there and grinned back, a slightly shorter, less heavily muscled version of myself. We even dressed much alike, with gold rings looping ears and nose, crimson and silver scarfs around our necks and heads. I wore a plain blue shirt and black silk pants that puffed out between waist and knee; he wore black and silver. Matching curved swords, gifts from our father before the Great Lord of Zelloque hanged him, dangled jauntily from our belts.

Father hadn't been able to tell us apart as children, so one day he'd given me a dueling wound on my right cheek that had left a jagged white scar. I stroked the scar and wished he'd given it to Nollin instead.

"You look well," Nollin said.

"Would've been better never to see your face again."

"Now, now, Hilan, you must have patience with your kid brother. Blood's thick, eh?"

"Thick enough I haven't killed you. Yet. What do you want?"

He laughed. "Drink up. Then we talk."

Casting a disappointed glance at the serving girl, who fluttered her long dark lashes coyly, I drained my mug then slammed it down. Then I tossed a copper coin onto the counter, stood, and followed my brother out to the cobbled street.

Midnight had scarcely come and passed. All the dockside taverns still rang with the boisterous sounds of sailors at ease. After two months at sea, I wished I were back inside Slab's place, away from the chilling night air and the monsters that haunted it. Still, it was my brother that had come . . . best to see what the boy wanted. . . . The two of us strolled silently past the inns and bars, through puddles of light and shadow cast by dim lamps and open windows, heading toward the long, dark piers stretching into the harbor. Small ships tied to the nearer pilings bobbed like corks on the low waves. Further out, tall, high-prowed, triple-masted sailing ships of the Viandas Mercenaries slowly rolled, proud banners fluttering against the wash of stars. And there were other ships, too, traders from Pethis and Coran, galleys from Lothaq and Zorvoon, even a few slavers on the long voyage between Losmuul and Volise. Scattered among the craft were a few unmarked ships belonging to lesser Lords of Zelloque or to privateers like Nollin and me.

Still silent, we passed onto the pier. Drunken sailors lolled on the decks of some ships, snoring, eyes rolled back, mouths open. I shook my head in disgust. Spirits of the night could enter a man's body through his mouth, stealing his heart and draining his blood.

"Whose ship?" I asked.

"Mine," Nollin said. "I have something to show you."

At last the two of us reached the *Serpent*, Nollin's ship, and crossed the rope gangway to its deck. A small, wiry man dressed in white breeches and shirt ran to Nollin while other sailors watched from the shadows, eyes wide and white as marble. Covertly, I studied his ship. The entire crew was present, to all appearances ready to sail at a moment's notice.

"Ship's tight, Captain," one of the mates called.

"Good," Nollin said. "We sail in an hour." He turned to me with a half-mocking gesture of welcome. "After you."

We went aft to the captain's cabin. Behind us, waves lapped at the *Serpent*'s sides like the pulse of a human heart.

*   *   *

A single lamp burned overhead. We sat at the chart table and watched each other warily for a moment. Then I gave up being patient and demanded, "Well?"

"We've never trusted each other," Nollin said, "and yet I feel responsible for you. Therefore I pass on this warning: soon, perhaps this very night, Zelloque will be destroyed. The Great Lord will be murdered and a tyrant will usurp the throne. Leave Zelloque or you will be killed and your ship taken."

I felt my face flush hot and red at the thought, and almost screamed back a challenge for anyone who'd dare to try. *Almost.* I knew my brother well enough to realize he thought he spoke the truth. But how could a tyrant kill the Great Lord of Zelloque, who lived apart from the world in his palace? The city guard would protect him—and the whole Zelloquan army, if necessary. It didn't make sense, the whole tale didn't make sense! No, someone had lied to Nollin. That was the truth.

I said as much.

"I knew you wouldn't believe me," Nollin said. He stood and strode to the door of his sleeping chamber, swinging it open.

An old woman sat quietly on the bed inside, her tear-streaked face a web of wrinkles, her eyes dark and downcast. She held herself with the humility of a peasant, yet dressed richly, as a noble might. The image disturbed me. I stared at her, forehead creased, until my brother shut the door again.

"Who is she?" I demanded.

"Loanu, once the High Priestess of the Shrine of Shon Atasha."

"Once?"

Nollin shrugged. "She dreamed of the coming tyrant and destroyed the shrine before he could debase it. Now that she is no longer touched by the god's power, she is half-blind. I found her wandering the streets in a daze, trying to warn people. They stoned her as a witch."

"You'd believe an old woman?" I snorted. "You're not my

brother!"

"Listen to me! She wept as she spoke—spoke not only of the coming Tyrant, but of great visions of far lands, of gods, of dead kings and their treasures! Her tales will set your heart afire as they have set mine. All you must do is listen to her!"

I shook my head. "No, Nollin. The witch is crazy. Turn her out for the nobles to take care of."

"Come with me. I'm sailing for Tázgul in an hour. Together we could win a kingdom!"

"Nollin . . ."

He sighed and I knew I'd won. "Very well," he said. "I can see you're not interested. Go, then, brother, but remember my warning. The Great Lord will soon be dead, and when he is, you must flee. Promise me that."

"I promise—*if* the Great Lord dies."

We stood and started for the door. There I made my mistake: I turned my back on Nollin. Brother or not, I never should've trusted him. I realized it the second I caught a flash of movement from the corner of my eye. He struck me in the head with something hard and heavy.

Darkness washed over me.

*   *   *

II: Nollin Lammiat

Nollin set the brass candlestick back on the table, then sighed as he looked at his brother's still form on the cabin floor. A trickle of blood ran from a shallow cut behind Hilan's left ear. A minor wound; he'd soon recover.

Quickly he stripped Hilan of clothes and jewelry, then bound him with heavy ropes taken from a chest next to the door. He changed into his brother's blue shirt and black pants, then stood in front of his looking glass, adjusting the scarves around his head. Satisfied, he turned and found Hilan glaring up at him with slitted eyes.

"I trust I won't have to gag you, brother?" Nollin asked.

Hilan spat.

"Not on the carpet, Hilan. Remember your manners."

"I'll kill you for this!"

"You'll thank me soon enough. You always were stubborn, and now I'm going to save your miserable life. Ah, how ironic!"

Hilan growled. "More of your talk. I'll see you in Hell!"

"I promised father that I'd look after you. I mean to keep that promise, whether you like it or not."

"You promised!" He laughed long and hard. "Promised!"

"What's wrong?" Nollin demanded.

"He made me promise the same thing! Never meant to keep it, though. I always hated you."

"Then keep hating me. It'll keep you alive." He opened the door and stepped into his sleeping chamber.

Loanu lay quietly now. He shook her awake. "Witch!"

Opening rheumy eyes, she peered up at him. "Who is it?"

"Nollin. You must help me, if we're to escape the Tyrant."

Her thoughts seemed to clear, for she looked at him with some measure of recognition. She sat up. "What do you ask of me?"

"Use your magic. Make me look like my brother for an hour!"

"I have seen your brother," she whispered, "in my

dreams . . ."

Nollin shook her again. "Do it!"

She stared at him. Her lips began to move. He heard nothing at first, then the barest trace of a whisper, then a low crooning song which jangled his nerves and made the hair on the back of his neck bristle. He shivered.

A blue glow surrounded her hands. She raised them to his face, touching his skin gently, tracing the line of his jaw, then his nose, then his forehead. Still she sang.

Nollin's vision grew cloudy and distant, as though he looked at the world through a mask. His cheeks felt heavy and numb.

Loanu sank back on her bed. "The magic is done."

Hurrying to his looking glass, Nollin stared at his image.

Hilan's face looked back at him. He smiled; Hilan's face smiled. He laughed; Hilan laughed. The illusion was perfect.

Turning to Loanu, he gently pushed her back on the bed and pulled the covers around her shoulders. "Sleep well, my witch," he said.

He opened the door and hurried through the chart room, ignoring Hilan's curses, and went on deck. A light breeze gusted from the east, heavy with moisture and electricity. Pausing, he studied the sky. The storm would soon break.

"Wait for my return," he called to the mate on deck, who knew his plan, "but have everything ready."

"Aye, sir," Klaff said. "Ready we'll be."

*   *   *

Nollin went to the *Falcon*, Hilan's ship, and strode up the gangplank like he owned the world. Just as Hilan would've done. He felt a moment's fear when one of the sailors ran forward, but thrust all thoughts of failure from his mind. Since he looked like Hilan, he was Hilan . . . at least to simpleminded fools like these.

"Sir?" the man said.

"Round up the crew. We sail in a half-hour.

"Sir?"

"You heard me. Get going!" Nollin sent him sprawling with a backhanded cuff, as he'd often seen Hilan do, then watched as the man climbed to his feet and bobbed his head nervously.

"Yes, sir!" He turned and ran.

Nollin called to the half-dozen other sailors on deck, and they put down whatever they were doing and gathered around.

"Most of you have seen my brother Nollin," he said. "We're joining up with him. Now jump to it!"

They jumped. Nollin watched for a minute, then grunted and turned to the captain's cabin. Removing a key from his waist pocket, he fitted it into the lock, turned, then pushed into the room.

He sat at the small desk and waited. His muscles knotted and he felt sick at his stomach. Time slipped by. How long would the witch's magic last? How long could he fool Hilan's crew? He stared at the looking glass on the wall as if daring it to betray him.

Feet pounded past his door from time to time; men shouted and swore as they climbed the rigging. The decks creaked and shifted against the waves.

He knew the time had come when a light knock sounded

on the door.

Opening it, he stepped out and found a tall, thin, square-jawed man standing there. He dressed in brown and black: Rilal, the first mate.

"Sir," Rilal said, "the ship's ready."

"Good." He looked across the deck at the men, nodding slowly. "You will follow the *Serpent*. Keep a close watch on her. Make sure no tricks are pulled. I trust my brother, but not far enough to risk my life. Eh?"

He nodded. "Yes, sir."

"I'll be aboard Nollin's ship. We sail in five minutes. You're in command until I get back. Any questions?"

He grinned. "No, Captain."

*   *   *

III: HILAN LAMMIAT

I heard a soft tread and looked up. My muscles ached from straining against the ropes, and though I hate to say it, I welcomed the excuse to stop.

It wasn't Nollin, returned to gloat, but the old woman . . . what had he called her? Loanu?

She knelt beside me and ran her soft fingers through my hair.

"Cut the ropes," I said.

"There are no ropes." Her voice was soft, almost sing-song, and she didn't look at me.

"Look—on my arms. See them?"

"The time has come. Do you not hear the winds? The end is here. The Tyrant has come."

I strained, but heard no more than the waves and the

creaking of the deck.

"He is near. I feel his presence. Shon Atasha protect me!"

Weeping, she collapsed at my side. Her sobs became hysterical. Again I strained at my bonds with no result. If nothing else, Nollin knew how to tie knots.

The door swung open and he stood there, sweating heavily, a knife in his hand. The *Serpent* lurched, suddenly, and I knew the moorings had been cast off. Then I noticed the scar on his face—my face!

"I'm going to kill you!" I screamed at him. "Nollin!"

"It's here," he said softly. There was a stunned look on his face.

"Let me loose!"

"Yes . . . yes." He looked down as if noticing me for the first time. "Yes—there's no time. You must help with the ship. We have to get out of port—the fighting's started!"

I stared at him as he bent and slit my ropes.

"Fighting?"

"All up and down the docks. We barely got away in time."

I stood, shoving him out of the way. *You bastard. Kill you later.*

Clambering out onto the deck, I stared in shock at Zelloque.

The entire city blazed with light. The houses burned. The shops burned. Flames danced among the tall, splendid buildings. Dark shapes moved through the smoke-filled streets and down the piers, throwing torches onto the vessels moored there. The proud ships flared brightly. Over the distant slap-slap of waves I heard screams from dying men.

I shivered. Nollin was suddenly standing beside me.

"Look," he said, pointing.

I turned. A hundred yards away the *Falcon* slipped through the darkness, as silent as a ghost, sails white and full. My ship. Nollin had saved it. If he'd allowed me to stay in Zelloque . . .

Suddenly I didn't know what to say. I turned and looked at him. His face shimmered for an instant in the starlight, then the scar faded and he was Nollin again, the same as ever. He grinned back like nothing had happened between us.

"Blood's thick," he said.

"Blood's thick," I agreed, and shivered again. The breeze had grown colder; I stood there in my undergarments. "I want my clothes back, though."

He turned toward his cabin. "They've too large for me, anyway."

I didn't follow him. Though we would never speak of this night again, I'd always remember what Nollin had done for me, and I'd never be the same.

I watched the city die, and with it, my hatred. I knew I should have burned there as well.

My brother, my brother. Why do you love me?

He came back and slipped a blanket around my shoulders. Together for the first time, we waited for dawn.

5.

Cleaning Up at Slab's

The day after the end of the world is never a pretty sight, I thought, as I stood in the doorway of my tavern and surveyed the damage.

The broken tables and chairs, the shattered glass where shelves of beer mugs had fallen, the gaping holes overhead where sections of the roof had blown away . . . I had never seen such a mess, not even after the wildest of parties. Worse yet, the room stank—not only with the cloying sweetness of wine gone sour, but the ranker odors of decaying cloth and wood. In the space of a week, rain and flood had ruined ten thousand gold royals' worth of rugs and tapestries.

I almost sobbed at the loss. That I, Ulander Rasym, craftiest of all tavernkeepers in Zelloque, should be reduced to such a sorry state! It was almost more than I could bear.

"Slab?" a low voice rumbled behind me.

I took another quick glance around the tavern, but saw no sign of Slab Vethiq, former owner of Slab's, whose spirit had haunted the place longer than I cared to remember. Good, I thought. Slab had made a habit of interfering in my affairs. Being dead hadn't slowed him down one whit.

"He's gone, too," I said.

The front door creaked as, with one finger, I pushed it open. Suddenly its hinges gave way and it fell with a whoof of displaced air.

Lur, my seven-foot-tall bodyguard, with muscles to match

and the sense of a good sheepdog, rumbled unhappily behind me.

I just stepped over the door and took another look at the damage, slower this time, lingering on all the little details, the warped floorboards, the stained plaster, the dirt and debris littering every surface. Underfoot, the residue of spilt wine made sucking noises and pulled at my feet. A deep ache grew in my chest; the shock of it all made breathing difficult.

I tried to convince myself it wouldn't be a complete loss. The walls looked sound; they'd weathered the tornadoes and hurricane winds without a crack. And most of the roof seemed intact; a few tiles had blown away, and some thatch had fallen in, but it could all be fixed readily enough. The huge oak beam that served as bar hadn't shifted an inch.

Pressed hard, I could have opened for business in an hour. If I'd had a customer. If I'd had the men to work at cleaning up.

But there wasn't much chance of that now, not after the storm. It had been as though all the primal forces had risen up at once and crashed down on Zelloque, poor old city, once the greatest ever to rise on Earth—but now more ruins than anything else. Most of her people had fled, or died, or still hid in their holes, afraid to come out lest the stormwinds return.

Something odd struck me: on the end of the bar sat a single glass goblet. I would have sworn it hadn't been there a moment before. Something green bubbled inside it.

I took a step forward. A bottle stood next to the goblet, and suddenly an ethereal hand raised it to pour more of its weird green contents.

"Slab," I said.

And suddenly he sat there, perched on the edge of the huge oak beam, looking smug in his immaculate green silk shirt, white silk pantaloons, and shiny sealskin boots. A gold earring dangled from his left ear, and the tatoos of monsters and naked women on his hands and arms seemed to dance to unheard rhythms. These were his best clothes. I knew; I'd buried him in them twenty years before.

"Slow day," he said.

"It's the end of the tavern," I wheezed. "It's the end of Zelloque."

He laughed, an awful sound that felt like fingernails dragging across slate. "Clean my place up."

"Why bother? No wine, no customers—"

"I'll take care of that." And then he was gone in the wink of an eye, bottle and goblet with him. I had an eerie feeling all over—as if I truly were alone. It was the first time I'd felt that way in Slab's Tavern since it came into my possession.

"Master?" Lur said.

I took a deep breath and pushed my pains away. "Might as well clean up," I said. "We'll open tonight. Perhaps a few of the regulars are still alive, poor wretches."

He grunted in his usual eloquent way and turned to the tables and chairs. Quickly he started sorting the broken from the whole, pitching trash through a window into the alley.

I watched for a moment, then headed for the winecellar. Perhaps all my wine hadn't been destroyed, I thought, as I pulled moldering tapestries from the doorway. But by the thick stench of wine from ahead, I had my doubts.

*   *   *

An afternoon's work brought forth six small kegs of Coranian brandy, two large kegs of good Zelloquan tablewine, and fifty-one assorted bottles of other, more exotic vintages from my private store. I lugged them up to the bar myself, wishing I were twenty years younger and still in shape. I hurt from the exertion.

When I'd brought the last crate up, panting and gasping for breath, two of my other servants chose to arrive. They'd probably come to loot the place, but I didn't have the strength or breath to yell at them as they deserved. I just turned them over to Lur, and he set to scrubbing the floor. Lur was a wonder at motivating workers, when he wanted to be.

By twilight, the worst of the debris had been cleared into the alley. My tavern had been scrubbed top to bottom, and with the newly-bare walls and floors, with the too-few-by-half tables and chairs, it seemed an entirely different place. Only the bar remained much the same.

"Light the lanterns," I said. We'd found three working lanterns and a plentiful supply of oil in one corner of the winecellar. "Put them in the windows, so people know we're here and open."

"Aye," said Lur, and did so.

And I sat back at the bar, watching my men polish and polish again the few clean mugs and goblets they'd salvaged.

And waited.

And kept waiting.

And still kept waiting.

Nobody came. It was the first night I could ever remember the place being so . . . quiet. Not a one of the ghostly apparitions that normally haunted the tavern showed up. No drunken disembodied heads singing wild songs, no beautiful women in glowing white dresses . . . not a single unearthly eye or hand or foot showed itself.

I might have wept, but I didn't have the strength. I finally got up, tottered to my private booth, and collapsed there, feeling sick as the minutes slipped away.

At some point, I began to drift off toward sleep. The tavern rippled in front of my eyes, dreamlike, a reflection in a pool of water. Through the ripples showed a thousand mirror images of my tavern, each slightly darker than the last, until the final few were so lost in shadows they seemed so insubstantial as to be naught but ghosts of reflections.

And in some of those taverns, patrons moved.

And in some of those taverns, the patrons weren't quite human anymore.

The world—I don't know the word—*shifted* somehow, as though Slab's Tavern had been picked up and turned sideways. It seemed to have different dimensions, depending on which way you faced.

I stood, and a thousand other Ulander Rasyms in a thousand other taverns stood with me, more ripples in the pool. I took a step forward, colliding with myself—himself?—and felt a cold shock, as though I'd suddenly plunged into a pool of icewater.

I shook my head. People bustled around me—I felt more than heard them—but saw no one. Invisible fingers touched my cheek, took my hands, pulled me forward. I heard myself cry out—pressed my eyes shut—

And suddenly I stood in a pleasantly warm room. Voices babbled around me, and I smelled fresh wine. Glasses clinked and someone began to sing a rousing old drinking song.

I opened my eyes to find a giant eye floating not a hand's width from my face. I gasped. It floated past, and behind it I saw three pirates hunched over a table, some treasure map spread before them. Then a buxom serving girl sauntered past, carrying a pitcher, her tresses long and silvery white, her gown shimmering ever so faintly. She winked at me, and I realized I knew her—had known her. She'd been one of Slab's barmaid's thirty years before . . . until a runaway wagon took her life.

Bewildered, I turned slowly to look across the whole of the tavern. Around me, movement rippled in all directions. In the blink of an eye my tavern had filled with colorfully dressed people, and things which once might have been people, and things which only could have come from a madman's nightmares.

A human heart, big as a dog and covered with little sucker mouths, pulsed softly in one corner. Overhead drifted the severed heads of sailors executed in the Great Lord of Zelloque's prisons. Their bodies sat at one of the corner tables—

Of a sudden, I realized the tavern's old furniture was back in place, even that which had been shattered and useless. The same tapestries hung the walls, showing great feasts in halls of forgotten kings, ancient hunts with dogs and horses, proud armies marching off to battle.

Lur stood calmly by the front door—the tavern had its thick oak door again—watching the stream of people and things passing in and out. He'd taken it all in stride and seemed completely unbothered by the change in patronage. Or perhaps he didn't have the brains to notice.

"Here, friend," I heard a smooth voice say.

I turned, and a spectral man I vaguely recognized as one of Slab's regulars in days long-gone pressed a few gold coins into my hand. I stared at them, felt them, even bit one. They were real.

"Thank you," I said instinctively, tucking them away. "Do come again."

"I will. I've been just dying for a drink." And he began to laugh, and still laughing, faded from view.

Slab did it, I realized suddenly, brought all his old friends.

"You don't look happy," Slab said. I looked up to find him sitting opposite me, feet up on the table, looking like he owned the place. He tipped back his goblet and drained the rest of his green bubbling wine. "Business good enough for you?"

"How can it be?" I said. "You just brought your friends here, and once they leave, nothing will have changed. Zelloque is gone, destroyed. Utterly ravaged. I doubt if there are five thousand people left in her. Once your friends go, what difference will they have made?"

Slab smiled. I never liked it when he smiled. It always meant trouble for me.

"But," he said, "all my friends are home. It's you who've come visiting." He threw back his head and laughed, and a sudden shivery jolt of dismay ran through me.

Standing, I bolted for the door. It had just opened to admit a pair of skeletons, hand in hand, both with glowing red eyes. And beyond them I saw—

Nothingness. Literal nothingness. I had a vague sense of swirling colors, of infinite depths in which creatures stirred. The lights in my tavern's windows seemed a beacon to the dead and undead. A creature with the head of a snake and the body of a man appeared, carrying a walkingstick. He entered and headed for the bar.

Slab had followed me.

"What have you done?" I whispered.

"A little bit of straightening up. There are rules to death, just as there are rules to life. The Mad God makes those rules. I simply told him my tavern had . . . died." Slab nodded. "That's the truth. The Mad God did the rest. A whim, perhaps. Or perhaps a part of some plan which we cannot fathom. This is your life now, or rather your death. Be grateful I need you, Ulander."

"My death?"

"You don't think you'd be here if you were still alive, do you?"

I suddenly remembered the pains in my chest, my shortness of breath, how every movement had been a labor. Perhaps my old heart had finally given out—but that still didn't explain everything.

"And what about Lur?" I said.

"Eh?" Slab glanced at the door, and a puzzled look crossed his face. "I don't know. He's not supposed to be here." Then he shrugged as though it didn't make any difference to him and he wasn't going to worry about it. "If he's too stupid to know the difference between life and death, it's not my fault. Just be glad: good help is so hard to find."

"I know what you mean," I said.

He laughed again, hard and nasty. "So you should be grateful I've put you back into my service."

The alternative outside seemed much less pleasant. I swallowed and forced myself to say, "Yes, I am grateful." And then I added, "Master." I hated myself then, almost as much as I hated him.

Still laughing, he drifted away from me, calling welcomes to old dead drinking buddies. Slab was back in business, it seemed, and completely on top of things. As always.

I stayed at the doorway a long time that night, staring out into the void. But finally the noise and the laughter and the clink of goblets got the better of me. I turned.

Drunken sailors raised their mugs and toasted everyone's unhealth. A barmaid handed me a goblet before I could ask, and I raised it with them. When I sipped, it tasted like nothing I'd ever had before. Better, somehow, than Earthly wines.

I went to Slab's private booth, and sat there, and watched the money pouring in.

Zelloquan royals or Coranian dzebs or Merindian kamaks—we took it all. The bottles never ran dry, and the crowds were always friendly, and Slab's Tavern had never been better. It was a cage, but what in life isn't?

And as the enormity of the change settled in, as I grew used to the dancing skeletons and the floating eyes and the heart with the sucker mouths that sat in the corner—and as I thought about the possibilities that awaited a crafty tavernkeeper here—I began to think that perhaps being dead wasn't so bad.

Existence goes on, after all.

ABOUT THE AUTHOR

JOHN GREGORY BETANCOURT is an editor, publisher, and bestselling author of science fiction and fantasy novels and short stories. He has had 37 books published, including the bestselling Star Trek novel, *Infection*, and three other Star Trek novels; a trilogy of mythic novels starring Hercules; the critically acclaimed *Born of Elven Blood*; *Rememory*; *Johnny Zed*; *The Blind Archer*; and many others. His fantasy novel *The Dragon Sorcerer* will be released by ibooks shortly. He is personally responsible for the revival of *Weird Tales*, the classic magazine of the fantastic, and has authored two critical works in conjunction with the Sci-Fi Channel: *The Sci-Fi Channel Trivia Book* and *The Sci-Fi Channel Encyclopedia of TV Science Fiction*. Visit his web site at:

http://www.wildsidepress.com/jgb.htm